DRAGON'S

SIMON AND SCHUSTER · NEW YORK

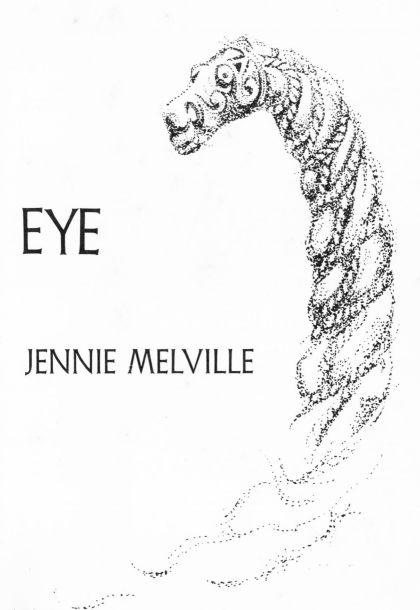

EYE

JENNIE MELVILLE

Library of Congress Cataloging in Publication Data

Melville, Jennie.
  Dragon's Eye.

  I. Title.
PZ4.M532Dr [PR6063.E44]   823'.9'14   76-15616
ISBN 0-671-22309-7

Never seek to tell thy love,
Love that never told can be;
For the gentle wind does move
Silently, invisibly.

I told my love, I told my love,
I told her all my heart,
Trembling, cold, in
ghastly fears—
Ah, she doth depart.

—WILLIAM BLAKE, *1757–1827*

PROLOGUE

A few weeks ago I went back to Markaby and Dragon's Eye—not to stay, although the house is open and ready for my use. No, I went to attend a memorial service in a small chapel near the village of Garrow. It was a fine, warm autumn day.

I went alone, bowing to the altar, then smiling a greeting at two nuns, one old, one young, who sat quietly waiting for the service to begin.

It was a beautiful service, if overlong. After the last note from the organ had died away I went to look at the inscribed stone set in the wall. Really, I was saying my private farewell. In my heart there was a mixture of sadness and pride.

As I stood remembering, an old countrywoman came up and looked too. I would swear there was a tear in her eye.

"I know he had his wrong side," she said. "So we all have, but take it all in all, he was good to the likes of us."

"He was," I agreed. I knew he had been much loved. I twisted my wedding ring on my hand.

"Ay. He was a gallant boy. And with an eye for the ladies." She looked at me, and observed my ring with interest. "When someone dies like that, I always say there's a broken heart somewhere."

"Very likely," I said.

"The sea's cruel. Ay, it is."

She was a sharp-eyed old woman, and she noticed that in addition to my wedding band, I wore an unusual heavy gold ring. She commented on it with the frank curiosity and unabashed critical faculty I had learned to expect hereabouts.

"Funny sort of ring, isn't it? What's that on it? Is it an animal's head?"

"A sheep," I said.

"Well, I never." She looked at me, sizing me up and waiting for the story to follow.

She didn't get it then, but later on I went over it all again for myself.

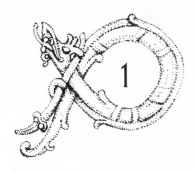

I was twelve years old when I first saw Markaby and twenty-two when it finally became mine. I would not like you to think those years had been completely taken up by an obsession with the house. I had other things to think about—growing up, for instance, and establishing myself in my chosen career—but still I had never forgotten it. The strength of my feeling for the place was peculiar, because I am not, in the usual way, a girl who desires things, not acquisitive at all. I suppose you would have to call me tenacious, though. Yes, tenacious and resourceful and quick with my tongue, not easily daunted. All of which were to serve me well. But even if I had wanted to forget Markaby, I would not have been allowed to do so. Every year, punctually and without fail, a reminder was delivered to me.

Markaby stands on an island off the Northumberland coast, looking out on the wild North Sea. The German Ocean, our forebears called it, and indeed, when you stand at Markaby and look out to sea, there is no land nearer than Jutland. The sea there is gray and cold and the waves white-fringed with foam, but it is so beautiful that once you have seen it you love it forever. Bamburgh, Craster,

Dunstanburgh, Alnwick, Warkworth, so the roll call runs, and then Markaby. Not a castle like the others, but a low range of stone buildings standing on an island in the sea with the feeling of great age about it.

The first time I saw it, the house was deserted and empty, but I think I knew even then, without being able to put it into words, that where I was standing had been a human settlement for many centuries. The feeling of history seemed to be absorbed through the soles of one's feet and through the hands and the skin and the eyes and the ears. I remember standing there and thinking the warmth was the sun, but it wasn't the sun at all; when I looked around there was no sun that day. What I was feeling came from perception nearly as old as the sun and closely related to it. I believe it is what a migrating bird must feel when it starts out on its flight and the whole history of its kind informs its body. I never had this feeling again—I suppose it is something only children can have—but I remember it.

Markaby was approached by a narrow coast road which ran parallel with the cliffs so that the sea was in sight all the time. Not much traffic came this way, as it seemed to lead from nowhere to nowhere. A few hundred yards out at sea and almost directly in line with the fishing village of Garrow was a small island. On it stood the house, lonely and beautiful. A narrow causeway joined the island and the mainland at low tide. It was at best a wet and slippery walk, because the sea had eaten away a lot of the rock which made up the path, tearing away a little more each year as it did everywhere along this coast. I always walked the path barefoot, my sandals slung around my neck, and traveled this route often that summer holiday, fascinated by the peace and decay of the island. I remember thinking then that the mainland and this island had once been a single unit, that they had grown up together in prosperity and fallen apart only with disuse.

From the island, as you looked down into deep water, there were fascinating outcroppings of rock. From above, it was like looking down into the remains of a submerged and ruined city. I was very fond of the legends of Atlantis and Lyonnesse and enjoyed the thought that a drowned city lay in the sea by the Northumbrian coast. Of course I knew it was natural rock formation, but you could always dream. I imagined swimming like a mermaid among those cool caverns. I loved to swim.

The country around Markaby was one of small hills with stone walls and narrow roads that wound up and down and in and out of the little rounded hills. It was a remote and silent landscape, full of wind and the light of the sea. An ancient church, a graveyard, a big house hidden by trees, and the tiny village of Garrow were the only signs that men had long been settled here. On the island, hard beside Markaby itself, was a steeply rising grass-covered mound, unlike any of the natural hills of the district. This was Dragon's Hill, and it had been so named on old maps for centuries, but before that it must have had another name that was older and truer. I didn't believe in the dragon, but the name had had some meaning, because the island on which Markaby stood was called Dragon's Eye.

There was a big notice stuck to the gatepost of Markaby that first day, the day after my twelfth birthday. In stolid archaic language it announced the auction of Markaby together with its tenements and messuages. I remember wondering what the words meant; I learned afterward that they simply referred to the lands with certain rights that went with the house. I don't believe even lawyers talk that way now. What an out-of-the-way, old-fashioned place Markaby was that they used such terms then! I stared at the notice and thought that it looked as though it had been there a long time, the wind and the rain had stained and torn at it so. But the sale was to be held that very day.

Markaby looked pretty run-down to me. I didn't think it would fetch much, not even with its tenements and messuages thrown in. It seemed to me that it might be in my power to own it. I knew that I had twelve hundred pounds belonging to me, because my guardian had told me so, assuring me that the money was for my very own use. When you are older, I think she said—but naturally I disregarded that provision.

The auction was held in the village hall, a shabby and sad-looking building which wouldn't have brought much in a sale either. To my surprise it was full of people— mostly men, but with a few women in sensible tweeds. Everyone was standing around talking (shouting, really, for they all had loud voices) and smoking. Not what I had expected at all. I wasn't daunted, however, and no one took much notice of me as I made my way through the crowd to the front, where the auctioneer stood on a platform. A table next to him held a glass of water and a hammer. As I reached him, he banged on the table with the hammer. The sale had begun.

One or two items were up for sale before Markaby. The auctioneer rattled off the names of a couple of cottages, and the bidding started. There was relative silence while the bidding went on, but at other times everyone was talking as loudly as ever and the auctioneer had once or twice to bang away with his hammer in order to get himself noticed. He took it all in good humor, though, as if he were used to it. The cottages were bid for more keenly than I had expected and became really quite expensive to my young ears, but I took it for granted that they were well-cared-for, opulent cottages for people who were rich enough to have afforded a proper house, but liked a cottagey feeling. I knew plenty of people like that in the part of London where I lived with my guardian. My guardian was not such a person; she had built herself a square modern house, which was, like her, a good deal more subtle than it looked at first.

Then Markaby came up for sale. No one seemed to take much notice. The auctioneer described the property and waited for the bidding to start. The level of the conversations going on all around dropped a bit, but it could hardly be called silence. Here goes, I thought. I cleared my throat and held my head high. No sense in beating about the bush. "Nine hundred pounds," I said loudly.

There was suddenly complete silence. Everyone was looking at me. I stood my ground. "Nine hundred pounds," I said again. This time there was no silence, but a murmur. I held my head up, stared straight ahead, and said nothing more.

Long afterward, when I knew Grace Beanley, who was there that afternoon, she told me about it. "You stood there bolt upright, like a young Daniel come to judgment, and called out your bid, and we none of us knew what to do about it. Staggered, we all was. Yes, staggered we were, love, and struck dumb with surprise. I could see Mr. Gregory, the auctioneer, didn't know what to do. He knew there was some rule that children under a certain age couldn't make a bid at an auction that was legally binding."

"I didn't know that," I murmured.

"No, of course you didn't, but you looked so proud and bold, he wasn't sure you might not do it, somehow."

"I wanted to."

"There you stood, and Robert Berwick looked at you hard. He wanted Markaby too. Never mind why, but he did. He wanted it as much as you did."

"I know that now."

"And so he bid higher than you."

"Yes, he did." I well remember that moment when a tall man, black-haired with a streak of white at each temple and with bright-blue eyes, had rapped out: "Nine hundred and fifty pounds." A wave of anger and possessiveness surged through me.

"A thousand pounds," I said stoutly. The audience murmured, and the auctioneer looked at me without acknowledging my bid, so I said it again. "A thousand pounds."

Robert Berwick glared at me. "Two thousand pounds," he said in a loud voice. There was a pause. Another voice took up the bidding, then another. The bidding passed on and obliterated me. I shall never forget the pain of hurt pride and disappointment that stung me. Two voices, Robert Berwick's and another's, stood out. Markaby went for twenty thousand pounds in the end; Robert Berwick (clearly identified by name, in a rather servile way, by the auctioneer) got the place.

I stumbled out, angry tears blinding me, and sank down on the grass. "That big man," I thought. "He's my enemy." I lay down and buried my face in the grass, which smelled of dogs and cats. I have noticed that grass has a very strong identity.

A hand touched my shoulder. I knew at once who it was, without being told. I had sharp, intuitive perception as a child; as I grew older, it faded.

"You made me feel a fool," I muttered, without looking up.

"Not me, no." I knew he was going to say something about it being life, or the way things were, or some other putting-off sort of thing that people do say at such times, and I raised my head to give him a sharp look. But I saw he wasn't looking at me at all, just staring into the distance.

"I wanted it," I said.

"I saw that." He stood over me, looking enormous. "Get up, young lady, you can't talk to me from down there. That's better. But you see I *had* to have it." When I stood up he still looked enormous; he was built big as well as tall. He was dressed in shabby tweeds and wearing that sort of tweed hat you call a deerstalker. It was a battered old hat that the years seemed to have shaped to his head. "Why do you want Markaby?" He was looking at my face, studying its shape and color. I was very fair. I am still fair, my hair a silver ashen color, but it was even paler then and it made my eyes seem a brighter blue. I supposed I was quite plain.

"I don't know," I said, turning my head away. But it wasn't true—I did know. Markaby seemed built for me. I felt at home with it. "It's on an island," I muttered, not wishing to share my real reasons with my enemy. "I've always wanted to own an island."

He believed that. It was a child's reason and I was a child. "Only a small one." He seemed almost relieved that I had had, after all, such a simple motivation. "Hardly one at all. So no one put you up to it?"

15

"I did it all on my own."

"I believe you. I'm Robert Berwick. I live at The Grange. What's your name?"

"Kate."

He was patient. "Kate what?"

"Kate Melrose," I said reluctantly. I was a rather cautious, suspicious child. I hadn't learned the sort of generosity that could spill out personal details.

"And where do you live?"

"London."

He waited, confident, I suppose, that his steady, re-assuring presence would get more response.

"I'm having a caravan holiday up here with my guardian," I said. "She's a schoolteacher." My lips closed again. Enough was enough.

"And where do you live in London, Kate Melrose?" he asked gravely.

I replied, still reluctantly, but clearly. "Number five, Snow Street, Pimlico." The words tripped roundly off my tongue. I rather liked them. Perhaps this was why I added an unsolicited detail. Or perhaps (who can tell?) I really wanted him to know. It was a fact that I found myself telling at surprising times, as if a compulsion was on me. "I'm an orphan."

I didn't tell him, although I knew it myself, that this was why I wanted Markaby. I sometimes had family fantasies, just as other children might have food fantasies, and imagined a family and a background for myself. I invented different parents to suit different moods. Sometimes my mother was an artist and my father a wild young man who ran away and left us both. She then died and I was left alone in the world. The background for this family was Paris, which then seemed to me foreign and appealing and romantic. I was always careful to weave in a bit of story to explain how it was I was not French. Another dream story gave me a heartless mother who had run away and left me and gone on to carve out a marvelous career on her own (I wasn't sure as what—sometimes as an actress, once as a distinguished surgeon), and I would one day meet her and she would know me and declare herself. I enjoyed that bit. Sometimes I welcomed her with open arms and at others I turned her down flat and told her to go off back into her own selfish world. It all depended on my mood. There were times when I had black, black dreams in which my mother was stupid and feckless and idle and simply mislaid me and never came looking, or other bad dreams in which my father was so cruel and brutal that she must lose me for my own sake. And occasionally, of course, I told myself that they were just an ordinary couple who had died.

Places came into this dream world, too. I would look at a house or a stretch of country or a town and wonder if I had come from it, sometimes actually pretending that I had. I had done this with Markaby, but Markaby had such a strong attraction for me that it did not even seem a pretense. I never told anyone of this game I played. It was my secret.

I think Robert Berwick saw a shutter come down in my face then, because he stopped asking me questions and drew a paper bag out of his pocket and offered me a toffee. They were strong peppermint toffees and they silenced us both while we chewed.

"Hmmm," he said, settling his hat firmly on his head. "You're a determined young woman, I can see that. Clever, too, probably. You look clever."

I supposed he meant I looked plain, homely, and as I

saw myself that way too, I wasn't put out. My ambition in those days was to have thick black curly hair and pink cheeks. I was pale-skinned and pale-haired, my eyes my only strong color.

"You look a man of substance," I said, thoughtfully, but without malice. I'd been reading a lot of Victorian novels, Dickens, Thackeray, George Eliot. Men of substance figured often in them and I had wondered what they looked like. Robert Berwick seemed to fit the phrase exactly.

"Yes, I'm pretty substantial," he said with a laugh. "I won't say the ground shakes as I walk, but it does notice I'm treading on it." He looked at his watch. "Well, good-bye, young lady, I'm glad to have met you." He touched his hat and walked away. He got into a Rolls Royce parked in the road. It was silver-gray and antique in appearance, but it suited him: they matched each other, Robert Berwick and his car. He waved his hand and drove off.

And that was the last I saw of Robert Berwick. Well, more or less.

I trailed back to my guardian, who was sitting placidly smoking and reading at the caravan door. When I told her a little of what had happened, she was very sympathetic. My guardian, Lydia Shelley, always accorded me full adult status.

There was a great moon that night and it was as warm as it ever is in that northern county. They had been hay-making in the farms near Markaby and the sweet smell of the new-cut hay lay over the countryside. Lydia was visiting friends in Newcastle and was to be back just before midnight. I took some fruit for my supper and sat by the sea to eat it, looking out toward Markaby on its island. Wine-dark, Homer had called his sea. Perhaps the Aegean is purple, but the North Sea is gray; that night it was made of silver. The tide was out and the old causeway stood out boldly. On the island the house and the little hill rising beside it were clearly silhouetted. On impulse I got up and started to walk across the causeway. The water lapped gently against the old stones, but did not touch my feet.

I scrambled up the path to where the house stood, aloof and slightly forbidding. For the first time I thought it would have been an uncomfortable place to own. Nevertheless, it still attracted me. It seemed the strangest, most sea-girt, most beautiful place there ever could be. I fancied myself walking through those quiet rooms. How would it feel to be inside, looking out?

Solemnly I approached the house. A low stone wall with a locked iron gate stood between me and the house. Markaby lay there before me, shuttered, enigmatic, asleep in the moonlight. It was as quiet as the palace of the Sleeping Princess. It might have been dormant for centuries.

As I searched, it seemed to me that one small square window reflected the moonlight like a mirror. I climbed over the wall and went nearer the house. Not too near. I kept my distance. The window did look like a mirror.

"Mirror, mirror on the wall," I chanted. "Who is the fairest of us all?"

It was a silly thing to say, because I could not even see my own reflection. It was a taunt, a shout of defiance, and I knew it.

Then the moon went behind a cloud and the mirror reverted to a dark window pane. At once it seemed to me I could see a face behind the window, a pale face which stared out at me for a moment, then retreated backward into the room and disappeared.

I was surprised, and I think I was a little abashed that I had been caught staring in, but I was not frightened. I knew what I had seen was human and I never for one moment thought of ghosts or apparitions.

I skipped back over the wall and down toward the causeway. I didn't like what I had seen very much, but I was not scared. There was a dreamlike quality to the episode which erased fear. "So somebody lives there, after all," I thought, and that was that. *Then.*

The tide, now coming in, touched my feet as I walked back across the causeway, and threw up a curious little pebble which I picked up. It had been so carved by the sea that it looked like a little crouching man with a pointed hat and a long nose.

I hurried back and slid between the sheets in my bunk, and when Lydia came back, smelling of cigarettes and jolly from her wine at dinner, I pretended to be asleep. In my hand I had something clasped. It was the pebble from the causeway. I still had it when, after our holiday, we drove south, back to our house in London, and my life there.

I did not forget about Markaby, but I suppose I didn't think about it as much as I had expected. It faded. The memory of it lay there, at the back of my mind, but I had a lot of other things to think about. I seemed to grow up very fast after that holiday in Northumberland, stepping into the adult world, at first cautiously, like one testing the water of a great new sea, then hurrying, hurrying.

Once, tidying a drawer, I came across a set of photographs my guardian had taken at Garrow and Markaby. Casual, idle little snapshots, they evoked that summer. I could very nearly smell the sea and the damp sands and the grass. It seemed long ago, though. I felt like a veteran of a long war, looking back at pictures of the first campaign of all.

The photographs spilled on the floor and I picked them up. "It was dull for you, that holiday, I'm afraid," said Lydia, rescuing one picture and staring at it. "I can see that now."

"Oh no, I loved it," I said truthfully.

"There was nothing to do but walk and look at the sea." She put the photograph on the table, face upward, and we both stared at it. There I was, younger, thinner, needing a haircut and frowning into the camera. "Goodness, you look cross."

"No, it was the sun." But it hadn't been entirely. I *had* been cross, I could remember, and the camera had captured the cause of my distress.

In the background of the picture, a small rowboat was visible and kneeling beside it, busy making a repair to it, was a dark-haired boy. His face was turned away from the camera, but his back, hunched over his task, was clearly visible.

Suddenly I was back inside the twelve-year-old, scowling into the camera. I was angry because I had offered him help, and had been refused with a few short words delivered in a strong Northumberland accent.

"I remember that day so well. You sat on the sand such a long time watching that boy, until I thought to myself, why on earth doesn't she speak to him and ask him if she can join in? But you never did."

"Yes, I did," I said briefly, "and the answer was no. A rude boy. He said girls couldn't work on boats."

Lydia looked at me hard. "Any minute now something is going to catch fire, and it might just be you."

I laughed. She was good for me. My guardian was a highly successful and accomplished educationalist, the headmistress of a respected girls' school, a brilliant woman, with a full and happy life of her own. As romantic and imaginative as I was about my birth, I had never for one moment suspected Lydia of being my natural mother. But I loved her and she loved me.

"Why did you take me on?" I asked. It seemed a perfect opportunity to explore my background for the hundredth time. "In the beginning, I mean?"

She smoked, and thought about it before she answered, as if it were the first time. "Little scrap of a thing you were, and no beauty, so it wasn't for your looks. But you needed a home, for the hospital where you were couldn't keep you much longer. My sister, Jessie, who worked there, told me about you. That was one reason. Then you know I've always loved children and wanted one, but there are some people for whom sex is simply not an option. I'm one, I think. So there seemed little chance of a natural child of my own. When you came along, I took you." She smiled her huge, charming smile, and lit another of her expensive Turkish cigarettes. A loving, worldly woman, my guardian.

"Why did we go to Northumberland?" I asked. "What made you choose it as a holiday place?" You who love the sun and the south, I thought.

"I thought you'd enjoy it," she said. Cigarette smoke floated into the air in a perfect ring and then melted away.

"My twelve hundred pounds, my nest egg, where did it come from?"

"You know that, my dear. I've never kept it a secret from you. You were born in the hospital where my sister had worked. When you were offered for adoption a small sum of money had already been deposited in a bank in

Newcastle in your name. The bankers were your trustees; they still are."

"Did my mother die?" I watched Lydia closely.

"Adoptive parents don't know very much about the identity of the real mother," she said gently. "That's how adoption agencies work it. All I knew is that she was young and couldn't keep you. She may be dead."

A cloud of smoke from her cigarette floated in the air, above her, then drifted slowly between us. "Still, I wish I knew"—but this I said quietly and to myself.

I put the photographs away, but the memory of Markaby was not so easily banished.

Every Christmas a card came for me from Robert Berwick. He had a conventional taste in cards, so that every year there was a robin and a sprig of holly on the card and a country scene with deep snow. It told me a good deal, not only about his taste, but also about the quiet persistence of his character. Having made a choice, he stuck to it. I was a bit like that myself, so I understood.

For ten successive years the cards arrived, always bearing the same message inside: From Robert Berwick, with his respects. I came to take its arrival for granted. Then one year it did not come. It was a year in which my whole life changed.

I had not been idle in those years. At seventeen I had won a scholarship to the College of Dramatic Arts. I was there three years and I departed with the Sarah Siddons Medal for the Best Student Actress of the Year firmly clutched in my hand, convinced that every producer of note in the country would shortly be banging on my door. No one came. I auditioned a good deal, and several times had the mortification of hearing a producer say, "We'd love to have you, dear, if you can get an Equity card." They knew and I knew, and they knew that I knew, that without work I could not get a card and without a card I could not get work. It was a vicious circle. It *could* be broken, but only if a producer wanted you enough to run, heart in hand, and say, "I *must* have her for this part. You *must* let her have her card." No one had wanted me that much.

The person whose magic wand changed my luck was, of course, a man, a producer and actor. I adored him then, I adore him now, but in between I've come near to hating him. Albert Reger—Bert to you and me and the world. He was and is tough, calculating, cunning and wheedling. Also brilliant and creative, and much loved in the theater. A tall man, always untidy, always in a hurry, he could nevertheless talk and gossip for hours if the mood took him and the talk was right.

I worked like a dog for him. I made friends, a girl called Toya from Japan by way of New York, a boy called Dickon; I made enemies, including a rival actress by the name of Julie Bell. And of course I fell in love with Bert, and of course it came unstuck. He was kind, though, Bert was, and when he saw how things were with me he got me a film contract with one hand and gave me a push with the other. He'd gone through it all before, no doubt, and perhaps the fact that Julie Bell was so beautiful and could walk into all my parts helped. I took it hard, but I made the film. I was glad I did later, because it helped finance what was to come.

The film, made in Spain, was called *Consort of Dracula*, and I was the consort. I enjoyed Spain in spite of my mood and my thwarted emotions. I added underwater swimming to my skills during breaks from work. It was fascinating exploring along the bottom of the sea. In my temporary state of riches I bought myself all the necessary equipment, including one of those suits that protect you from the cold. Swimming was discovery, always discovery.

It was Christmas by the time I had finished my blood-thirsty activities as Dracula's chosen, and I spent most of the holiday sleeping off a deep fatigue that had fallen on me. I was depressed and uneasy. In the future and still unknown to me lay the success of the film I had just made and a contract for three more. All I knew then was that I was the actress whom Bert had tried out and cast aside for being beyond the pale of contemporary taste. I hadn't written to Dickon or to any of my friends; neither had they tried to get in touch with me. I felt strange and neglected and at odds with myself; full of self-pity, I felt unloved.

I was still sleeping fitfully on the day after Christmas when Lydia came into the room and handed me a drink in a tall, cold glass which, eyes shut, I took to be orange juice till I tasted its sharp, stimulating contents. "Tastes like champagne," I said sleepily. "What is it really?"

"Champagne." She sat down on the bed beside me.

"Champagne before breakfast?" I said. "How decadent."

"It may be before breakfast to you, my love, but it's before lunch to me, and it's my birthday. I'm celebrating." She gave me a long look. "Also I wanted to wake you up."

"You've done that, all right." I leaned forward and gave her a hug. "Many happy returns. I forgot you were a Christmas baby."

"Many long yules," Lydia said cheerfully.

That day I examined my Christmas mail, turning it over

idly. Christmas cards viewed after Christmas cease to appeal. "None from Robert Berwick. The first Christmas for years that he has forgotten me."

"Perhaps he's ill," suggested my guardian. She was stroking Tiger, her lean and serious tomcat, now virtually retired from active service, but full of scars of honor.

There was a card from Bert and, written inside, in his neat, precise hand, the words "Love from Bert and Happy Landings, Darling." He always used that out-of-date early-thirties slang; it was his trademark and we had all copied it. Once it had seemed clever and funny; now it annoyed me. I threw the card away, and my guardian retrieved it. "A lovely view of London painted by Canaletto. You should keep it for a while." And she propped it up on a table.

I picked up the next piece of mail, a thick, expensive white envelope. The missive inside was typewritten and I unfolded it with curiosity. "Oh!" My exclamation made my guardian look up. "He's dead. Robert Berwick is dead."

"I was afraid he might be," said Lydia sadly, "when you didn't get a card."

I handed the letter to her in some bewilderment. "It's from his solicitors in Berwick-on-Tweed. He's left me Markaby if I still want it. He died some months ago but he didn't tell them my address. They had to find me. It's so strange."

"I believe he was a very rich man. My friend Michael Sars has a cottage up there." Lydia was studying the letter. "The house and island are yours if you want them, but they revert to his other heirs if you don't want them, or if you die without heirs. Seems straightforward." She handed the letter back.

"Of course, I can't take it," I said.

"Oh no, it was just a childish whim." Her voice was innocent, too innocent.

"You're not deceived for a minute. You know that I want the place."

"I know how tenacious you are," she said slowly. "Perhaps I don't know everything about you, my dear, but I do know that. And I've seen your face each Christmas as his card came. It had your *remembering* look, and I used to think: she hasn't forgotten, nor given up."

"No, I never had," I admitted. "I don't know why, but it has been so."

We sat looking at each other.

"The upkeep would be a drain," she said. "Could you manage it? I could help, if you like."

"No." I was fierce. "If I do it, then it must be all me. Markaby must be mine and I must owe it to no one."

Lydia did not answer. She put down the cat, who strolled off, and lit a cigarette. "No doubt you're right," she said. "One should always be independent, if possible. It pays in the end. Look at me: the completely happy woman."

There was a mildly ironic tone to the last part, but I chose to take it at face value.

"I believe you are," I said seriously, "but it's built into you—happiness, I mean. Not me, I've got something else. I don't know what, but it rules out happiness and gives me some other motivation instead. Ambition, perhaps."

"And pride, and possessiveness, and sheer cussedness," said Lydia, cocking one eyebrow at me. "As a baby you always wanted to lean forward to grab the lollipop, and I don't think you've changed."

"Not as much as I'd like," I admitted. "Tell me more about me as a baby."

Lydia retreated a little, as she always did on this subject. "My sister looked after you when you were very small, you know. Jess had young children herself."

"Please go on," I urged.

Lydia took a deep breath. "Yes, well, we've never talked much about all that. My fault. It seemed better so. It's only lately that I've realized how much it has always been there with you, in your mind, eating into it."

"You've noticed?" I was surprised.

"Of course." She dismissed my surprise, as if she had always seen more than I had guessed, which was very likely true. "Although I know next to nothing about your mother, I do know that she had lived in the country near Markaby. The money you were endowed with had been deposited in a bank at Newcastle, which is not far away. I did ask a few questions but got short shrift for the answers. I *have* wondered if you were related to Robert Berwick. Or if he thought you were. Now you know as much as I do." She lit another cigarette. "The champagne has gone flat."

"My grandfather?" I queried thoughtfully. "Robert Berwick had grandchildren, I know."

"Perhaps," said Lydia. "Pity about the champagne. I'll drink it all the same, but I like the bubbles."

"But what a strange family to have a grandchild and let it be adopted. I suppose I was illegitimate? Which of his children was thought to have produced me?"

"It's all speculation," said Lydia. "I wish I hadn't put it in your mind. Forget it. You are yourself, that's what counts."

I ignored this. "One thing is settled, anyway." I picked up the lawyer's letter. "I accept the legacy. I shall have Markaby."

Lydia seemed to sense that I needed time to think. Abruptly, she exclaimed, "Oh, by the way, a fat package came by hand for you today. I kept it." She got up to get it for me. "Here you are." She kissed my cheek and hugged me warmly. "I have to run. I'll be out for the rest of the day. See you in the morning."

I took the package. It was thick and heavy, the address in a familiar typescript. With barely controlled excitement, I opened it. Inside was a note from Bert, clipped to a bulky sheaf of typed papers.

"I know, my dearest love," he wrote, "that you never believe a word I say, but to prove I do sometimes think of you, I enclose a play with a part for you. I can't promise anything, but work hard on it. Come back in two months' time and give me a beautiful reading of it."

I took out the script and sat down at the table and began to read. It was a new play, a modern play, by someone whose name meant nothing to me, but I knew before I had finished the first scene that it was everything I could have hoped for and like nothing the stage had seen for years. I could just hear Bert saying, "This play has got *class*, dear, class and style." The play was a comedy, but, like all good comedies, it had its serious side. The chief character was a young married woman by the name of Clara—but I won't go on; you will already have recognized the play. Everyone knows it now, and you will understand my enthusiasm for the part of Clara.

I got up, made some coffee and returned to the play. I read it once, then went back and read it again. It was almost midnight by the time I leaned back and took a deep breath. The last act was not perhaps as brilliant as the first, but with Bert producing it, any weakness would disappear. I already thought of myself as Clara, though the part was long and difficult. I should need to study, really work on it.

I came to a decision without even being conscious that I had reached it. I would go to Markaby. I would study my part there.

"See you in the morning," Lydia had said, but by the morrow I was gone. I left a note on the kitchen table for Lydia and took an early train to Northumberland. My destination was Berwick-upon-Tweed, the town not far from Markaby where Naseby and Son, the firm of solicitors used by Robert Berwick, aptly lived.

"Seems silly to possess a house I haven't seen for years," I wrote. "I'm off to have a look around." Lydia would understand. It was what she would have done herself. "Will also drop in to see Robert Berwick's solicitors."

The train was crowded with Scots returning home to celebrate their New Year, but I walked its length and found a seat in the first compartment, which was empty except for a young man. He was asleep. I settled myself comfortably in a corner facing the direction of travel and took out a pocket volume of Shakespeare's plays. I was reading *Cymbeline*. I had heard a major production was being planned, and (who knew?) I might get a look-in.

It was a lovely day, one of those pale, quiet days that sometimes come in the English midwinter—a day on which it is possible, whatever one's troubles, to be very, very happy and peaceful at heart. The sunlight shone on fields which were bare and earthy, but which already offered a hint of spring. I read *Cymbeline* and relaxed. The fat woman who had boarded the train at our first stop leaned forward and said, "It's unnatural, this mild weather. We shall pay for it later, you'll see. A green December always means a full kirkyard." Her mission of alarm accomplished, she leaned back in her seat and got on with her knitting. The young man in the corner slept on.

After a while I came out of my own preoccupations to observe him. His face looked white and tired. He must be even more tired than I am, I thought.

Suddenly, as if he felt my eyes upon him, he awoke, and he didn't look tired at all, but very alert and somewhat older than I had imagined. Not so young as I had thought, but older than I. The sun was streaming into the carriage, and he took a pair of dark glasses from his pocket and put them on. They performed their usual magic of transforming the face. I noticed how suntanned he was, as if a lot of his life was spent in the open air, and how the laugh lines of the mouth were deep. A more sophisticated face than I had thought.

Our fellow traveler put down her knitting and shook her head at him. "I hope you don't mind me saying so," she said, "but you'll damage your eyes with those spectacles. They do harm in the long run, you know."

"No, I don't mind your saying so at all," he said in a pleasant deep voice. "But you mustn't mind if I take no notice."

"Oh no, I don't care. People never do take notice, but I was right to speak. It's always right to speak." And she gazed out of the window, satisfied, duty temporarily done.

I think I must have slept a long time after that, because when I looked around once again, we were crossing the Tyne and drawing into Newcastle station and the woman was packing away the knitting and preparing herself to get off the train. The man was reading a thick paperback called *The Viking Invasions.*

He looked up as the woman left the carriage, and

31

although his eyes were still masked by his dark lenses, I saw his mouth turn down in a half-smile. "Good," he said, and removed the glasses. "Now I can take these off. I don't know why it is, but helpful advice always makes me awkward."

"I wondered if she'd have some for me," I admitted.

"She looked at you once or twice, as if she was thinking of something, but you were sleeping like a baby." He laughed. "It put her off for a bit, but she had a try, though. She leaned forward, gave you a good look and said: 'Sleep in the morning, wakeful come night.'"

"What an old witch," I said. "I need advice as much as anyone, I expect, but not from her." I watched the plump figure of our late companion disappear down the length of the platform. She was weighted down by a heavy coat and two bags, but she was light on her feet and made haste. A kind old thing, really, but quite wrong in her advice to me—I stayed that night in a Berwick hotel and slept like a log. Perhaps, however, in the long run she was not so far wrong, for I was to know many wakeful nights.

I went back to *Cymbeline*, and he to the Vikings. We did not speak again. But it would not be true to say I ceased to notice him, because I remained acutely conscious of the figure sitting quietly opposite. I watched with pleasure as the train swept across the graceful bridge over the Tweed, and the red roofs, old town walls and battlements of Berwick came close. As we both got off at Berwick-upon-Tweed, I sensed my fellow passenger looking at me with considerably more interest.

He was met by a striking, tall girl, hair tied up in a silk scarf, casual in a dark fur coat; they drove off together in a small Fiat. As far as I could see they hadn't spoken a word to each other, but acted silently and with co-ordination. I mutely saluted a good performance.

As a matter of fact I had already been silently allotting him a part. Well, he wasn't difficult to cast. Whether he could act or not, he was built for big parts. He had the sort of face every producer hoped to get for Hamlet. Also Richard II, Romeo too, and, yes, definitely costume, with a strong romantic appeal and a lot of poetry. No comedy, though, unless I was much mistaken. The girl who had met him was a beauty. The way they had moved together they ought to be dancers, but living up here they were more likely to be farmers. As I hailed a cab to take me to the King's Head Hotel, I remembered the book on the Vikings and wondered. Still, I knew my England and knew that many people attended courses on local history and read books about the archaeology of their own district. I decided to dismiss thoughts of my traveling companion and directed my attention to the beauty of the just-setting sun.

The hotel seemed almost empty. A notice above the entrance reported that Charles Dickens had stayed here while on a lecture tour. The days when Berwick-on-Tweed was a posting place between London and Edinburgh and when coaches and travelers were in and out of the King's Head daily were long in the past. They now seemed as distant as the days when the town had been a border stronghold, bitterly contested between Scots and English, and when the thick fortified walls around it had served a real purpose.

I was given a pretty, old-fashioned room, with a window seat overlooking the main street, and a four-poster bed, trimmed with faded chintz. A pink-cheeked girl in a starched apron brought me a laden tray, and I sat in the window seat, sipping my tea. The street before me sloped gently downward to the old town gate. Across the road an old gray stone house let a stream of light from an un-curtained upper window fall across the paving stones and cobbles. Inside, I could see a comfortable room, a leaping fire and a child playing with a kitten. I felt as though I had slipped back a century—I imagined myself as young Ellen Ternan, actress and child of actors, come up here secretly with her lover and patron, the distinguished novelist Charles Dickens, and left sitting alone while the great man appeared in public. Young, pretty, mercenary Ellen. How well I could understand her relationship with her magnetic lover. God knows what the Victorian stage must have been like for any girl; it certainly could not have been a place of romance for Ellen, born to strolling players and thrust onto the stage to act with Fanny and Maria, her sisters, as soon as she could talk.

I turned back into the lighted room, shutting out the dark and the past. My bag waited to be unpacked. I took out my nightgown and laid it over the bed. My book of Shakespeare plays I put on the bed table.

On the wall above was a framed map, an old one. In the corner were the date, 1838, and the words "Joseph Royal, Cartographer to the University of Durham." With interest I noted that it was a map of the coastline nearby and also the hinterland. I could identify the site of Markaby by the island: Dragon's Eye, it was named. The mapmaker had drawn a strange creature in the sea by the island. I was looking at it closely and thinking it looked vaguely like a dragon, when the maid came in to collect the tea tray.

"What a nice old map," I said.

"Oh yes, we've got lots of lovely old things here. You *have* finished, miss? You never touched the scones."

"I couldn't manage those, but I ate the toast. And the shortbread."

"A London appetite," sighed the girl. "I could eat twice that much and think nothing of it." She was piling things on the tray. "I shouldn't take any notice of that old map, miss, it's bound to be wrong."

"Oh no, Joseph did a beautiful, careful job, but I wonder why he drew this little monster in the sea? Can you see?" I pointed it out to her.

She put down the tray and came over and had a look.

"Oh yes, that's toward Dunstanburgh. I used to live near there. Craster, I come from. Oh well, that'll be their monster." Having settled the matter to her own satisfaction, she picked up the tray and prepared to depart.

"What monster?"

"Oh, a fat little monster with a big head and a tail that pops in and out of the sea, so we used to say at school when we were kids," she said placidly. She carried the tray to the door and opened it expertly with a quick bump from her rear, then stood there talking to me, holding the door with one hand, the tray with the other. "It's only a story, miss. Just one of those tales."

"Yes." I nodded at her. Indeed, I could see that with a name like Dragon's Eye, the countryside would have to invent a monster to fit the name. Still, the name meant *something*. I was studying the map. "As a matter of fact, the shape of the coast just there *could* look like the outline of a dragon and the little island would be his eye. I suppose that's how it started."

"Oh yes, miss, that'll be it. We used to frighten ourselves by saying it ate young girls, but it never ate one that I know of. No one was ever missing about there that I heard of, except one, and he were called Billy English, and plenty to run away from by all accounts."

I nodded, not much interested in her old school friend who had run away from home. "Before you go—" She paused, waiting. "Is there someplace to rent a car?"

"Grover's Garage, 'twixt the Sandgate and the Bastion, will let you have one, I expect. Grover's hire 'em out. Not much choice, though. Take it or leave it, it'll be with them."

"Where is the Sandgate?"

"Just down the hill. You can't miss it."

When someone tells you that a place can't be missed, you can be sure you are going to have a job finding it. This time was no exception. Grover's Garage proved elusive. I found the Sandgate and I found the Bastion, but the garage which was supposed to lie between them was nowhere to be seen. Or so it seemed the next morning, when I went into the old town.

I was out early, and the shops were just opening. A greengrocer was arranging a box of cabbage, great white-hearted things, next to a tray of red and green peppers. From a baker's shop came the smell of warm bread. In a little dry-goods shop a tortoiseshell cat slept in the sun among the skeins of knitting wool and the reels of thread.

Behind a high wall was a red brick building from which floated girlish voices singing a hymn. The Convent of the Sacred Heart contained a girls' school run by the nuns. Even as I watched, a tiny, aged nun crept along the street and let herself in by a side gate. It was a step backward into the past. I thought of the lover of Ellen Ternan and wondered if he had stood here and seen such a view. Then a wind laden with auto fumes and diesel oil blew southward down the street, and I was back in the present again.

I went into a grocer's shop and bought a few provisions so that I could have a picnic lunch if I wanted one. Plans for exploration were beginning to take shape in my mind.

Farther down the street was a shop selling newspapers and cigarettes and ice cream. I went in and asked for a guidebook to the county. A woman was standing behind the counter, straightening the already neat shelves laden with chocolate boxes and toffees.

"Oh, this one is useful and not expensive." She produced a paperback called *Northumbrian Walks*. "We sell quite a number. I recommend it."

"Thanks. And some cigarettes, please, and a block of plain chocolate." I might be out all day and supplies were always useful. "I'm looking for Grover's Garage," I said as I paid.

She gave me a radiant smile. "Oh, just around the corner. You can't miss it."

"Perhaps not, but I seem to manage it."

"I'll show you." She came to the door of her shop and pointed. "There—away with you, then."

I saw a narrow alley at the curve of the street, and on the wall of the corner building an arrow and the word "Grover's," and there was Grover's Garage, almost inaccessibly placed in a court behind the street. I walked around and spoke to a man washing down a sedate black Rolls on which was a little flag. He raised his head from his work.

"Morning."

"Good morning. Mr. Grover?"

"No. He's been dead these thirty years. Jackson's the name."

"I want to hire a car for the day. Anything will do."

He looked thoughtful and seemed to be studying my appearance.

"The King's Head suggested you," I said hastily.

His face cleared. "Let you have an old Daimler," he said. "Bit heavy on fuel, but drives like a dream."

"I was thinking of something smaller," I said.

"Nay. It's the Daimler or nothing." He went back to his polishing.

Take it or leave it, the maid had said of Grover's, and she evidently knew what she was talking about.

"I'll take it, then," I said quickly, before he could forget I was there altogether—a process which already seemed to have begun.

He threw down his rag. "I'll go and get it out for you, then." And he disappeared behind a great double door.

In a few minutes he appeared at the other side of the courtyard, at the wheel of a high, elegant, but ancient Daimler, silver in color and upholstered in powder blue.

"Lady that sold me this used to buy her clothes regular in Paris," he announced with satisfaction. "Went over, twice a year, regular as clockwork, till she died."

"I can believe it," I said, wondering how many decades had passed since the fashionable lady had died. It was a car such as a duchess, more at home in London, Paris or New York than Northumberland, might have used. I placed it about 1937. I should certainly not have an unnoticed journey about the countryside in this machine.

"Everyone'll know you're from Grover's," said Jackson cheerfully, revealing an unexpected interest in publicity. "Well known, that car is."

Considering what luxury he was providing, he asked a reasonable charge. I paid, showing him my driver's license and banker's card. He checked both with the frank interest of those who like a new face and don't see many.

"Bit difficult for you to run a garage tucked away around here, isn't it?" I asked, when I was in the driving seat.

"Everyone knows us," he said. "Used to be a livery stable where the gentry kept their horses when they were in town. Lots of big families used to keep a town house here to spend the winter in, you know, in the old days."

"An excellent practice," I said absently; I was studying the controls of the car.

"Old ways die hard around here," he said. "Take this Rolls, for instance: belongs to the Lord Lieutenant of Northumberland. We used to keep his carriage for him when he was in town and now we keep his car." He gave a final polish to the Rolls and turned around to look at me again. "Up here on holiday then? That's right, enjoy it. You'll be comfortable in the car; and she'll give you a lovely ride."

He was right about the car; she moved like a dream. I sat, high above the rest of the traffic, as if in a bus, and sailed through the countryside in state. I enjoyed it, so he was half right about the holiday.

I drove south rapidly, avoiding the main roads, and making my way through narrow winding country lanes. A thin mist lay over the top of the hills, but the sun was breaking through. It would be a fine day. I passed Holy Island; Bamburgh Castle rose up on the horizon and dropped behind me; then the noble outline of Dustanburgh appeared. I saw the word "Craster" on a signpost. I slowed my speed. Suddenly I did not want to get to Markaby too soon.

It was ten years since I had seen the house. In that time, I had changed from a child to a woman. To all that crowd who had been at the auction when I had bid for Markaby I would now be unrecognizable. What would Markaby seem to me? If I had changed, why not the village and the house? I was altered inside, as well as in appearance. I might hate it all now. And if I did, a dream would be gone. Something that had fed and nourished me for years would have dissipated. I was frightened.

I stopped the car and got out. I took a deep breath of pure, cold air with a salty smell of the sea about it. I crossed the rough turf and found I could look down on the sea. There it was, curling away roughly beneath me, thundering down upon an edge of pale sand. The beach was quite deserted. On the skyline was the mighty ruin of Dustanburgh Castle, perched on its cliff with the sea dashing against the rocks below. All but impregnable from attack, only time had defeated it. Still it stood there, massively defiant.

I turned away from the sea to look inland. Here and there on the hills I spotted sheep grazing. It was too early yet in the year for lambing, but it would start soon, bringing with it the promise of spring. The hardy Cheviot sheep dotted across the distant hills looked much as they must have when the Scots swept south, looting and marauding.

I went back to the car, satisfied. On all sides I had seen evidence of continuity. Without any more hesitation, I drove to Markaby.

The village of Garrow, which lies so close to Markaby, was all laid out along one main street. It appeared unchanged, although I could see one or two newer houses that must have been built since my last visit. But they had been carefully designed to fit in with the rest of the village. The post office was open and doing business; the village store still had a Christmas tree in the window.

I drove straight through, identifying without any trouble the field where Lydia and I had camped in our caravan. It was empty, but I knew it by the great oak tree that stood in one corner. I stopped the car here, parked it in the exact spot where we had always parked, and took the path toward Dragon's Eye, my food in a shoulder bag.

The path rose and then sloped gently down toward the causeway. At its crest I halted for my first view of Markaby. There it was, smaller than I had remembered— but I liked it just as much as I ever had.

The tide was ebbing fast now, leaving a wide band of gleaming sand on which an early rider had left hoof prints. The causeway was uncovered, which pleased me. Ten years ago I wouldn't have much minded a paddle in the cold North Sea. Today, I was wearing smart black boots. For the first time, I wondered who had been living in Markaby all these years, if, indeed, anyone had. I supposed I could find all that out from the lawyers.

The round, irregular stones that formed the path through the sea were still shining wet. Here and there a trail of seaweed was flopped across the way, still fresh and alive-looking, as if the sea had only just dropped it there. I had to walk carefully, keeping an eye on where my feet were going.

Thus preoccupied, it was not until I was scrambling up the track that led to Markaby itself that I saw that someone was there before me.

Standing by the house and looking up at it was a man. He had his back to me, and the collar of his jacket was pulled up against the wind. A lean old collie dog stood by his side, and a piebald horse was tied up to the gatepost of Markaby. Unlike me, he had neither walked nor come by car.

He turned toward me as I approached; at once I recognized him as the man on the train. He knew me too, and gave me a faint smile, accompanied with the sketch of a bow. It was an old-fashioned gesture that was oddly attractive. He was wearing riding breeches, and this fact, together with the aged dog and the horse's ugly face, suggested to me that he was a vet who took over animals no one else would keep.

"You'll have a wet walk," he said, eyeing my guidebook. "There'll be rain before midday."

"Rain's nothing to me," I returned. If he wanted to know what I was doing here, I thought, he could go on wondering. It was my business.

"Nice house, isn't it?" he said, turning back to look at Markaby. "Pity it's going to be pulled down."

"What!"

"Oh yes, have to be. No one's lived here for years. No one ever will again. No, it'll have to go." I thought I heard a certain satisfaction in his voice.

There was something puzzling here. "Is it your property, then?" I queried cautiously. I knew it could not be.

He frowned. "No," he said briefly. "It's part of an estate at present in probate. . . . The will's not yet proved, you understand." I nodded. "But in the end, yes, I expect the property to become mine. And then, well, we shall see." He gave the stone gatepost a kick and some powdery dust floated down. He shook his head. "It's in a bad state."

I looked at the house. "I think it looks good for another

hundred years," I said firmly. "It does *look* shut up and empty, though." I managed to sound detached and not overinterested. "I wonder why?"

I thought he wasn't going to answer at first, then he said, "It belonged to someone who's now dead, and he never leased it out."

"It looks furnished." I had been studying the house. The curtains were not drawn and I could see furniture.

"He had a reason for keeping it partly furnished. It's not been lived in. I didn't say it hadn't been used," he said tersely.

"I like the island very much." It was time to change the subject, from the sound of his voice.

"Oh, it's a nice enough place. Lonely, of course, but beautiful."

"What a strange name: Dragon's Eye." I allowed myself, falsely, to sound a little nervous. "And it says 'Monsters' on an old map I saw."

He smiled. "No dragon. Not as far as I know. No monsters either, with feet to set on Dragon's Eye, save for human ones. Take no notice of anything you hear. The name is really Dragonsey—it's a Viking place name. So is Markaby. The Vikings came here from Norway, settled, built a homestead and farmed it. They're still here."

He was interrupted by a wail from the dog. "Quiet, Thisbe," he said, patting her head and adding affectionately, "Silly bitch." She rolled her eyes at him and pawed him fondly. "She hates it here, says it makes her nervous." Not a vet after all, I thought.

"Is the horse all right?" I asked, casting my eyes toward the piebald that stood there grazing, one foot moving restlessly.

"No nerves about that one. She'd eat if her tail was on fire," he said. "The faster, probably, to see she got the food before the fire did."

"I noticed on the train that you were reading a book about the Vikings."

"And you were reading Shakespeare."

"So I was." We confronted each other. It was out now, the truth that yesterday we had spent a good part of the journey quietly studying each other.

"I'm interested in the Viking settlement in this county," he said. The black look that had been on his face while he talked about the house lifted. He had an expressive face; his moods could be clearly read as they appeared and passed. His enthusiasms, loves and hates would always be revealed in his face. After Bert, who could look one thing and mean another, I found this refreshing. "Are you interested, too?" I could see the light in his face.

"I'm an actress."

"Oh." I saw him admit the fact and handle it cautiously. For some reason it gave him trouble. Doesn't like actresses, I thought. Ah well, I hadn't expected spontaneous joy.

While I talked, my eyes had been on the horse; there was something about her that worried me. Now I drew his attention to her: "She's lame, I think."

"What?" He jerked around, stood looking at his mount for a second, then dropped on one knee and lifted a hoof. She continued grazing. "Blast, you're right. The shoe's loose. It's new, too. That blacksmith ought to be shot. All right, girl, you can put your foot down." He stood up. "You seem to know about horses."

"No. Just observant."

"I'll have to walk her home. I'll miss lunch." He sounded hungry and suddenly much younger.

"I've brought a picnic. I was going to stay and eat here. There's plenty if you'd like to stay too."

"Love it," he said wistfully. "Wonder if I ought, though."

"Cheese, ham, and fruit. And wine. I've got some wine." I dug about in the bag and produced a bottle of Rhine wine. Suddenly I felt it ought to be champagne. "Will your horse mind if you drink? I mustn't take much, on account of the car I've got on hire. It takes some driving." I was being positively garrulous.

"Yes, I saw it. I know that car. Everyone hires it. It's famous, or infamous."

"It's a beautiful car," I said indignantly. "Fit for a queen. Or a queen mother."

He laughed. "There's a tale she *did* drive in it once. Years ago, when she was Duchess of York. It's probably untrue."

"I'll imagine it when I drive back to Berwick."

"Yes, I knew from the car you must be staying in Berwick. The King's Head?"

"Where else?"

I poured a glass of wine and held it out to him. "The glass is borrowed from there. We'll have to share. You have first turn."

"Sure?"

"I'm more hungry than thirsty." I sat down on the grass and stared out to sea. I felt excited, as though some unexpected and happy event was about to happen.

"Do you often picnic like this?" he asked.

I knew what he meant: Do you often picnic with someone you've only met once? "Only with strangers I meet in trains," I said. "But after all, it's a long journey between London and Berwick."

He looked away. "You have to watch the tides on this

coast. But don't worry, I am watching." Then he turned back to me. "Sorry, I didn't mean that question about the picnic the way it obviously sounded. I'm clumsy sometimes. Almost always, really. I'm enjoying myself."

"So am I."

We drank the wine and finished the meal by giving what remained to the dog. Not much conversation passed between us, but the silence was friendly. The dog came up and laid her head on his knee and he stroked it absently. It was the most gentle and revealing of gestures.

Complete silence fell, the only noise the lapping of the water. I began to be conscious of the cold air. A wind was blowing up. Everything comes to an end; the picnic was over.

"Tide's coming in," he said, standing up and holding out a hand to me. "Time to be gone."

I let him draw me up. Standing up, I was almost as tall as he was. He leaned forward and kissed me softly on the hair. I knew now how the dog had felt when it was stroked. It was a gentle, quiet movement and I stood there, absolutely still. Then I moved. I knew I had to tell him about the island, that the moment had come.

"I'm the owner of Markaby," I announced. "Robert Berwick left it to me in his will."

Instant fury exploded in his face. "So that's who you are. One of my grandfather's preposterous girl friends. The last in the line. The one mentioned in the will. He had a succession of you."

I'm not speechless often—it's not my trade to be—but I was then. Finally, I said, "I don't believe it."

"Oh yes. One after the other. All more or less like you. Sometimes he brought them to visit Markaby, sometimes he didn't. It was some sort of test, I believe, but I don't know of what." There was great bitterness in his tone. He turned away to untether the horse, and mounted.

"I only saw Robert Berwick once in my life," I said crisply.

"See if I believe you," he said and touched the horse with his whip.

"I own Markaby," I shouted. "And I was twelve years old when I saw him." The rising wind carried away my voice like a sob.

I felt part of the wind myself as I ran across the causeway and then drove away. I didn't know his name, who he was or where he came from, but for better or worse we should surely meet again.

I was haunted by the image of Markaby. It seemed to me a house asleep. I wanted more than ever to wake it up. This was part of my emotion. But I was also puzzled and disconcerted about the new light thrown on Robert Berwick. It clashed so strongly with my childhood memory of him that I wanted to reject it. But I couldn't quite throw it away. The force and feeling in the young man's voice had rung true. *He* believed what he had said, and, to a certain extent, I believed him.

This did not stop my being angry with him. I retained the anger inside me, and to a degree relished it. The strange thing was that I remained tenaciously attached to my idea of owning Markaby. The mere notion of a check or impediment to the plan made me want to establish my claim more quickly. And as for standing by and allowing this remote, romantic house to be knocked down, turned into a heap of stones and—ultimately—a mere mark on the ground to be turfed over, I felt physically sick.

The rest of that short winter's day, while daylight lasted,

I drove like the wind around the county in that antique car, devouring everything with greedy eyes, observing ancient churches, small gray manor houses, and sedate country market towns. I ate my chocolate as I drove and occasionally I sang. I felt angry, wild and free. I stopped only once, and then just to get some fuel. Finally I roared back to Berwick, returned the car to Grover's Garage and went back to the hotel.

I swept into the hotel. I walked through the hall to the room with the log fire leaping in its grate and warmed my hands. One of the luxuries denied the beautiful antique in which I had floated about the countryside was an adequate system of heating. The wealthy and fashionable lady who had owned it had presumably wrapped herself up well in her sables and put up with the cold. Lacking a fur, I was, as they said in the north country, "starved."

Above the fireplace was a great mirror framed in gilt, with gilded swags of mock drapery and grimacing cherubs, a magnificent piece of Victorian furniture which had probably been there for generations. I looked at my image in it and saw a girl with pale hair and eyes that looked dark in the firelight, but which I knew to be blue. In the past few years I had learned that I could pass, with a breath, from something near plainness to beauty. With me it depended on the mood. Well, my luck was in: I seemed to be in looks.

Behind me in the mirror, I saw the door open. I stayed for a minute staring into the mirror, breath held.

"Oh, it's you," I said, releasing my breath.

He stood there, a neater and tidier figure than the one I had met on Dragon's Eye. He had changed his clothes and brushed his hair and mended his manners.

"James Berwick," he said, giving a hint of a bow.

I turned around slowly.

"You were the child at the auction, I realize now. Please forgive me."

"I might," I said.

"I apologize."

He wasn't, obviously, a man to whom apologies came easy, but he offered them well when necessary. On the table beside him he had placed a small parcel. Now he picked it up and handed it to me. "I might have added flowers to my apologies, but I'm not the sort of person who gives flowers. And to be quite honest, in Northumberland in midwinter, I found it hard to find you anything you deserve. So I give you this. Please take it."

I began to undo the paper wrapping. "I wonder what flowers I would deserve."

"I don't know . . . violets, primroses and daffodils, perhaps," he said slowly.

"Perdita's flowers? So you read Shakespeare, too. Oh . . ." I had the parcel open. He had given me a picture of Markaby. It was a small watercolor, painted in precise delicate shades, creating a tiny, clear image of the house and island, like a world seen through a child's telescope. "Oh, you can't give me this, it must be valuable."

He shook his head. "My great-grandmother did it. She couldn't really draw, you know; the perspective's all wrong."

"It's enchanting."

"For the house's new occupant," he said, raising his hand in a kind of mock salute.

"I haven't moved in yet," I protested.

"But you will," he said. "Won't you?"

"Yes." I thought about it for a minute. "Yes, I will."

He left almost immediately after that; from the window I watched him get into the same car which he had used at the railway station the day before. He seemed to drive the Fiat much the same way he had ridden the horse: apply pressure and move away with a rush. Of the two, the horse had made the more elegant business of it.

"Fancy *him* coming here." Behind me a tea tray had arrived, and my friend the maid was standing holding it. Her eyes were round and amazed as she watched the Fiat depart. "What brought him here?"

"Who?"

"Jaimie Berwick." She put the tray down and started to arrange the meal on a round table by the fire. "I heard you come in and thought you might want a bite to eat. There's no one here but you, so make yourself comfortable. Here's some hot scones, and I did you a nice bit of smoked fish. I'll pour some tea first." With comfortable wonder she repeated: "Fancy him coming here."

"You know him, then?"

"Everyone knows Jaimie Berwick. Here's your tea. Him and his cousin Angel. She's a Berwick, too."

"Angel?" I sat down at the well-spread table, realizing suddenly that I was starved in another way. "He looks as if *he* should be called Lucifer."

"Lucifer?" Her eyes went round again. "Like the devil?"

"Lucifer was an angel, too," I reminded her. "A beautiful angel. A magnificent angel."

Her eyes remained wide. She planted the teapot back on the tray with a firm ring. "Still, better not think of that Angel as being too angelic," she murmured cryptically, and when I raised my eyes in query all she said was, "We none of us are, are we?"

I met Angel Berwick soon. The next day was market day, and I was strolling around, surveying the stalls of fruit and vegetables and fish. I was on my way to visit Mr. Naseby, the solicitor, and was filling in time because I was early. Her tall figure stood out in the crowd. She was bending down talking to someone, a child, I thought. I was startled to notice then that her companion was the nun I had seen the day before, letting herself into the Convent of the Sacred Heart. She was the tiniest, oldest, frailest creature I had ever seen. Angel was carrying a basket of fruit and vegetables to which, every so often, another cauliflower or cabbage was added by the nun. The nun was talking and Angel was listening. Finally a boy appeared at their side, the laden basket was handed over to him, he and the nun departed, and Angel was released.

She saw me and came straight up to me.

"I'm Angel Berwick. You're the girl who's getting my house."

"You know?"

"Of course. This is a small town. Things get about. I loved Markaby. I used to ride my horse over there. I called it my house."

"So that's why your cousin Jaimie doesn't want me there. He wants it to belong to you."

She smiled. "He knows I can't have it, though. Anyway, I've grown up now, and I'm not so sure I want it. I think it's haunted. Possessed. Don't you feel it?"

I shook my head. "No."

"Grandpa did. He looked prosaic, ordinary, but he felt something about the house. I know he did. He always seemed to be looking for the perfect occupant for it. I suppose he finally found her." She eyed me.

"And it was me," I said uneasily.

"It was because of what you did at the auction years and years ago. Oh yes, I know about that, too. It's a famous incident. I was jealous of you for being so brave."

"It didn't seem brave at the time. Only reasonable."

"Yes, I think that's what I meant; that's what I call brave." She smiled. "Come and have some coffee." She pointed to where tables were laid out in a covered court in the old market hall.

I hesitated. "I'm really on my way to see someone called Naseby. I was going there when I saw you."

"Oh yes, you saw me with Sister Agnes." She pulled a long face. "Don't let her looks deceive you. She looks as frail as a kitling, but she's tough. She teaches French at the Convent; she taught me," Angel sighed. "She doesn't forget it, either. She *chastises* me."

"I thought perhaps she did the cooking."

"She does the marketing because she's half French and she loves to shop. Oh, she knows a grozer from a neep."

"Grozer?" I queried.

"Gooseberry. Neep is turnip. You're near Scotland here, you know. You'll have to get used to the way we talk if you're going to be a local landowner."

"Hardly that," I protested.

"Well, get along to Pip Naseby. We used to go to dancing class together. Don't give him my love, though. He doesn't want it."

This was my first taste of the quality of Angel Berwick, and the episode contained a touch of her wry, ironic self-possession, as dry and fresh as verbena.

Thoughtfully, perplexed and fascinated by her, I continued on my way to the offices of Naseby and Son. "Son" meant Pip Naseby, I supposed. My business was transacted briskly by a young man who looked about my own age, wearing country tweeds and a country-fresh complexion. "Our Mr. Phillip" he was called. A spaniel slept at his feet and I could see a shotgun and the sort of bag a hunter slings over his back lying on a table behind him. Not much doubt about where *his* true interests lay, I thought. But he dealt with me expeditiously and told me that, although the will was not yet through probate, there was no reason why I should not take possession of my inheritance immediately.

"The house has been cared for, but not lived in for some years," he told me. "Robert Berwick looked after the property, naturally, but he never took a tenant for it. Several people offered, but he always refused. I'll check that the electricity and water and so on are working for you, so that you can just take over." He made a note on a pad in front of him. "A woman from the village cleaned there once a week."

"Is it furnished?" I asked.

"Partly so," he said. "Some of the stuff is nice; I'll let you have an inventory. You don't inherit the furniture, but the estate will probably sell it to you, once it's valued. If you want it, that is."

"I'll think about it," I said. "But it's all right to use it in the meantime?"

He nodded. "Yes, certainly. I don't know how much china and linen there is, though. Better arrange to bring some with you when you come. Will it be soon?" He looked at me with curiosity. I suppose I *was* an interesting and curious person to him, this strange girl who had inherited a home.

"Very soon, I hope," I said, holding out my hand to say goodbye.

He rose to see me to the door. "And now you're going back to London?"

"Yes, but not for long."

He said, as if the idea had suddenly come to him, "There's no need to go, you know. You could move in now if you like. It might be a good idea. It's a strange house. Not everyone likes it, or feels at home there. Test your strength against it."

He smiled as if he was making a joke; but I felt it was only partly a joke.

"I ought to go back," I said.

"Ought?" He raised his eyebrows. I was beginning to like Pip Naseby.

"There's my guardian. And clothes. I didn't bring much with me."

I wanted to stay. The work I had brought with me, the puzzling but agreeable presence of Jaimie Berwick, the island itself—they all tugged at me.

He nodded toward the telephone. "There's the telephone. Use that, why don't you? Have everything sent by rail."

"Could I?"

"Of course. Give me the number and I'll have my secretary get it for you." He settled back in his chair. "It might take a bit of time. Have a glass of sherry while we wait." He produced a bottle from a cupboard and poured some sherry into slender, fine old glasses. "I'm glad you've decided to stay. You'll be in possession. Lawyers like possession; it makes a hard fact."

He smiled again, but I felt he was warning me.

2

Lydia was easy on the telephone and made no difficulties. I think she was glad for me to be in North-umberland. She had one or two worries.

"You'll be all right at Markaby. Is it livable, by the way? Aired, dry and clean?" Lydia could be very old-fashioned about that sort of thing; she really did think I'd suffer if I slept in a damp bed. I'd slept in a sleeping bag in a theater dressing room sometimes, under Bert's regime, and come to no harm.

"Oh yes, apparently a woman has gone in and kept things in order. I will probably buy what furniture is in the house. Only a few of the rooms are furnished. And I might ring up Toya and see if she could come to stay."

"I hope it's heated, my dear," said Lydia gravely.

"Oh yes," I answered; in fact, I had no idea.

"Well, I suppose you're old enough to know how to keep your feet warm. And what are you going to do up there besides study your part and lick your wounds?"

"Oh, look around. Get to know the countryside."

After a pause for thought, "I'll lend you my motor car," she said. "I don't like to think of you stuck. You might need movement."

So she *was* nervous about me. "I can't afford that car," I said. "Just to keep it in fuel would impoverish me. Besides, I'd have to come and get it. No, you send my motor bike up. The railway can handle it and I can collect it at Berwick station." I had owned the bike for three years and enjoyed scooting around on it. "I don't know why you have a car like the Bentley." I knew she loved it, really, and that next to me it was her treasure.

"I like to show off." She laughed. "Besides, a crash helmet would not suit me the way it suits you."

"The bike's just right for me."

"Oh, that bike!" she cried in despair, half mock, half real.

"It's a good little bike," I said indignantly.

"Are you going to wear that yellow windbreaker on it?"

"I expect so." And I added, because this was news: "And I have had the bike painted yellow, too."

"The traveling canary," said Lydia. "I do admire you, darling. My dear little bird."

There were tears in her voice. To my utter surprise she was crying. "Lydia," I said. "Please, Lydia."

"It's nothing. Take no notice. But look after yourself, dear, silly little bird. And goodbye. It *is* a sort of goodbye, perhaps the hardest one of all to say. You're free, absolutely free, dear child." Deliberately she kept her voice light. "Anyway, I'm planning to take a sabbatical term's leave myself. Consider yourself turned out."

She had offered me my freedom, but I thought she wanted her own freedom, too. Lately she had been restless, very unlike herself. I wondered if, after all these years of being heart-free, she had not found someone she cared for. I thought there were signs. Perhaps it comes to every woman at some time.

"I'll organize it all today if I can," she said, "seeing that we're both in a hurry; and I'll send you a telegram telling you which train to meet. Berwick station, you say? Right. And the telegram? Where shall I send that?"

"Better make it the hotel," I said.

"First thing tomorrow, then," she threatened, and I knew Lydia, she'd do it somehow, railway procrastination or not. "Your things will probably arrive before the telegram."

"You're probably right," I said. "And I won't get a wink of sleep worrying over whether I'll be there in time to meet the train."

In fact, I had to stay a day extra at the hotel while Lydia organized the dispatch of my motor bike and the old-fashioned theatrical hamper which contained all my possessions. The latter was a treasured object with me, because it had once belonged to Sarah Bernhardt. But it was true enough—I was in a panic at the last as to whether I would get to the station, which lies a little way out of the town, in time.

As luck would have it, my noble yellow bike and the hamper arrived at Berwick station at the same time as I did, and putting the hamper and the rest of my things into a taxi to follow me, I set off at last to ride over the Northumberland countryside to Markaby.

I thought we made a gay little procession, the taxicab and I. It was a late winter's day with a gray sky, but the air was calm and sweet. A lovely pearly light lay over the fields and woods. Such days have a beauty all their own; no wonder gardeners call them "growing" days, during which the first small start toward spring is taken.

We came to a narrow bridge over a small fast-flowing stream, and followed the road for a few miles, and then a crossroads with a sign saying in one direction "The

Grange" and in the other "Garrow." I waved to the taxi driver, and he waved back and we sailed down the Garrow turn. It was on the hill just here that I stopped my Honda for a while to stare down at Garrow and Dragon's Eye. Garrow was as quiet as ever with its shops and the local inn spaced out down the main street. A church lay a little apart, while a gaunt-faced mansion overlooked the village from a slight eminence. We went through the village, where I stopped to arrange to pick up mail in the post office. I arrived at the causeway ahead of the rest of my little caravan and drew to a halt. I paused for a second time to look across at Markaby and to wait for the taxi to catch up once more.

"You'll kill yourself one day, miss, the way you ride," said the taxi driver, when he finally caught up with me. "Frightened the life out of me, you did."

"I like to go fast."

"I noticed that. Mind you, you're good," he said. "I'll admit you handle the machine well. Just as good with a car?"

"Not quite so fast," I admitted.

"That's something to be thankful for. You nearly had the toes of those two men sitting outside the post office. Got a bonny gliff, the pair of them did." He grinned at me, explaining. "A good fright, in the Queen's English." He was chuckling as he dragged out my theater basket, its bright labels from Crewe and Wigan and Harrogate and Brighton, dating back to the nineteenth century, reminding me of my long, hard search in the Portobello Market in London for just such a basket. For a moment I doubted the wisdom of leaving such treasured London opportunities behind to bury myself in this forsaken, unknown part of England, and I shivered in the damp sea wind. I eyed the causeway with misgiving. Of course, the tiresome thing was already an inch or two under water. The side road down to the causeway looked unpleasantly steep with a sharp bend just where no road planner should ever have put a bend. You'd need to be sure of yourself, riding down that slope, then swinging a sharp right and over the causeway.

"You thinking of going that way, miss?" worried the driver, giving the sea a disapproving look. "You believe in doing things the hard way, don't you? Over there?" He gave an exaggerated shudder.

"It's my house," I said proudly, glad again of my resolution.

He gave a low whistle and shouldered the basket—no light task either, in view of all I had in it—and said, "You like living cut off from the world, I can see that." He marched forward to the causeway. "Good job I'm wearing thick boots." He splashed determinedly across and I followed, pushing the bike. On the other side, he lowered his load and took his first close look at Markaby.

The house looked big and quiet and dark. I can never explain the fluctuation in the color of the stones of Markaby. Sometimes it is silver-bright, sometimes a clear gray, and at others dark, like anthracite. Today was such a somber day.

"Won't you be nervous all on your own?"

"Oh no. I'm looking forward to it. And of course I'm going to have many visitors." It wasn't true, but there was no point in telling him that.

"They'll have to swim across," he said, looking seaward, where the tide was coming in. I made a note that I would have to remember how fast the tide rose here. "Young Lochinvar, and all that."

"No lovers," I said firmly.

He brought the rest of my luggage across, helped me to the door of the house with everything, accepted his payment and tip, and cheerfully departed. I was too excited to watch him go. Instead I took out the bunch of keys, picked out the right one and put it into the lock.

The solicitors had sent me a plan of the house and a detailed list of its contents, so that I knew it without ever having set foot inside. I paused on the threshold and looked up. Carved on the lintel stone I read the words "The Riders sleep, the Heroes in the Grave." Immediately above, carved in low relief, was a tremendous face—a visage of glaring eyes, with great broken teeth and a ferocious smile. I could hardly tell whether it was man or beast, monster or dragon. The face had a penetrating, archaic fury; the lettering, although old, seemed comparatively modern by contrast. The face could have been a thousand years old, the letters a hundred or less. If this was the household god of Markaby, it was an alarming one. Then I took a deep breath, turned the key and pushed the door. It moved easily.

At once a current of air moved out toward me. Houses do have a breath, I swear, and Markaby's breath was cold but dry, not a trace of damp; it was a smell of old wood, long-ago log fires, and a scented spiciness very faint and far away, a memory of the days when it had been lived in. It was a smell which had built up over many years and it spoke of the past.

Then a burst of cold sea air blew in and the past was gone. But I never forgot that first moment.

I consulted my plan. Kitchen to the right, living room to the left. Up the stairs bedrooms and a bathroom. I dragged my things into the hall and made immediately for the kitchen. I was hungry and cold. I had plenty of food with me, in tins, jars, and packages. My theatrical experiences had made me an old soldier. I knew what to bring with me and how to make myself comfortable.

The kitchen proved to be a long low-ceilinged room, with an old-fashioned Welsh dresser and a big kitchen range with an oven that looked as though it could have cooked an ox. But further investigations, prompted by my list, which said simply "electric cooker," turned up a small electric hotplate with two burners placed close by. I pressed a switch and saw a red light appear. Good, I had electricity.

I set my store of food out on the shelves. I ran my finger along one shelf and found it dust-free. Indeed, everything was scrupulously clean, and even the window curtains appeared to have been freshly laundered. You got a good view of Dragon's Hill from the kitchen window. I had not realized before how close it was. Seen now, it seemed to loom up taller and more forbidding than I had remembered.

Before I did anything else I made myself some coffee. After drinking it gratefully, I felt prepared to explore the rest of my domain. A narrow box stairway ran off the kitchen up to the first floor. Designed for the use of servants, it had an unused look, and beyond a look up I ignored it.

The living room across the hall had paneled walls painted white and a creamy marble fireplace with a recess on either side. Though it was now dull, it was apparent that the wooden floor had once been highly polished. A desk, a sofa, and a few upright chairs were the entire contents of the lovely, elegant room. I closed the door without reluctance.

But next to it was a smaller room which instantly won my heart. Some former owner had chosen a pretty wallpaper with tulips and flying parrots and had hung curtains to match. There was a worn but still pretty carpet, a desk, a curving buttoned sofa, and an upright chair that looked like a Hepplewhite.

Upstairs was one bedroom, large like the paneled room beneath, and like it almost empty. Four smaller rooms were on this floor, and a narrow box staircase led to an upper floor of attics, according to my floor plan. The door to the stairs was locked. I shook it, but it would not give. My keys were downstairs.

I selected a room with a view out to sea for my bedroom. Denmark and Norway lay across the ocean. I ran downstairs and dragged my case and wicker hamper up to this room. The high old bed, white enamel and brass, faced the windows. I would be able to lie on my pillows and look out to sea. The room was no bigger than a snuff box, but it was, like the one below, a room with a good character.

I arranged my things and was about to return to the main floor. The short winter's day was drawing in. I had brought candles as a precaution, in case the house lights did not work, but when I pressed a switch by the door, a lamp by the bed at once shone cheerfully. I looked from the lighted room to the sea outside. The color there was thickening and darkening with every minute. As I stood there, I could hear the sea sighing and grumbling below me. It was going to be like living in a ship.

Perhaps I did feel a flicker of anxiety then, but I waved it away.

I headed for the stairs slowly, because I was tired. Without warning, somewhere in that empty house a telephone began to ring. I went galloping down the stairs. It didn't occur to me that it couldn't somehow be a welcome. At the bottom, in the hall, I stood listening, trying to locate the instrument. I realized then that it was ringing both above and all around me. That gave me a clue: there must be a telephone in the big white-paneled room and one in what had been the main bedroom above. It seemed logical.

But in spite of my intuition it took me some time to find the telephone—it was not on the desk, not on the floor, not on any of the chairs. The room seemed so empty in the dusk. I could hear the phone ringing but I couldn't find it. I was on the point of running back upstairs and looking for the telephone there, when I saw a small china knob in the paneling, pulled it hard, and found a small cupboard in which the telephone was still merrily trilling away.

I picked it up and said "Hello" hopefully, cheerfully, questioningly. At that precise moment the line went dead, as if the caller, having hung on so long, had tired of trying just as there was an answer. "Hello?" I said again, on a falling note. I was disappointed, almost cross. A call now would have been just *right*, just what I wanted. Come on now, I said to myself, replacing the receiver, you're not going to be much good at living on an island if you're lonely already.

But at least I knew where my telephone was and that it was connected, and if I wanted I could pick it up and telephone Lydia. Only she wouldn't be back home yet, and in any case I wasn't going to ring her. There was a strong link between Lydia and me. Nothing was going to break it, but I didn't want to call upon it quite yet.

I compromised by calling Toya to invite her up to Markaby. She was unreservedly impressed by my legacy.

"What, a whole *island*? You *are* marvelous. Oh, I envy you. I don't even own half a bed-sit." As she spoke, I imagined her lovely, narrow eyes sparkling with pleasure. Her parents were in fact extremely well-to-do, but Toya was a refugee from the closely knit family circle back in Tokyo. Some people are natural cosmopolitans, adapting immediately to any city, rooting themselves easily. Toya was such a one.

Cosmopolitan or not, my friend accepted my invitation with alacrity. More relieved than I cared to admit, I listened as she rapidly made plans to arrive the very next day. I was laughing gaily as we rang off.

By way of making quite clear to myself that I was here to stay, I went outside to find a home for my bike. Walking out the front door, I confronted the causeway and the mainland, where lights were beginning to spring up in the cottages. The causeway had disappeared beneath the water and would not be seen again until the tide fell. I pushed my bike along the side of the house and opened the door of what seemed to be a byre. I thought an animal had once lived there, because there was a sort of manger at one end and a big ring to which it could have been tethered. Perhaps Markaby had once kept its own cow. From the past I seemed to hear the distant voice of Robert Berwick saying, "But the grazing is let." So far I had seen no animals on my little island.

I pushed my bike in, shut the door and made my way back to the house. The lights I had left on, shining through the windows, gave the place a cozy, welcoming look. The wind was rising and I had to struggle against it. It was biting, blowing as it did from the east. It had come to me across Scandinavia from the Arctic. High in the darkening sky I could see the pale crescent of the moon with the

North Star close by. Once, hundreds of years ago, men had traveled through this sea in longboats, guiding themselves by that star from Trondheim and Skiringsal, from the Sognefjord and Hordaland through the safe fiords out to a wilder sea and then across it to the coast of Northumbria.

Lost in my Viking fantasies, my gaze wandered toward the mainland. To my surprise, a motorboat was battling its way from there to my island. As it came closer and closer, I could make out only one man inside. It was that strange dusky time between night and day when the light can play tricks. The silvery light reflected back from the sea was making him more visible to me than I could possibly be to him. Daylight was shrinking with every second that passed. I moved away from the house a few yards and hid behind a bush, keeping my eye on the boat every instant.

The pilot maneuvered the craft close to the island. This much I saw, then he disappeared from view. Suddenly the engine was cut. I listened. Nothing. The evening was quiet, even the sea birds were silent.

Still I stood where I was, prompted by goodness knows what unconscious reasoning to behave as effacingly as possible. Five minutes passed, no more, and I heard him. He didn't make much noise, but I heard his feet on the path. He walked right past me and toward the house. For a second he stood looking at it. The lights still shone out; I might even have left the front door slightly open, though I couldn't remember, but he did not go any nearer. After standing there looking, he walked on. I saw him disappear around the side of the hill.

At this point I moved out quietly to get a better view. The island was small; at any minute I must get another sight of him.

But he did not reappear. I waited. Only the wind blowing through the trees and the gathering dusk were my apparent companions.

For what seemed a long time I stood there listening, then I moved softly forward, following the path that led around the island. It was darker now, but I could see where I was going. If he were there I would have to have seen him. After all, I saw a few sheep huddled together against the wind. But there was no one. He seemed to have disappeared.

If I seem calm, I was not that night! I was puzzled and alarmed. I was alone on the island, out of touch with help.

Below me I saw the motorboat. It had been neatly tied up by a projection of rock which served as a sort of landing stage. I lowered myself carefully onto this slab of rock. From here I could see that the motorboat was tethered to a solid-looking iron staple that looked as if it had been driven into the rock face for this purpose. It appeared to be new.

I was in the boat before I had time to think. I remember landing in it and feeling it rock on the water beneath me, but I do not remember making a conscious decision to get in. If I *had*, I probably wouldn't have done it.

It was a tidy affair, this boat, with bare, empty seats that looked as if they had been vacuumed recently. On the air was a faint lemony scent, dry and astringent, which I could not identify. But although someone had cleaned it carefully, certain traces remained. I could see sand glittering on the deck, and some dried seaweed underneath a seat. Somehow, a distinct impression of a hard-working craft that had seen good service was made by the combination. I suppose it was the way the floor covering was worn in patches, with the bare metal showing through, where the paint had worn off around the structure of the seats.

On a small shelf was a large flashlight. I picked it up and switched it on. A powerful beam lit up a segment of the island and then, as I turned, illuminated the sea. The water diffused the light where the land had somehow concentrated it. The sea stirred and rippled, as if the light had disturbed something. I thought I saw a blunt head and a long sluggishly moving shape. I stared in disbelief. Too large for a fish, and the wrong shape for a man, yet, if it were a thing of substance at all and not a chimera, it was alive, and no piece of driftwood or clump of floating sea-weed. But it melted away into the water, as evanescent as a nightmare, and I dismissed it as an illusion.

Switching off the torch and replacing it, I jumped out of the boat and clambered back up the rock, where Providence or the hand of man had left neat little projections like steps to make the climb easy, and ran back to the house.

The door was closed, the lights still shone. Inside, all was exactly as I had left it. I went from room to room, upstairs and down, even giving the locked attic door a shake. No one, nothing met my searching gaze.

I stood by my bedroom window, thinking. The man must still be somewhere on the island. The best thing to do would be to telephone the police. I opened my bedroom window for one last look around. At that moment, through the open window came the unmistakable sound of the motorboat being started. My visitor was leaving.

I never did telephone the police. What could I have said? That a man had been on the island and was now gone?

Back inside the house it was easy to chalk up to

imagination my uneasy belief that I had seen something swimming in the water near the motorboat. I made myself some coffee and an omelette. The house seemed very big and empty about me. I wasn't frightened, exactly, but for the first time I did ask myself what I planned to do with Markaby in the future. It no longer seemed the safe and peaceful refuge I had dreamed of finding. Suppose I grew to be afraid of staying there?

"Lick your wounds," Lydia had said. I had denied the need for this, vehemently. Still, there was a certain element of truth in it. So what should I do with Markaby? I didn't know.

I meditated as I finished my coffee. When no answer was forthcoming, I sighed and rose to draw the curtains, which were so thin and old they almost tore in my hands. Washed and starched stiff, they had hung there so long that the strong sunlight and the salt air had destroyed them.

Then the telephone rang again. I stood there for a moment, listening to it, then moved toward the hall. I had only the light streaming from the kitchen to guide me to the telephone, but I made my way with happy confident speed. It was Bert. This time I knew it was Bert.

"Hello?" A man's voice.

I gripped the receiver. "Darling, at last," I said breathlessly.

He cleared his voice. "It's me, Dickon."

I made my surprise embarrassingly clear to both of us. "You? What do you want?"

"How are you? All right? Are you all right, Kate?"

"Yes, of course." I was firm. "I always am. Why shouldn't I be?"

Dickon did not answer for a moment, then he said, "Toya

gave me your phone number. I don't know why, but I felt worried about you all on your own. Not like me, is it?"

"I'm fine. Have you been reading the tea leaves again?" Dickon, like a lot of theater people, was very superstitious (a sign of their insecurity, you might say, and you'd be right), and was always ready to look for signs and portents.

"No, I've not been casting the runes this time. Been behaving quite normally for me."

The runes, he'd said, the secret Viking writing they used for important and sacred inscriptions. Unconsciously Dickon had plucked the phrase from the air. He really must have some form of telepathy, I thought.

"I'm all right," I said, perhaps a little irritably.

"You sound quite cheerful, I must say. Glad to hear it. Look after yourself. Don't ring me, I'll ring you."

And he was gone. I think I knew then that I no longer loved Bert as I had. The emotion was fading, but it had taken this call from Dickon to reveal it to me.

I lay that night for a long while without sleeping. All about me the old house creaked and moved and spoke. The wind blew through the open window. Silently I was doing what Pip Naseby had suggested: I was pitting my strength against Markaby.

I was also experiencing the last of the countless shocks of revelation that had occurred during this most remarkable day: Jaimie Berwick was part of Markaby and Dragon's Eye. The unexpected surge of joy accompanying this realization sent the blood racing through my veins.

I was under no illusions about what would become of me if I got too involved with Jaimie Berwick. I was tinder to his spark. And yet my feeling about Dragon's Eye—my sense that my past and my future were there—all these drew me to Jaimie.

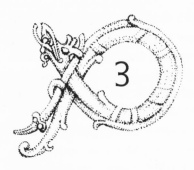

3

In the night I was roused.

Markaby wasn't a quiet house; it creaked and groaned like a ship at sea. The simile was not inappropriate, because a strong wind had blown up and the window frames were rattling. Awakened in the middle of the night, I rose to fasten them more closely. The moon was clear and I could see high clouds passing quickly over it. The sky looked like another sea, infinitely remote and limitless. I stood a long time at the window.

Finally I went back to bed and slept. When I awoke again the sun was shining brilliantly into the room and the wind had dropped. I ran to the window and looked out. My island was bare and peaceful, just as it should be. The tide was low, so the causeway stood out boldly.

I got up and dressed quickly, because today Toya arrived and I wanted to be all settled in with my goods and chattels bestowed about the place just where I wanted them. I knew from experience that Toya had a great gift for appropriating the best places first, if you didn't bestir yourself. Ordinarily I didn't mind, but this was *my* house. I unpacked all my clothes and hung them in a huge sycamore-wood wardrobe. There was enough room inside for me as well, I thought. Several me's, in fact. A faint smell of cedarwood floated out, which pleased me. Knowing that fine-quality old furniture was often lined with cedar or sandalwood, I could already tell that people of taste and discrimination had lived in Markaby. A woman had lived here. A beautiful woman—the presence of many mirrors testified to that. I thought she might have been fair-haired, too, because she had chosen so much pale, blond wood. It had darkened a little with age, but it was still lovely. Now that daylight was here I could see that the house glowed.

Downstairs I piled my books and papers on the desk that stood in the window. I would put them away later. I fancied my possession of this desk. It was a nice piece, a man's desk. I would sit at this desk and study my part and be very intelligent and hardworking. I could see it already. I rested at the desk for a moment and daydreamed as I looked outside. From here you could see straight across to the village of Garrow and the countryside behind it. I wondered about the man who had last sat at this desk and studied this view, and what his relationship had been with the woman. A loving one, I felt somehow. In spite of all its alarming undertones, there was a feeling of love at Markaby.

I ran my hands over the desk top, admiring the delicate inlay of different-colored woods. I gave a drawer a slight tug and it moved like silk. I've always been good with my hands and I admire craftsmanship when I meet it. I enjoy making things and I used to contribute a lot on the scenery and sets at the theater. Bert said I'd make a first-class stage designer if nothing else. Bert! I'd have to stop thinking about him. I pushed the drawer back swiftly and stood up.

I had arranged to have my letters sent to the post office,

and I thought I'd go in and introduce myself. I didn't want to turn myself into a local personality, but I knew enough about village life to guess that I was already an object of interest and observation. I might just as well offer them a little information to get on with. A little and not too much, I thought.

I locked the door behind me and trotted down the path to the shed which housed my bike. A gull swooped overhead and eyed me speculatively. I wondered if the island claimed any land birds like thrushes and finches and blackbirds. I hadn't seen any. Perhaps the sea birds felt they owned the island. The gulls laughed and screamed in the air as if they knew what I was thinking. One sailed right past. Seen up close, they had curved beaks and sneaky eyes.

I wheeled my yellow bike out. I was dressed to match in a shiny yellow jacket. They'd notice me coming, all right, but that was the intention. I gave the bike a quick polish; I liked to keep it bright. Then I pushed the bike down the path and across the causeway.

I took one backward look at Markaby. I was always doing that in those first days, as if I couldn't see enough of it. One window had been left open by me on purpose to give the house a "lived-in" look. It had not quite succeeded in its purpose. Markaby retained its air of aloofness, but it was waking up. In the roof was a slanting window I had not noticed before. I realized I must possess large attics. Strange, even ridiculous, to own a house and know so little about it. But I had admittedly come by my property in a most unusual manner.

The sunlight shone on the roof window and was reflected back, so that, oddly, a small arrow of gold seemed to shoot upward to the sun. It was a pretty illusion and I watched, fascinated. I wondered if there was a mirror in the attic that was turning back the light. Then the sun disappeared behind a belt of cirrus cloud and the light was gone.

I watched for a minute more, but, with the sun gone, it was cold. I got on my bike and departed.

Behind me I know now that Markaby stirred to life.

The village store, which also housed the post office, was the old-fashioned sort of shop which stocks everything from bedsocks to kerosene. I knew it sold the latter by the strong smell of oil that hit me as I pushed the door, which gave a little tinkle as it opened. And I knew about the bedsocks because there was an old lady at the counter buying a blue-and-white pair from the proprietor of the shop, a thin bespectacled woman with tightly curled gray hair. Her name was written in beautiful copperplate above the door: Mary Ann Ogle, licensed to sell tobacco. They both studied me as I came in. The bell on the door was unnecessary: there never was a time when Mrs. Ogle was not on duty in her shop, bright-eyed and alert, ready to intercept all comers.

"I won't make up my mind about the socks just now, thank you, Mrs. Ogle." The old lady pushed the rejected objects back across the counter. "They won't run away."

"Last pair in stock," retorted Mrs. Ogle, with automatic expertise, never taking her eyes off me. "Don't make 'em any more. Not with electric blankets so popular."

Both faces were turned toward me, waiting expectantly while I made my way to the post-office section. At this moment another figure appeared behind the grille that protected the post-office area of the counter. The grille was so stuck about with official notices, some yellowing with age, and various advertisements, that only a small hole was vacant for a face to be seen, but this man's was immediately recognizable as in relationship with Mary Ann Ogle. In features different, in expression they were the same: marriage had marked them.

"I'm Kate Melrose. I arranged for all my letters to come here for me to collect."

At once the look of interest was interrupted. "That's right. I had word of it. So you're Miss Melrose."

"Is there anything for me?"

He shuffled over to a table set against the further wall and pretended to look, although, of course, he knew already. "No letters," he announced.

"I'll come in every day and ask," I promised.

"But there's a telegram come." He pretended to look for this too, though he had it under his hand.

I held out my hand. He finally handed the telegram over and I tore it open. The two women made no bones about having a good look.

It was from Toya. SORRY TO LET YOU DOWN BUT MUST CANCEL. PARENTS ARRIVING LONDON TODAY. SENDING YOU SOMETHING TO KEEP YOU COMPANY, ARRIVING MORNING TRAIN. PLEASE COLLECT. FONDEST LOVE TOYA.

I felt a sharp dip of disappointment situated somewhere in my diaphragm. Without realizing it, I had counted on Toya.

"Not bad news, I hope?" probed Mr. Ogle.

I shook my head. "No." I won't say he looked disappointed—to say that would be unkind—but he did look as if he knew better. "Where's the station, though?"

"Railway station?" He shook his head. "None in Garrow. Closed it down six years ago. Berwick will be your best bet."

I nodded. "And when does the London train get in?"

He frowned. "You've missed the *early* one. The midday train'll be the next."

Blast Toya, I thought, why couldn't she be explicit about the train? And what exactly was she sending me to keep me company? I hoped it didn't have four legs and a tail. I didn't trust Toya's sense of humor.

"Thank you for telling me," I said politely. "And can I buy a pint of milk? Oh, and some butter."

"Yes, indeed, Mother will serve you. Mother!" he called across to Mrs. Ogle. "The young lady wants some milk and butter."

She'd heard, of course, and had them ready on the counter before her husband finished his sentence. "Must be lonely on that island," she said, eyes bright and inquisitive.

"No," I said.

"Well, you haven't been there long enough to find out," she contradicted.

"I came yesterday," I replied.

"I know." She nodded. "Comfortable, is it?"

"I think so."

"He did keep that house properly nice," she said. "Mr. Berwick never neglected it."

"No? And yet the island has a deserted air, as if no one ever went there."

"Billy English kept a few sheep there," Mr. Ogle volunteered. "They nearly all died, though. A few are left still, gone wild."

"What a shame," I commented politely. "I fancy I saw them. Doesn't he mind? Mr. English, I mean?"

"Not around himself, now." He shrugged.

"Dead, you mean?"

"Just went off," he said vaguely.

"Never trust a red-haired man," said the old lady.

I remembered then that Billy English was the name of the young man who had disappeared from these parts and about whose character the maid in the hotel at Berwick had offered dark hints. "I think I've heard of him," I said.

Mrs. Ogle cut in. "You can't say the island's been neglected since Mr. Berwick took over. Before that, maybe, yes; but he visited it regular. Didn't he now?" She put a loaf on the counter. It looked crisp and fresh. "Better have a loaf, my dear. Never can tell."

"I suppose I should take a can of dog food," I said gloomily.

"Oh, you've got a dog, then?" She was pleased. A new fact had been extracted painlessly from me.

"I might have."

"Well, either you has or you hasn't," said the old lady, who had been silent all this time. "You ought to know." She didn't sound very friendly. Neither had the other two, come to think of it. Curious, but not friendly.

"I am just about to find out," I said, picking up my purchases and taking my leave. "Tell me, who lives in that great gaunt barracks of a house you can see from here?" Mrs. Ogle murmured something about it being his lordship's house, but someone was coming into the shop with the same impetus as I was departing with.

We collided, and my parcels slid from my arms. The newcomer fielded the milk with a neat movement. "Oh, thanks," I stammered in admiration.

The man's agility was impressive. "Sorry if I hit you."

He was slender and dark-haired, clad in a thick blue sweater and old-fashioned trousers. They seemed the sort of clothes a fisherman might wear. He nodded politely and held the door open for me to leave. I heard Mary Ann Ogle explaining on my behalf that I was in a hurry. I think the word "dog" floated in the air behind me as I left.

"And how are the fish prices over at Seahouses?" began Mr. Ogle, his speech falling at once into a stronger Northumberland burr, as if it were demanded of him. Many people are bilingual, I've found, talking the Queen's English to outsiders and falling into a vernacular with their own kind. We all do it, more or less, but my actress's ear made me sensitive to such variations. "Prices tolerable, eh? But you fishermen are never satisfied." The r's were specially rolling and vibrant, like a Frenchman's. So that's how you talk when you feel friendly, I thought, letting the door shut with a bang behind me.

I left my bike parked against the curb and crossed the road. I had noticed a shop selling vegetables and fruit and I wanted to buy some tomatoes.

I was served by a younger woman. She was short, with dark, curly hair, and might have been a sister of Mary Ann Ogle, also of the old woman who had been studying the bedsocks. There was a kinship somewhere, I could swear. She gave me what I wanted without a smile or a word of greeting. Not a friendly lot, these villagers, I thought. Or else they didn't like the looks of me.

"Nice morning," I said, tentatively.

"For some," came the answer. Not only unfriendly, I thought, but actually hostile. Yet she'd never seen me before; she really couldn't dislike me as much as she seemed to. Indeed, her tone, though surly, was also detached, as though her grudge was impersonal, directed against me but not because of me. She probably had a headache or indigestion. Perhaps the whole village had.

I paid for the tomatoes, bought a bunch of daffodils and carried all my purchases out into the village street. I had a bag at the back of the bike which managed to hold every-thing I entrusted to it. I just prayed that the milk bottle would not break.

Then, since I had some time to kill before meeting the train and because I did not plan to cut myself off entirely from the outside world, I went into the next shop, which sold newspapers. Here I bought *The Times* and a copy of the local newspaper. I glanced over the main news stories before I tucked the papers under my arm. A seamen's strike, a menacing rumble along the China-USSR frontier, alarms in the Middle East rated the front pages. Inside, a new wonder drug to control viral infection had been de-vised, a hitherto undiscovered and totally new animal had been encountered hiding in a damp jungle in Brazil, and a conference of archaeologists was discussing and dismissing the possibility of a settled colony of Vikings in North America. "Vinland the Good" the Norsemen had ap-parently called the land in the west, but where it was and how long it had existed seemed a matter for dispute. I felt a brief touch of sympathy for the unlucky animal now doomed to publicity.

A rack of magazines and another of paperbacks were so arranged that they created an alcove into which I now wandered. I chose a couple of books, a spy thriller and a Victorian romance, and I was studying a book on dog management, when two people came in. I knew there were two, although I had my back to them. I myself was hidden away behind the racks of books.

There was a mutter of conversation. It did not attract my attention at once. I just noticed two men—quietly talking. Then the pair moved away. I stood reading for a few minutes, then walked around the stand of books. My nose wrinkled. For a moment I thought I caught a whiff of the dry scent I'd noticed on the motorboat. It's not true, I thought. It's an illusion. But the illusion persisted.

I hurried forward. Without being conscious of it, I had decided to follow the two men.

"Do you want those books, miss?" inquired a polite voice behind me.

I had been on the point of departing, still clutching the unpaid-for paperbacks. "Oh yes." Hurriedly I handed over the cash, waited impatiently for the change, and hastened out.

The delay had been crucial. The street outside was empty. I walked toward my Honda. There were a few cars parked up and down the street. They were the usual shabby motors you expect in a farming community, but one pale-blue vehicle with a foreign look caught my eye. It was moving away. I watched it thoughtfully.

At this moment, the young fisherman left the post office, stood at the curb for a second, and then, apparently recognizing the driver of the blue car, waved. The driver slowed down and must have spoken. The fisherman turned his head and looked down the road, as if they had been talking about me. I had the strange feeling that sides were being picked for some game no one had told me about. I hurried along to see who was in the car when the driver put his foot down and the car moved away smartly. I was left well behind.

I didn't wait any longer. I got on my bike and sailed off.

The road was bad, flints and sharp stones; I jolted over them, slowing down as a precaution. It might not be a bad idea to learn how to mend a puncture, I mused. But I got to Berwick in record time and rode triumphantly into the town. I could see a flash of my reflection in a large mirror placed in the window of an antique shop and I thought I looked good. I roared into the station yard. "London train in yet?" I called to a lad unloading a railway van.

"No. Signaled, though."

"Can I leave my bike here?"

"Sure. Leave it where you like. Safe enough. Going on the train, are you?"

I shook my head. "No, just picking something up."

He cocked his head. "That's the train now."

I heard it too. I settled the bike, gave it a pat, assured it that no dog would ever take its place in my heart, and walked on to the Berwick station platform.

The London train rumbled in, and a few passengers got out. The station was not busy, and the guard in the mail car and the station's two porters and the lad who had been at work in the station yard were able to devote their full attention to me and my problem.

"I haven't got any animal for you here, miss," said the guard, scratching his head.

"Was it put off at Newcastle, maybe?" asked one of the porters.

"No, it was not," said the guard shortly.

"When is the next train?" I asked.

"Afternoon," said the other porter.

"There's a fast train, stopping only at Newcastle and Berwick then through to Edinburgh," suggested the guard. "Due in an hour."

"Best go into Berwick for a bit, miss," advise the lad. "Have a cup of coffee. I'll look after the little dog if it arrives before you do."

"But supposing the dog's been put off at Newcastle," said the first porter, who seemed worried about this possibility.

"You ring through and tell 'em not," retorted the guard, "and let this young lady set off now."

There was a chorus of agreement, and I let them convince me. It was a pleasant morning, and I looked forward to exploring the town some more. It was not a disagreeable proposition, although I was beginning to shape a few sharp sentences that I would put in a letter to my friend Toya.

The first thing I saw as I came into the main street of Berwick, the place where the road widened into a market place, was the blue car. It was parked at the curb, empty.

Hard at hand were the public library and the town museum. The library was on the first floor with a small art gallery in the back. On the next floor were two rooms devoted to a collection of objects of local interest.

I strolled through these two rooms, idly studying one showcase after another. In the front room a large window overlooked the street, so I could keep an eye on the car. I wasn't much interested in what I saw; it seemed a mixed collection, nothing greatly to my taste. I was bored and preoccupied, there only to fill in time. I was not anticipating anything—which was why the shock of what I suddenly encountered brought me up short. I remember I jumped. It was a physical reaction. I was actually shocked into movement.

Before me in a glass-fronted cabinet was a selection of weapons; I recognized a sword, an axhead and a shield boss. The neatly lettered notice underneath read: "Norse weapons: Found in a grave at Beal: Ninth century." But what mesmerized me rested on a shelf beneath.

Two wooden carvings were placed side by side. The wood was so ancient and weathered it had acquired the appearance of stone. It looked as if it would crumble at a touch, yet it seemed immensely enduring.

The first object was a bearded man's face with piercing eyes, a long straight nose, and a mouth opened as if in the midst of a shout. It was labeled: "A Viking head: Beal: Ninth century." Striking and even terrible as it was, it was not this object which had made me jump, but its companion. There it was—carved now in wood and three-dimensional, not in stone and in relief, the self-same animal head that I had above the door at Markaby: the nose, the eyes, the fanglike teeth. I could not mistake it. Here the inscription read: "Animal's head from a Viking warrior's sleigh: Ninth century: Found near Garrow."

Now that I could see the head in profile I thought I understood the explanation of the name Dragon's Eye. Here was the dragon; here too was the monster. The stone now built into my house had probably been dug up either on the island or near at hand. The sight of it had given birth to country tales of monsters from the sea. Or even, I thought, the very memory of the Vikings coming from nowhere out of the sea in their terrible ships had lingered on to create the legend.

I believed I had solved one of my mysteries. Never without a notebook and pencil in my pocket, I sat on the windowsill to sketch the monster, all the while keeping a discreet eye on the blue car. No one else seemed interested in the museum, which was quiet and cold.

Lion, dog, man, bear, fish? What was the ancestry of my monster? He seemed to derive from all and yet resembled none closely. But whatever he was, he had endured a long time, and had left his mark on Markaby.

I worked away quietly for a minute, still checking now and then for the car. After a while I realized that without my noticing someone else had come in and was quietly studying the Viking weapons. He had his hands in his pockets. From his posture he looked slumped in gloom.

At last he turned and saw me. "Hello." Jaimie Berwick. He looked tired, thinner than when we had last met. "How are you? Nice to see you again. Studying our sacred relics?"

"I suppose you come here often?"

He laughed. "Oh, you think so? Well, no, not so very often. I'm just filling in time before a business appointment."

"Me too." I showed him what I had drawn. "You see, it's exactly the same image as the one on the stone at Markaby. I'm living there now, you know. And it's one of the first things I noticed."

"What a clever girl you are."

My spirits plummeted. He had spoken just as if I were an enthusiastic child. "I suppose it's not an important parallel. Probably lots of people know."

He made an effort. "No. No one has noticed. Markaby is not well known. No, it's really quick of you. And you've done a fine drawing, too."

"Oh, it's nothing, not good at all. I just wanted it for the record." I put my drawing in my pocket. "What strange people they were. And imagine them being at Markaby. Of course, I knew they invaded the south of England— King Alfred and all that. I didn't realize how far north they came."

"They got everywhere. Up the Danube, into Russia, to Samarkand, to Byzantium. They even got as far west as L'Anse aux Meadows."

"Where's that?"

"Newfoundland."

"Oh yes, Vinland—I've just read about that."

Intrepid voyagers they had been, these men who had created my monster and who had decorated the prows of their ships with wild, fierce faces such as the carved wooden one I saw here.

"What made them travel so far?"

He shrugged. "They came from a poor country with few resources. If they wanted to prosper, perhaps survive at all, they had to sail out toward the richer world. And they were traders, too. They brought home furs and ivory and wax and honey, as well as spices and silk. The luxury goods of the Dark Ages, in fact. All the silk there was in the world then came from China. Someone had to bring it in."

"They must have been marvelous sailors."

"They were. Remember they didn't have a compass; they had to steer by the stars. But, in fact, they hugged the coastlines and went from landmark to landmark."

"Still . . ." I suddenly remembered and I looked quickly out the window. The blue car was still there.

"Yes, we don't know and can only guess how many ships set out on a voyage and failed to return," Jaimie continued. "Generations were short then. Very few men and probably fewer women witnessed anything like old age."

"They believed in an afterlife, though."

His eyebrows shot up. "How do you know that?"

I wondered suddenly how I did, and then it came to me. I pointed to the swords and weapons in the other display cabinet. "Surely you only take your weapons into the grave with you if you expect to come through the door of death and use them on the other side?"

"Their burial customs weren't what we'd call pretty, although they had a validity for the users. When a rich man died they drew his ship onto the shore and built a funeral pyre. Then they summoned an old woman whom they called the Angel of Death and she dressed the body. And then she prepared the girl who was to be burnt with the dead man, dressed her, and drugged her too, I guess. He had to take a girl with him. It was a man's world. They didn't burn a man when a woman died. The Angel of Death dressed the girl up in her death finery and veiled her, and led her through to where the body was and laid her down, too; then six of the dead man's closest friends came and made love to her, one after the other. Then two of the men seized her legs, two her arms, and the Angel of Death put the veil around the girl's neck and gave one end to each of the other two men and they pulled it tight. Then they burned boat, ship, man and girl."

The picture he drew was bizarre and frightening. "Was it always like that?"

"No, they practiced inhumation, burying the ship, with the bodies and grave-goods on board."

"How did they choose the girl?"

He shrugged. "Perhaps it was some poor creature who happened to be around. Or perhaps she volunteered. There are women like that, who set out to be victims."

I blushed; it was a shock, in a way, the hardness in his voice as he spoke. He seemed almost to be laughing at me. I wanted to say: It's nothing to do with me, I'm not a natural victim, and the only Angel I know is beautiful and young.

I think he saw this in my face, some feeling, however inexplicable and unwarranted, of personal involvement, for he said, "You know, I've been thinking that my grandfather must have had some reason for leaving you the house. It may be he thought you were one of us. Related."

"I've thought that too," I admitted.

"It must be the answer."

"One of the answers."

"Makes a difference, doesn't it?" He smiled at me charmingly. "You and I might be cousins. Very remote, of course."

"Of course." I glanced away.

"There's no real likeness, but you're tall and fair, like us. I suppose one day we might find out what evidence my grandfather had. If any. Unless you have some. You keep looking out of that window, did you know?"

"I'm watching a car outside. It's the blue car," I admitted.

"Oh, why?" His face was serious, but his voice sounded amused.

Feeling defensive, I found myself trying to explain. "I have had uninvited guests on Dragon's Eye. Or one, at least. At night, too—not exactly the time I want strangers prowling around the island. A motorboat arrived one night, someone landed and walked around, and then went away. It was nasty."

"Yes, I can see it would be alarming. Have you told the police?"

"No, and I'm not going to." I could just imagine a skeptical Northumberland policeman listening to me. Especially when it became known that I had acted in a horror film.

"Have you got a gun?"

"No." I was startled. "I'd rather find out who is taking an interest in me than shoot them. That's why I'm watching the car."

"What makes you think the car will be a help?"

"Oh, just a guess." I did not tell him about the smell of lemony scent in the shop. Its value as a clue seemed nebulous and vague.

"I think you may have guessed wrong. I hope you have."
His face was still serious, but now there was undeniable
amusement in his voice.

"Why?"

"The car's mine."

"What? Was it *you* on the island then?"

"It was not. Was there anything there at all? Dragon's
Eye is famous for producing all sorts of illusions. It must
be the prototype of Caliban's island, I should think—full
of strange sounds and noises."

"So it was you I've been shadowing over the Northumberland roads?" I was only half pleased, a bit ashamed
really.

Our eyes met and I began to laugh. But I was glad I
hadn't told him about the scent of lemons I smelled among
the paperbacks, and that I hadn't asked about the conversation with the young fisherman.

"But there *was* someone on the island. I won't be driven
away, and I'll get to the bottom of it," I said obstinately.
"Pip Naseby told me to measure my strength against the
strength of the island and I will. Oh, I'd love to stay and
talk of it all to you, but I've got to meet a train."

"I would never have suspected Pip Naseby of such
poetic imagery," he said. "You get off to meet your train.
Whom are you meeting, by the way?"

"It's not a whom," I said. "I believe it could be a dog.
It's a sort of surprise." I looked at my watch. "I really
ought to go and collect this animal."

"You go." He actually gave me a little push. "Go *now*."
He called after me, "They always put dogs in the mail
car in the middle of the train. Try there first, remember."

On the way downstairs, I passed the librarian going up,
arms full of books. Behind me I heard her say, "Oh, Mr.

Berwick, here are the books on the Viking invasions you ordered."

The mail car seemed bare of dogs, however. No kennel, box or tethered puppy met my eyes.

"You haven't got a dog here for me?" I asked, addressing a porter carrying out parcels. "My name's Melrose."

"No dog." He shook his head.

"It *might* be a cat."

"No cat either."

I hoped it wasn't a donkey or a lion cub or a baby elephant. But no, even Toya would have failed to persuade the railway to carry something so exotic for her unescorted. "I've met the wrong train, then," I said, turning away. I was half relieved. With any luck the animal and I would fail to meet, ever.

"Wait a minute." He put down his parcel and consulted a list. "Melrose, did you say?"

"Yes."

"Well, I have got something for you. Put me off you did, talking about a dog or a cat." He went behind a stack of newspapers and magazines. "Got it." His voice was triumphant. "Here we are."

He emerged carrying a large bird cage. Inside, I saw a hunched, dejected form, eyes mournful, beak lowered against the chest. "Pretty Poll," said the man encouragingly.

"A parrot!" I cried. "I never expected a parrot."

"Got a word on it to say it talks nicely," said the railwayman, reading the label attached to the cage. "Called Cromwell. Come on, Crom, then, say something."

Cromwell gave him a baleful look and remained silent.

"Tired, I expect," said his friend. "Here you are then, miss. He's all yours. Just sign for him in the office."

I picked up the cage, which was surprisingly heavy, and carried Cromwell away. It would be wrong to say we were pleased to see each other, Cromwell and I. We approached each other warily. He didn't speak; I didn't speak. The label on Cromwell's cage was in Toya's writing. It said: "Cromwell—to keep you company. Eats the usual things. Guaranteed to talk freely." The word was "freely," I noted, and not "nicely." There might be a difference. Cromwell didn't look as though the words stored up inside were necessarily nice at all, but they might well be very free. I thought Cromwell looked a licentious old bird. And the usual things to eat? I wondered what they were. Raw meat, perhaps? There was a vulturous look to that beak.

Weighed down by the cage, I went to the stationmaster's office and paid Cromwell's fare from London, which Toya had omitted. He hadn't cost much. Then, helped by the stationmaster's assistant, I roped the cage to the back of my bike and prepared to set off. I made a detour back to the town and circled the market place.

Jaimie Berwick's sports car was gone.

I made good time back to Markaby, found the causeway still free but the tide coming in fast, and hurried bike and bird across and up to the house, where I stood the cage on the kitchen table.

The bird did say something then. He raised one bleak eye and managed to lower the other. "Bugger," he said.

"I knew you were a bad old bird," I triumphed. "Say that again and I'll cover you with the kitchen table cloth."

He was silent. Round One to me.

I unpacked all my purchases and stowed them away in the kitchen cupboards. I was missing Toya already. I had looked forward to her cheerful company. Although she always had lots of problems of her own to recount, sad sagas of what had happened to her or what was about to descend, the crises were largely imagined and Toya didn't really care much anyway. Consequently, she was always entertaining and amusing. Then again, we could have worked together. It's handy sometimes to have another person with you when you are working on a part.

At least I could work on my own. It was what I had come here for, after all. Or was it what I had *pretended* to come here for? Inside me a little voice was beginning to ask why I had truly come to Markaby, what I had really sought. A hiding place, a refuge, a place to sort myself out and get over Bert? Yes, there was an element of that in it. Wasn't there something else I was seeking as well? In my heart I knew there was.

I wanted a place and a history; I had wanted it all my life. This was the origin of my obsession with Markaby. I wanted its past. I had always known that I was adopted. In the accepted manner, Lydia had told me as soon as I had asked questions. What she did was kind and truthful and right, but it had left a hole inside me. Soon I found I was always inventing places and stories for myself. Markaby seemed to appear out of one of my stories and claim me as its own. Its past could be my past, the family that had lived there could have been my family, and I could be Markaby's future. I knew it had to have one. It didn't look like a house that had come to an end. There was a life to be lived in it. I wanted it to be mine.

I don't know if Lydia guessed much of this, but she was clever and knew a lot about girls, so she probably did. If she did read minds, I hope my dream didn't seem ungrateful to her, for she gave me so much. I was Kate Melrose of Markaby now, and I was where I had long wanted to be.

With fresh perspective, I took a slow walk through the house, going through empty room after empty room, noticing where the sunlight fell and where the darkest shadows lay, savoring the peace and the loneliness. After all, it didn't matter about Toya. My mood changed. Solitude would give me best what I wanted.

Into this solitude came the sound of the telephone, that modern tocsin, to remind me that solitude is relative.

"Hello?"

"Jaimie Berwick here. How are you? I've been thinking about you on Dragon's Eye, frightened by strangers. I didn't really think it all such a joke as it may have seemed when we were talking."

"You didn't make a joke of it. And I'm beginning to agree with you. Dragon's Eye *is* a strange place. I don't know about noises, but the atmosphere gets through to you. Yet I feel at home here. I suppose you find that odd?"

"No. You're a Viking. I've always known that, haven't you?"

"I'm glad I wasn't one, in any event," I replied. I was floundering a bit, feeling tension and some inexplicable excitement in his voice—wondering, really, what the conversation was all about.

"Oh, but they gave a very high place to women in their society. Unless they were slaves, of course. Many were, spoils of victory."

"Exactly," I said.

He laughed. "How's your pulse?"

"Quite steady," I answered. Not true; it was racing.

"You're not afraid?"

"No." No, alas, no. I felt alive with a dangerous excitement. It was nothing he had said, just a message that came through his voice. People's voices, his especially, can tell you so much.

"You ought to be. You're trembling, though."

"How do you know?"

"It's in your voice." He too could read voices. Perhaps it was the telephone, magnifying nuances and inflections. I have noticed before that it does.

"Not fear," I mumbled; I suppose he hardly heard, because he was still talking to me.

"I want you to know all this: I don't pay my bills. I am extravagant. In many ways a despicable character. Not to be relied upon."

"Do you think I believe all this?" I wondered if he'd been drinking. I knew he hadn't. It was not drink speaking through his voice.

"It is a strange way of ingratiating myself with you, isn't it? A funny way of making love."

"Is that what you're doing?"

" 'Never seek to tell thy love,' " he quoted. "The poet gave good advice."

"Oh, Jaimie."

" 'Trembling, cold, in ghastly fears— Ah, she doth depart.' Do you depart, Kate?"

I was silent, utterly overthrown, deeply moved. I *wanted* to speak, but I was paralyzed by happiness. Words, any words of mine, would have burst the golden bubble.

"I've been in love myself," I said, thinking of Bert. "So I know what you mean. I told my love all right, and you and the poet spoke truly: it's a bad idea. But there is your cousin, Angel. No, don't interrupt. Were you talking to her just now or to me?"

"To you, I think," he said slowly.

"Make sure," I said. "Get it clear. See you later, Jaimie."

Briskly, I went back to the kitchen, made some lunch, fed the parrot the same menu. He picked thoughtfully at the bread and butter, and rejected the cheese by throwing it in one corner of the cage with an angry noise. Then I went to the big drawing room, where I had already laid out my script, and started work.

I read quietly over the words, just mechanically absorbing them. This was always the first stage of all with me, when I just let the words wash over me. I read everyone's part. I could never be one of those actresses who knows only her cues. I don't believe they exist any more. So I read the play and I read the play and then I read it again. One of the things about being a poor out-of-work actress is that you have time to do this sort of thing. I have a good memory and learn extremely easily, but as a matter of fact it doesn't always do to be word-perfect with all directors. Bert, for instance, liked all his cast to start off reading and only slowly get the words by heart. He claimed that he could impose his pattern on the play better this way. I often had to pretend to him that I didn't know my lines.

It was as I was sitting there that I realized I had already moved away from Bert. The misery I had felt over him was spent. The memory of it was still there in my mind, but the reality was gone. No longer was it a mountain of despair. Perhaps it never had been so, really. Perhaps it was a mirage which when you faced it bravely shrank and died away—I was learning that a lot of emotions, mine anyway, were as fragile as that. I was learning something else, too—that there were some feelings that were so strong and vital nothing could diminish them. Oddly enough, it was my feeling for Markaby that was proving to be one of the latter. Whatever spring inside me fed it, the stream ran deep and pure.

All this time I felt that Bert and my acting world, Theater Street, represented one side of my life, and Markaby another, distinct and separate. Even inside myself I kept the two apart, by deliberate effort. I liked it this way. I thought, mistakenly no doubt, that I was free to choose.

I switched off the Markaby self now, dismissed speculations about Jaimie Berwick, fishermen and Vikings and got down to the script. I am the sort of actress who likes to work from the outside in. I daresay that sounds strange, back to front, but it's the way I do it. So I have to decide how my character walks and what she wears before I can tell you who she is.

My character was a young woman about my own age, married, with a child. I decided to concentrate for the moment on her feet. In the script she talked a lot about dancing, and I thought this would *show* in the way she walked and what she wore on her feet. And the way she moved would influence the way she talked. She had a lot to say, most of it aggressive and a bit flashy (I loved that side of her), and she'd say it fast. I was off.

At this stage I was doing all the visualizing inside and trying to keep it to a minimum, because Bert—and I was assuming it *was* Bert who would do the production—would have ideas himself. All the same I couldn't help seeing the stage clearly as I read the words slowly over to myself. Moves were forming themselves in my mind's eye. Some might have to be discarded, but some would get through. A lot of work I was doing now might have to be thrown away, one had to accept that idea, but nothing was wasted. All the work gave solidity to what was left.

My work world was shattered and Kate of Theater Street was suddenly terrified by a high scream. It was a terrible noise, a bit like a train whistle. For a moment I thought it *was* a train, running straight through the house.

Then I remembered and laughed. I got up and raced into the kitchen, where the parrot's cage still rested on the table. "Lonely then, are you?" I lifted up the cage. "You can come with me. Only no more of that screaming." Cromwell's eyes watched me beadily, saying nothing.

I put him by one of the big windows and let him look out. He stayed there quietly, occasionally moving around in his cage and looking over his shoulder at me. Toya was quite right: he was company. I wondered what his history was, where he'd come from and what he had learned. It might be amusing to try to put together his past from the things he said. Judging by his performance as the old-time train whistle he was either over twenty or had traveled abroad—perhaps in Russia, where they still have trains that whistle. I'd have to work out his diet. I could not expect him to live on bread and no cheese for long. "Pretty Poll," I called out, trying to be friendly, but he did not answer. However, he moved his head from side to side to let me know he had heard and didn't resent the words.

I worked on, letting the time run by. After a while I began to feel cold. The sun had faded and the room was chilly. In the big hearth was a pile of logs, already laid to form a fire. I put a match to them and they were so old and dry that they flared up at once. Soon the room was filled with leaping shadows and a golden light. I crouched by the blaze, enjoying the flames and the warmth. I wondered who had cut these logs and how long ago, and whose hands had laid this fire and for whom. The wood smelled sweet, even spicy, as if it were apple wood or pine, and here and there it burned with a blue flame where the salt sea had been dried into it. Driftwood, perhaps; the island was sparse of trees. Bare, too; little seemed to grow except grass. I would go out tomorrow and inspect my territory. You could walk completely around the grounds in ten minutes—a little, little world, but I was so proud of it!

Meanwhile I went out into the kitchen and made some tea. I drink a lot of tea when I am working. Cromwell was drowsing quietly in the window. I moved his cage over to the fire and gave him a sugar biscuit. Then I sat down on the floor and sipped my tea while I stared into the flames. I felt at peace. I thought dreamily, as I sat there, that I must keep up my voice exercises. I knew I moved well on the stage and projected powerfully, but I wasn't satisfied with my voice. It was sometimes too light and needed deeper, richer tones brought in. I was working on it. Lydia hated my voice-production exercises. She said I was ageing my voice, and I knew exactly what she meant. I *did* sound a much older woman when I was using my dark-purple voice. I hadn't got the balance quite right yet, with the result that the tones were part of my voice but not the whole of it. Lydia said it desexed me, too, and there was a point of truth in this, inasmuch as one of my exercises was to "use my voice like a man." I had been sounding like a man, letting my tones fairly boom round the room, feeling like Chaliapin himself for some minutes, when the telephone rang.

I went over to the cupboard where the instrument was

housed. "Hello." My tones were at their very deepest; there was always a hangover for a time which I couldn't control. Then sometimes my voice would shoot up. "Hello?" I made it a question.

Dead silence was the answer.

"Hello," I repeated, my voice, by some freak of nature, coming over even lower.

A whisper, soft and husky, a woman's voice, came across the line. "But I thought you were dead. They told me you were dead. Robert, Robert, where are you?"

Swinging back to normal, I said, "Who's that speaking?" But again there was only silence. The connection had been broken.

I went back and sat by the fire, my mood broken. It was a silly episode, but an uncomfortable one. No one likes to be mistaken for a ghost.

"Say something cheerful, Cromwell," I commanded, not expecting any response. To my surprise he announced in a grave voice, "All nice girls love a sailor."

I giggled. "You've been to sea by the sound of you, Cromwell. No doubt what you say is true. I'll remember it. Thanks, Cromwell." I gave him another biscuit and stirred the fire up, so that a shower of sparks flew out. The telephone rang again. I sat still for a moment, reluctant to answer, then dragged myself over and picked up the receiver.

"Hello?" It was the same voice again, gentle and unmistakable, but under control now. "Markaby?"

"It is."

"I am sorry, I'm afraid I gave you a fright just now."

"Yes," I said bleakly.

"I gave myself one." She had a sweet voice. "It was you speaking? It was just that you sounded so like an old friend. I've been away a good deal. But, just for a moment —it was silly of me."

"I understand," I said. I didn't really, but I wanted to say something.

"I was only deceived for a moment, you realize? Forgive me, won't you? And please forget it."

"It's forgotten."

"I wouldn't like anyone to think I was mad," she said sadly.

I didn't know what to say, so chilling and pitiful was her tone.

She continued, "I'm Stephanie Lyon. Jaimie Berwick asked me to get in touch with you. You've inherited Markaby." It was a statement, not a question. "It's a long time since I've been there."

"I don't think it's changed very much."

"No," she said politely, as if she knew better.

I cleared my voice. "I owe you an apology. My voice, I mean. I was doing my voice exercises and it sometimes has a strange effect for a while. I expect I did sound odd."

There was a moment's pause. "You mean . . . it wasn't all my imagination? I wasn't just being, well, a little mad?"

Again that word, *mad*; it dropped into the conversation like a splinter of ice. "No, no, you weren't. It was quite real, the change in my voice. I apologize for alarming you. I'm Kate Melrose."

"Thank you for your charming explanation, Kate. It was charming, may I say so?" The diffident, soft voice went on. "I blame myself a little. Just for a moment, you know, I wanted to believe in the past living again. There are . . ." She hesitated. "There are reasons. But thank you, Kate." Then she seemed to give herself a shake, because her voice became crisper and more matter-of-fact. "Jaimie asked me to telephone you and introduce myself and ask you to visit me. Will you come, Kate? I live about four miles away, on the coast. I can see your house from here, see the windows at night when they are lighted up." Her voice was getting dreamy again. "Last night I saw lights there again. The first time for years."

"Yes, it was me. I arrived yesterday."

"It's lovely to think of Markaby having life in it again. Although I sometimes wonder if it is ever empty."

As with other remarks of hers, I didn't know what to make of it, so I didn't answer directly. "I'd love to come and see you some time," I said.

"Lunch on Sunday, then? I'll write and tell you how to get to me. Have you a car?"

"I have transport," I said cautiously.

"You can walk across the sands, if the tide is right. Or ride," she sighed softly. "My horse used to love it. Do you ride?"

"Sort of," I replied, thinking of my beloved yellow bike.

"Sunday, then?" She sounded quite bright as she rang off.

I put the telephone back in its hiding place and closed the door. As I did so I looked out the window. The tide was right in now, the causeway covered, my island completely detached from the mainland. The sea looked gray and the waves had little whitecaps. If I wanted to get to Garrow anytime from now until low tide, I would have to wade or swim.

From his fireside seat the parrot said, "Let's all be beside the seaside." And then he gave an uncanny imitation of a man laughing.

"Oh, be quiet, you old wretch," I said. "A plague on Toya for sending you." I went back to the fire, which had burned down to a red heart, fragrant and warm. Stephanie Lyon sounded as if she both knew and loved Markaby. But at least she had made a welcoming noise to me, whereas the villagers of Garrow seemed to will me away.

I moved from the fire to sit down at the desk in the window, which had figured in the inventory given me by Mr. Naseby as a "gentleman's library table, satinwood with inlay." I let my fingers rest on it lovingly, then opened a drawer to put away my script. The drawer moved easily to a touch. But it was not, as I had supposed, empty.

Inside was a square white envelope addressed in what I knew to be Robert Berwick's hand. Had I not seen it on ten years of Christmas cards? In his bold handwriting the letter was addressed to me. I pulled it out, and sat for a moment with it before me. It took some courage, I can tell you, to open it, Robert Berwick then having been dead nearly a year.

It began with no more of a preamble than "Dear Kate," and said:

"I sought no contact, made no bargain when I left you Markaby, but weakness makes suppliants of us all. I have let you have what you wanted. Do something for Robert Berwick in return. I have seen you act, and you are the girl to do it. Save Jaimie for me." He ended the letter formally: "Yours sincerely, Robert Berwick."

I put the brief letter down. The writing grew weaker toward the end, as if the writer were already ill.

I had no idea what he meant. He asked me to save Jaimie, but he had neglected to tell me from what. Perhaps he had thought it so obvious that I could see for myself. I had seen Jaimie with his cousin Angel and it seemed to me that he might need saving from her. No one ought to own anyone as totally as Angel seemed to own Jaimie. It was that name. If you call a girl Angel, of course she isn't the same as a girl called Mary or Joan or Kate. I didn't take to Angel. She was so beautiful, too beautiful. Beauty, when self-adoring, as hers might be, can be repellent.

There was one other thing which occupied my mind; he had seen me act. As if to underline the thought, I pulled a slim, glossy, colored booklet from the back of the drawer. It was a program from the theater where I had worked with Bert. *Hedda Gabler*. I had been Hedda.

It took a little while for the implication to sink in, but when it did, it was both pleasure and pain. Robert Berwick had seen me act and I had never known. I wished he had got in touch with me—I should have been so proud. He had chosen not to, but he had left me Markaby and asked me to save Jaimie. And I meant to try.

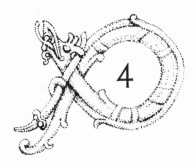

4

Even more than the usual assortment of noises plagued Markaby that night. The old boards were creaking and moaning as if someone were walking around overhead. The evening wind had risen, causing windows to rattle and doors to bang. I drew the curtains to shut out the dusk.

The kitchen looked cozy enough with its red brick floor and red-checked curtains. Like those in the other rooms, they were very old and had been washed and starched till they were thin and frail. In fact, almost everything in this house gave the impression of having been put there years ago, and used and used, and then almost forgotten. Markaby was a real Sleeping Beauty's castle, in its way.

I was no candidate for the title myself, though, for I felt wide awake. The same wakefulness was true of my companion. I had moved the bird's cage back to the kitchen and he sat there contemplating me, wide-eyed and alert. "A little bit of bread and *no* cheese," he said appositely. Never say parrots are not intelligent! He banged his beak imperiously against the bars of the cage.

"Supper's coming," I promised. I made myself an omelette and mixed up a bowl of muesli for the bird; it was the best I could offer him. I opened the cage and put the bowl inside. At once he hopped down from his swing and started to poke at the bowl of oats, apples, nuts and fruit. Briskly he threw out the slices of candied cherry I had added for color; the rest he tasted thoughtfully, raising his beak and rolling the food around in his mouth. Eventually he decided that it was good; he then put his head down and rapidly cleared out the bowl. At least now I knew what he would eat.

I ate my omelette sitting at the same table, with my book propped up in front of me. I was reading Jane Austen. Shakespeare had seen me through the grand storm of passion after Bert. But for gentle support or comfortable, everyday good cheer I relied upon Jane Austen. Music, too, had a similar calming effect on me, and the look of the sky and the feel of a smooth pebble from the beach, or even, as now, the simple act of making a good cup of coffee. I drank the coffee black, since there didn't seem as much milk left as I had expected. I must have used more for my tea and the muesli than I had realized.

From nowhere it occurred to me that Stephanie Lyon was very likely looking out of her windows and could see my lighted kitchen in Markaby. How odd to realize that she might be wondering about me, just as I was wondering about her. What did she look like, what did she do with herself—for that matter, how old was she? She hadn't sounded old, but not young either. There was a quality to her voice that only time and experience could bring. It was nice of her to ask me for lunch, even if it was only because Jaimie Berwick had asked her to do so. What was their relationship? And Jaimie—whether for himself or for my benefactor, I wasn't sure, but I was determined to protect him. . . .

"Only from what, Cromwell dear?" I shook myself from my reverie to consult the bird fondly. "From what am I saving him?"

"Do have a drink, my dear boy." Now sophisticated and masculine, the parrot's voice was so unexpected that I jumped. "Let's have a drink." Abruptly his voice was feminine, coarse and already more than a little drunk.

"What company you've kept," I murmured reproachfully. I got up to fetch him a bowl of water, just in case.

I was walking across the dark hall, just as on my first evening, when the telephone rang again, and this time I didn't think it was Bert. I was certain it was Dickon. I was right.

"Hello. It's me again. With felicitations on making that horror film we're beginning to hear about."

"Oh, are you?" I couldn't help being intrigued.

"Yes, word's getting out that it's good and that you're the best thing in it. I'm happy for you, Kate." It cost him something to say that: we watched each other's professional progress like hawks. Success for one came almost like a blow for the others. I was growing out of that adolescent attitude now. I owed that advance to Bert; what a lot of good Bert had done me, really.

"Thank you, Dickon. I haven't seen anything in the newspapers." But then until today I had ignored the newspapers. I must remember not to withdraw too far.

"There's not been much publicity yet, but it's coming." Then his voice became curious. "And what about you? What are you *really* doing up there?"

"Working," I said. "Just working."

"We heard you were so rich you'd bought an estate with a mansion on it."

"A house only," I said, suppressing the island.

"It'll corrupt you," he said gloomily. "Artists shouldn't own property."

"You don't truly think that, Dickon. Remember, I've seen you driving a dark-green Rolls."

"I don't own one, though," he said virtuously. "I only went for a ride in it. They knew I wouldn't buy it, really."

"You looked lovely in it, though. Just your style, Dickon."

"That's generous of you, Kate. Yes, it suited me. It was the contrast between me, all young and slender, and that great machine." No one admired Dickon's appearance more than Dickon. "It had such class with its power, didn't it? I mean, one couldn't be vulgar in a Rolls." Without either pause or change of tone, he continued: "Got over Bert, have you? I believe you have." He sounded envious. "You've profited from it, I expect. You're just the sort that would."

"I'm looking forward to working with Bert again," I said, truthfully.

"Yes, and now you'll be a match for him. In five years you'll be beyond him. Way above and beyond. I can see it coming. Don't think I don't envy you, because I do. But you're going to be out in a class of your own." It was a strange and touching profession of faith coming from Dickon, and, because it was wrenched from him almost grudgingly, I believed it. "I can say this on the phone. I couldn't say it face to face."

"Thanks," I mumbled.

"Remember I said it when the time comes, will you?" he went on briskly. "And if you want a good supporting actor for a long run, I'll be around."

Trust Dickon to have an eye to his own interests. "I'll remember," I said, "and I'd be delighted." I said goodbye to him, and rang off.

I went to the window and looked out. I could see the lights of the village of Garrow, with little points of brilliance in the darkness which surrounded the village indicating farmhouses and isolated homes. Somewhere out there were the Berwicks and Stephanie Lyon. I opened the window and listened to the wind and the waves. Even the wind was dropping.

It was still blowing a little, though, and as I stood there I could hear a door banging somewhere. It sounded sufficiently loud to worry me. I thought it might come from one of the sheds and outbuildings attached to the house. Although the only one that mattered was the one which housed my bike, I was worried already about the sea air and salt making it rusty. I wanted to be sure I had it safely shut up for the night. It was as precious to me as a horse.

I put on a thick coat, picked up my torch and went out. As I closed the front door behind me, I reflected that I seemed to be making a habit of night walking, and that it might be wise to lay in a supply of torch batteries. Moisture seemed suspended in the air as if the sea would shortly draw the island into itself.

I found I could see well enough as soon as my eyes adjusted to the moonlight. I hurried down the path and toward the sheds. Even from a distance I could see a darker patch against the darkness of the outbuildings. The door *was* open. I was annoyed with myself for not having closed it more firmly. There was no lock on it worthy of the name, but I could have latched it more securely. Strangely enough, the sound of banging that had brought me to investigate was gone now, and when I came to pull it forward I had to give it a hard tug. In some way it must have wedged itself.

Automatically I glanced at my bike with the usual pride

of possession. I saw at once that something was wrong, or at any rate, strange. The silhouette of the bike looked different. Perhaps it had been moved. I set the torch on the floor where it could give me light and knelt down to look. One tire was quite flat. I put my hand out to verify by feel what my eyes had told me already.

I crouched there, not moving. I had ridden over a rough, stony road that day, and I had feared for my tires, but not seriously. Apparently I had damaged this one after all. I was angry.

I shut the door behind me, closing it with care, and walked back into the house. For the first time I began to appreciate the enormity of what I had done in coming to Markaby. I had cut myself off from Lydia, who, of all people, loved me most, and isolated myself in a place where my arrival caused resentment. The people of Garrow seemed cold and unwelcoming, as if they didn't like me. Jaimie Berwick's instinctive reaction to my appearance had been anger. He had explained it away, but the emotion had been there. Only Stephanie Lyon had held out a welcoming hand. And she was a puzzle herself, considering the strange undertones in her conversation. I felt I wanted to see her before I passed judgment. But it was only Wednesday night; Sunday's lunch was a long four days away.

I walked up the path to the front door, which I had left wide open. Light streamed out. There was a toad sitting on the step; he looked at me for a moment, bright-eyed, expressionless, and then hopped away. He was no more disposed to be friendly to me than the rest of the natives.

I locked and bolted the front door behind me. Then I trudged wearily upstairs and went to bed. High up as I was, I could look out to sea. I did so for a long time, overwhelmed by my strange mood. Markaby was a place with which I had felt an identity; now it seemed to reject me. Eventually I drifted to sleep, my last conscious thought being that the door I supposed I had closed was still banging.

Thud, thud, thud, it punctuated my slumbers.

I woke up with a start. It was dawn and a gray light was blanching all the color out of the room. But it was not the light that had waked me. I had heard a noise. As I lay there I tried to make out what the noise had been. Evanescent as a dream, the memory was fast disappearing. Not that thudding door, which I now recalled clearly as disturbing my sleep. No, this had been a different noise.

Suddenly it came back to me, and I sat up quickly. It had sounded like someone moving about downstairs. Even now I could not say precisely what had alerted me— whether something had been knocked over, or whether I had heard footsteps.

I jumped out of bed, hastily put on a robe and ran downstairs. At the bottom of the stairs I halted. The door to the big drawing room was firmly closed. So was the door to the little sitting room I had made my own. I tried each door. Both were still locked, as I had left them last night.

Across the hall the kitchen door stood wide open. Slowly I walked across and into the room. It was empty. I looked from the clean, empty sink to the bare table. Everything was as orderly and ordinary as I had left it last night. On the table the bird sat in his cage dozing. Or was he *quite* asleep? True, his eyes were closed, but his feathers had a ruffled look, as if something had recently disturbed him.

Defenses are low so early in the morning, and images and visions which would be dismissed as ridiculous at full noon crowd in on the mind and find easy entrance. Dawn has its own peculiar terrors, as many as midnight. I remembered what Stephanie Lyon had said. I couldn't remember her exact phrase, but wasn't it something about never being "alone" at Markaby? And Jaimie Berwick, too, although he had tried to laugh it off, had made an ambiguous remark about monsters with no feet. I didn't believe yet that Markaby was haunted, or possessed by a monster, but for a minute I wondered if *something* did not walk here. I shook my head, put the kettle on and made a pot of tea.

Sanity returned gradually as I drank it; I was reluctant to admit that Markaby was an odd house. I sipped my tea and began to feel warm again. It was admittedly a house with warm and cold areas which never seemed directly related to the heating arrangements. The kitchen was warm always. I never came into it and found it cold. My bedroom, on the other hand, always struck chill. I told myself that I was a rational person who did not believe in the irrational, the inexplicable.

Still, there it was: mystery hung in the air at Markaby, lending warmth and scent to some rooms and bestowing a deadly chill on others. Dismiss the notion as I might, I also welcomed it. I pushed it away with one hand and held it close with another. Markaby was bringing out a side of me that I had never guessed existed. I began to ask myself what drama had been enacted in Markaby. I was sure one had been born there, had reached a climax, and had been played out to its end.

The day became one of pearly delicacy. The sky stretched above the island in a silvery haze melting imperceptibly into the sea. No wind, no bright sunlight disturbed this extraordinary day.

I walked on the island that day, for it was a day to be in the open air. My territory was bare of trees, except for a few small birches that grew on Dragon's Hill, and on this account quiet; there were few birds. Underfoot the grass was coarse, but flowering plants and ferns were profuse. I saw greater meadow rue and sweet milk vetch and hairy violet. Hornbeam-leaved bramble stretched across my path, and maiden pinks and burnet roses scrambled where they could find a hold. Even the sheep gone wild were tame that day and let me come close. I felt sorry for them, so skinny and scrawny were they.

I climbed up Dragon's Hill, although "climb" is too grand a word for my stroll up the gentle slope. I wondered idly what accident of fate had created this tiny pudding basin of a hill on this rocky place. From here I could see just that much deeper into the sea. The ramifications of rock spread out around the island, making narrow gullies and hinting at underwater caverns and mysteries. I remembered my childhood visions of drowned cities. My adult eye, less romantic, could not deceive me into seeing a drowned cathedral, but still, the rocks did have a strange workmanlike air, not wholly natural.

In the depths something was moving. I just saw a shadow pass and noticed the displacement of the water. A large fish. A very large fish. It must be very cold and dark down there. For a moment my happiness wavered. But when I looked again the water was still, and I could only make out the shapes of rocks and seaweed.

It was a day of great sweetness and peace, the memory of which I treasure still. I felt healthy and happy. I wandered around, tranquil and delighted. From everywhere you went on my tiny island you could see Dragon's Hill and Markaby. House and hill were paired.

Hunger eventually drove me back toward the house. I had never been very far away and it had never been out of my sight. But I knew the minute I set foot inside the door that another person was there.

I halted on the threshold to listen, wondering what had alerted me. There must have been some deep subliminal noise, or perhaps it was the parrot. Then I heard it again, and hearing it clearly now recognized it for what it was: the chink of china. I didn't find this reassuring but at least it told me where to look.

I made straight for the kitchen. By the refrigerator a boy was standing. He was small of stature, dark and sturdy, and he was looking over his shoulder at me with bright, intelligent, anxious eyes. In one hand he had a bottle of milk. For a moment we stared at each other in silence.

"It's not really stealing," he offered by way of explanation, wiping a ring of milk around his mouth with the back of his hand. "I was thirsty. And I often come here. 'Course, there's never been milk before."

"No, I suppose not."

"While the house was empty, it seemed all right," he said shyly. "No one said it was wrong. And I like it here."

"So do I." We had something in common. "Where do you come from, and who are you?"

"Kenny. I'm Kenny Beanley." He smiled. "We live near the village. Grace Beanley is my mum. Everyone knows her. Me too."

"And what are you doing here?"

He hesitated. "Mr. Berwick, old Mr. Berwick, never minded me coming. He knew how I like the island. And there's rabbits. I catch one or two and take 'em home for the pot."

He looked small to be a poacher, I thought.

"There's a lot of us, you see, and we gets precious hungry."

"Do the people in the village know you come here?" But of course, probably almost everyone knew. No one would tell me, though; I had been left to find out.

He grinned. A cheerful, unembarrassed smile. "Some do, but they'd never say. We're one of them, see."

"One of them." Silently I took in the significance of the phrase. "You mean you were born here?"

"Yes." But it wasn't just what he had meant, or not entirely. He labored to express his point. "We're the dark lot." He thought again. "There's *them* and there's *us*."

I looked down at him from my own tall, fair height. It was true, there was a family likeness between him and the villagers of Garrow. Not tall now, he would never be a tall adult; he would always be short and thick-boned, with a pale-skinned, dark-haired, sturdy look. Compared with his, my own skin had a ruddy glow. I thought that in him I did see a member of the older stock, still living in the countryside it had inhabited for thousands of years, but overshadowed by a taller, fair-haired invading race. No wonder I had sensed hostility from the villagers. Of course they disliked me. In fact, the source of their dislike must be deeply rooted, handed down through the years. I felt relief to know there was no personal animosity.

"I suppose I am one of the fair ones?" I said, half amused, half convinced by my own imaginings. No doubt I was romanticizing this division between the old peoples and the invaders.

"Well, you are, aren't you?"

"I'd better take you home," I said.

"No need, miss," he answered uneasily. "I know my way."

"Of course you do. But I'll feel happier."

"Safer, you mean," he answered glumly, as if he knew the signs, and this sort of dispatch homeward had happened to him before. He hitched his clothes around him. "People are always taking me home. Teacher says I ought to be put on a lead like a dog, but 'tis no good, I'm a wanderer, I am, always have been and always will be. 'Tis in the blood."

Our walk to the village was silent. Kenny looked miserable and I was perplexed. He was weighed down by a clumsy coat, miles too big for him.

"How many in your family?" I asked.

"Six. Counting Mum."

"What about your father?"

A shadow passed across his face. "Dead. Drowned. The sea's terrible dangerous around about here." He pointed. "That's our house. We can go on around the back to the scullery." He led the way in, calling out, "Mum? I'm back."

The Beanley home was a tiny cottage, one room upstairs and one room down, I guessed. I wondered if they had any money at all, and what I had better do about it. Social services existed, I knew, to help people like them, but some families always fall through whatever nets are held out, and the Beanleys might be a pretty intractable lot. Kenny Beanley was a born kicker of holes in nets if I ever saw one. I suppose I was a bit that way myself, so I sympathized.

I found reason to modify this view later on, as I watched Kenny Beanley unload his pockets onto the kitchen table. Out came potatoes, cabbages, an unlabeled bottle, an unskinned rabbit, a roll of paper, a loaf of brown bread; it explained a little his uncouth, bulky appearance.

"I allus was a good shifter." He spoke with satisfaction. "Shifting" in Northumberland parlance means the power to transfer quietly to yourself what other people don't want. You can't call it stealing quite, it's more a sort of poaching. I recognized that in Kenny Beanley I had met a prize shifter. No doubt the Beanley clan had lived a sort of tinker's life, moving around the country, doing odd jobs, poaching and "shifting" for generations. Tinkers they had been for centuries, I had no doubt, but did not tinkers trace their descent backward through the millennia to the ironsmiths of the heroic ages, taking their mysteries, now degraded, around the countryside?

Grace Beanley came downstairs, followed by a large and ugly striped cat. One ear was bent forward, and a scratch across the nose had healed with a scar. Unmistakably masculine, he looked like a battered, half-pay captain from Marlborough's wars. The long face was patient and experienced. "That's our old Timmy," said Mrs. Beanley. "Take no notice of him, he wouldn't harm a fly." The paws and teeth that had never harmed a fly looked to me alarmingly capable and practiced.

"Who's this then, Kenny?" She did not really need an answer; she knew. "Miss Melrose, is it?"

"I brought Kenny back," I said, feeling awkward. Behind her surged a troop of young children, staring and silent.

"I'll see he don't get in your way, miss." I could see she was unobtrusively studying the goods her son had deposited on the kitchen table. "Young rogue, isn't he?"

I never got entirely used to the appearance of Grace Beanley, but the first sight of her was a shock. Small of stature, very plump, she was the most unkempt woman I had ever seen. Girt about with garments rather than clothed, her dark hair standing up around her head in a startling halo, usually a bruise or two somewhere—there was a gleam of aggression ever ready in her eye. Boadicea herself was not more warlike in appearance.

"I hope he'll come again. I really mean that. I like him." I looked around the tiny room now crowded with Kenny's brothers and sisters. They looked a friendly, wild tribe. "You'll come, Kenny?"

He nodded eagerly.

"I never had a family," I said wistfully, looking perhaps for an easy touch of sympathy.

"We've got too much," came the reply. No sentiment there.

"I'm lonely," I said, as if I had made a discovery. This didn't get me any false sympathy, either.

"Better than being crowded out," he said with feeling. Then, surprisingly, his heart melted. "Oh, but you are pretty. I do love a pretty girl."

"Thank you." Our eyes met; I knew I had a friend. I was no longer a stranger in Markaby. I ventured a question. "Since Mr. Berwick died, have you ever seen a man walking on the island? Or a boat near it?"

He shook his head. "We've all had measles, and Mum kept us in." He thought for a minute. "I *did* see a boat tied up one day, but I thought it was Jaimie Berwick. He comes over sometimes. Or Charlie Guise. He comes to look at the sheep."

I turned to his mother. "Have you seen anyone on the island?" I asked. "Any strangers?"

She shook her head. "I minds my business and lets other folk mind theirs," she said, unhelpfully.

I was persistent. "There was a man there the other night, and I think he came back secretly on another occasion when it was dark. I just wonder what he was after there on Dragon's Eye. There may be more than one man involved."

"I never seen anything on the island myself. But then I don't go to look," she replied stoutly.

"A good rule," I said drily.

"It's one I allus follows."

"Oh, Ma," protested Kenny.

I didn't believe her for a minute. She looked to me exactly the sort of person who kept a sharp eye on all that went on around her. However, I was reluctant to press her too much right away, especially since it was getting me nowhere. Hoping to learn as much as I could about my newfound neighbors, I glanced quickly around the room.

With the help of an oil stove, a length of carpet, a sofa and several mattresses, the room had been made cozy enough. The baby sat in a highchair and glared at us, mouth open, cry silenced by the interest she took in us. Three other children had crowded into the room. All were younger than Kenny. They were untidily dressed, but a look of health and energy was apparent in each child. Nor did Grace Beanley look exhausted by her family responsibilities.

On the table an old clock ticked away merrily, then suddenly and eccentrically it sounded the hour.

"Take no notice of that," said Grace. "It's crackers, like us."

"You knew me," I pointed out, thinking that I'd never looked into a saner pair of eyes, regardless of what she said. "You called me Miss Melrose straight away."

"Ah well," she said, apparently conceding this point.

"Good sort, Mr. Berwick was. Him and us have allus dealt well together."

"I'll deal well with you, if you'll give me a chance," I said.

"Yes, I dare say."

"She will, Ma, she will," said Kenny. "She's a lady, you can tell."

A faint smile appeared. "He likes your face," she announced. "Can't resist a pretty face, Kenny can't. Just like his dad."

"I'm here to stay. And I want to be happy. I won't be happy if I don't feel safe on Dragon's Eye." Ignoring the compliment, I let her know gently but firmly that I hadn't given up on the topic of my intruders.

"Ah, you're safe enough there."

"I hope so. But if not I shall certainly go to the police." I thought it as well to spell it out to her. It seemed to me she was just the woman to get the word around the county for me.

"You don't want to do that. No good ever came of that." She looked at me with anxious dark eyes.

"Perhaps not, but there seems to be something on the island those men are interested in and I'd like to know what it is."

"Smugglers' place this was in the old days, but not any longer." She shook her head. " 'Twas too dangerous even for those booty men. The sea's terrible greedy about here, terrible hungry. Not many winters go by without the lifeboat going out." Her voice changed. "I hates the sea and yet it does seem I can't get away from it. Took my man, it did."

"I'm sorry."

"He was out with the boat. Markaby owes a man to the

boat. One man, that's Markaby's share. Did they tell you that?"

"I don't understand what you mean."

"One man, that's Markaby's share," she repeated. "You owe a man to the boat."

"You mean the house provides someone for the lifeboat?"

"From time past that's been Markaby's share."

"But I haven't got a man."

"Then you pays someone to do it for you," she said impatiently. " 'Tis your obligation."

"I don't know anyone to pay."

"Charlie Guise'll do it for you."

"Charlie Guise?" I looked at the boy's face. Surely he had just used that name. Yes, it was the man who looked after the sheep. "All right, Charlie Guise it is. How do I find him?"

"Oh, he'll find you," she said vaguely, so that I concluded that Charlie, as well as looking after the sheep, was one of her ilk.

"I hope he's honest," I said, not without apprehension.

"Oh ay," she laughed. "Except with the girls."

I slept well that night, and later the next day as soon as the tide was down and the causeway was clear, I got my bike, wheeled it across to Garrow and pushed it to the garage at the edge of the village to have the puncture repaired. It was very cold and I took off my helmet to tie a scarf around my head and another around my throat. I left the bike while I went to the post office to see if there were any letters. There were none, so I bought a newspaper and some groceries. Mrs. Ogle served me and I sensed her observing me with the same mixture of curiosity and dislike as before. Except for her the shop was empty.

Then I went across the road and bought fruit and vegetables. The young woman who weighed them out for me was no less and no more friendly than before, but I minded less. I thought I had an explanation.

The weather had changed; it was a bitterly cold day with a lowering sky. Thick gray clouds tinged with the yellow that speaks of snow were lined up overhead. Sky and sea met and moved into each other. I think it was already snowing out at sea. Darkness would come soon, I thought.

The man in the garage hadn't been more than polite to me either. I had been there once before, on my first adult visit to Markaby, the day I had hired the Daimler in Berwick and swept around the countryside. I had bought gas. I wondered if he remembered and recognized me. It was not very likely, although he might have remembered the car. I remembered him, though; I had thought him surly then and I still did.

The cycle was not ready when I first went back for it, laden with my shopping. "About another ten minutes till I get around to it," said the man, eyeing me without pleasure. "Been busy on another job. Come back in about half an hour."

"You said that when I left it here," I protested. "And where is it, anyway?"

"Half an hour," he repeated. In the shed behind him I saw a car that seemed familiar. It looked like Jaimie Berwick's. "The bike's out back," he said, following my gaze. "Give me half an hour."

I gathered up my parcels and went to the Percy Arms, where I ordered some tea. I took it over to a seat by the window overlooking the village street.

A voice came from a figure sitting hunched over a tray of coffee in a corner.

"Hello." It was Jaimie Berwick.

I stared, without speaking. His face looked tired and drawn, as if he had been up all night without enjoying it.

"Hello," he said again. "I'm glad it's you. Come and join me."

I carried my tea over and sat down, still without speaking. He wasn't drunk or anywhere near it, but the coffee he was now drinking had not been his first choice. "What's wrong?" I asked.

"You can tell, can you? That something's wrong, I mean, and I'm not just tipsy? Yes, I suppose it's obvious. They all know me around here; anyway, they expect it of me. I'm expected to act wildly." He added, "I'm trying to sober up before I drive home. It was their idea here."

"A good one," I said; I waited, eyes on his face.

"La Belle Dame sans Merci hath me in thrall," he said. "And it's a fatal condition."

"Oh, Jaimie, not unless you let it be."

"Poor old John Keats knew all about it, didn't he? It killed him."

"He died of tuberculosis," I said. "It wouldn't happen now."

"Consumption, they called it then, didn't they? He was consumed, eaten up. The same will happen to me. She'll have me mouthful by mouthful. A nice bite went today." He looked at me, eyes blue and serious. "I've done something terrible, Kate. I almost killed Angel."

"What did she do?"

"I hit her in the face. I wanted to go on hitting her. I don't know how I stopped myself."

"What did she do?" I repeated. "Why were you angry with her?"

"I hit her hard and she fell on the floor. I *needed* to go

on hitting her. I did, only she screamed." He buried his face in his hands. I waited. "Then I went outside and got my gun. I was going shooting later. I loaded it. I don't know what stopped me from using it, but, thank God, something did." He swallowed. "She was still lying on the floor, but I put the gun down and came away." He took a deep breath and sat still for a moment. "Thank you for letting me say that. I'm steadier now. Thanks."

"What did she *do*?"

"She spent a lot of money she shouldn't have spent, but that wasn't it. Angel's done as much often before. Every time she goes shopping, almost. It wasn't that, it was something she said." He gave his head a shake to blow away the memory. "Forget it. I ought to. I will forget it."

"No trouble to me at all," I said. "I've forgotten it."

"I shouldn't have troubled you really—after all, you're . . ." he stopped. He put out a hand blindly, and I took it. Little you know, I thought, but your grandfather asked me to make you my business. "Not so much of a stranger as all that. After all, I now own Markaby, and that puts me bang in the middle of everything," I said.

"Yes, doesn't it? In the old days the possession of particular houses brought with it a certain social position. My grandmother would have said it gave you a position in 'the county.'"

We both laughed. I don't know what picture he was seeing, but into my own mind flashed a picture, like a colored still from a film, of a tea tray graciously laid with white linen and a silver tea urn and hands elegantly poised to pour the tea. Then I thought of the parrot and Kenny Beanley and it was all so unlike the reality of Markaby that my laughter rippled on till Jaimie looked at me uncertainly.

"And what about Angel?"

"I won't try to kill her again." He smiled with embarrassment. "I'll go home and I'll probably apologize humbly."

"It might be wise," I agreed. "By the way, someone called Stephanie Lyon has asked me to lunch on Sunday."

"We'll meet there, then. You'll meet Angel." He still couldn't stop talking about her.

I did not say that I had met Angel once, and talked to her. Instead I said, "Of course, you asked Stephanie, Mrs. Lyon, to invite me, so thank you."

"Well, I was keen to arrange a meeting. The second time we met, not the first, I was extremely rude and now . . . You've become important to me. I won't say thank you again, because I can see a look rising in your eyes. Do you know you have a very expressive face?"

"I'm an actress," I reminded him.

He thought about this in silence. "I suppose you'd say I was a farmer. Anyway, that's what I do—I look after the farms that belonged to my grandfather and now belong to me. Angel has her share; our fathers were brothers. Yes, I'm a farmer."

"And a historian," I reminded him.

He raised his eyebrows.

"The book about the Vikings," I said. "I noticed you reading it on the train. And then we met in the museum."

"Oh yes, of course. That's a hobby only." He dismissed it and got back to me. "But you're not acting now? Does that mean you won't always be at Markaby?"

"At the moment I'm what the profession calls 'resting.' I don't know about Markaby," I admitted. "I'm here for a bit anyway. Perhaps I shall stay forever."

"On that dream island?" he laughed. "You'd better

watch out. I'm not sure Markaby brings luck. The last chap who lived there drowned."

"I know your grandfather bought it at auction," I said slowly. "I was there. I don't know why he bought it. And never lived in it."

"He was a friend of the last owner, Jocelyn Lyon. He was drowned in a storm. Stephanie is his widow."

"So your grandfather bought the house as a sort of memorial to his friend?" I thought that if this were so, it explained the loving disuse of Markaby, which was both kept up and yet neglected at the same time. I had the atmosphere exactly now—it *was* like a museum.

"You could call it that. He also liked the idea of buying land, though. He had little parcels of it all over the country, most let on very low leases, all bringing in nothing much and carrying very high death duties." He spoke with feeling. I could see that a landowner's life was not an easy one nor one especially to his taste. "I didn't understand my grandfather very well. Perhaps he didn't mean for me to."

He loved you, though, I thought, but judged it wiser not to speak.

"He left me all his landed property, but what cash and investments there were he left to Angel—or most of it. I supposed it seemed fair on paper."

"And it is if you're going to marry her," I said gently.

"Did I say that?" He sounded suddenly angry. "Yes, I suppose that was the idea. An understanding, people used to call it, didn't they? We've always understood, Angel and I, that we were to be married. Or so I thought. She's older than I. One year older. Not much, but enough. Apparently just after I was born, she was lifted up to see me in my cradle. She stared at me and I stared back. The first human face I'd really looked at. That's called imprint-ing, isn't it? Anyway, Angel's face was imprinted on me, all right."

"You'd better go on home," I said, thinking that perhaps brandy and deep emotions were too powerful a mix.

"We've always married among ourselves, or, if outside, among a very small group of families. Much more than we should." He was looking toward me, but not really seeing me now. "It's made us all so close, too close. But that's over now. Something broke when I met you. You've freed me. You've given me freedom from Angel, Kate."

It was the other side of the coin from me, I thought. I had no family, he had too much. Like Kenny, only with Kenny it was his family's present problems that weighed on him, whereas it was the whole past of his family that pressed upon Jaimie. I had never conceived of a family background as a burden before, only as a support. It was a new idea, something to be pondered.

"Of course, we are of the old religion; that's been the thing binding us and separating us." Noticing my surprise, he laughed. "Don't worry, we aren't Druids. I mean the old Catholic religion. The Church has always kept its strength up here. But the families that kept the old ways tend to hang together. Sometimes literally," he added grimly. "One of my ancestors was executed by Henry VIII. Another was executed by Cromwell, and we were out with the Old Pretender in 1715 and again with his son in '45."

"You're proud of it," I said.

"Yes, I believe I am. Part of our romantic past. Anyway, that explains Angel. And, to a lesser extent, me."

"Yes." I nodded, and indeed it did illuminate that air they had of a pair apart.

He didn't mention his telephone call to me, although he

continued to hold my hand. I understood now some of the emotion behind it: he was torn between Angel and me. He had probably been quarreling with her when he telephoned me.

"Angel always gets what she wants," he brooded. "If she doesn't get it one way she gets it another."

"And one of the things she wants is Markaby?" I guessed, remembering her calling it *her* house. "I suppose she wouldn't actually harm me to get what she wanted?"

He looked at me, his eyes expressionless, then shook his head. "Not herself. Angel doesn't behave like that. She'd ask for help." He gave an ironic laugh. "Not from me, though. Not like that."

"I don't understand you."

"Don't try."

I said gently, "But I want to, Jaimie."

He stood up. "Let me drive you home. Heads we go, tails we don't."

"No." I wanted very much to invite him to come with me, but I knew it might encourage a scene from which there might be no going back. I wasn't ready. "I'll go alone. I want time, Jaimie."

"Are you sure? Will you let me go with you?"

I stuck to it. "No."

What seemed like a long minute passed. "So be it. Let the gods decide."

I waited for him to kiss me. But he did not.

He left before I did; I watched him walk away, back to apologize to Angel. Compared with him, I felt weightless and free. He turned just before he reached the corner, and waved. I think he called a goodbye. From the door of the shop opposite appeared the figure of the young fisherman I had seen the day before. He stood there, watching

Jaimie. I caught for a moment then that faint change in the note of the motor that tells you the whole machine is swinging into danger. Then it was gone. Not intuition, nor imagination, but a genuine, physical perception, quick as a bird's wing and as quickly flown away.

I took it in, experiencing a touch of alarm, but did not know what to make of it, except that I associated it with these two men.

Slowly I went off to collect my bike. It was ready as arranged. I paid the bill: an astonishingly small amount, it seemed. Then I packed my shopping away and mounted. The bike started easily, and I responded, as I always did, to the sweet pleasure of motion. The village street was quiet, with hardly any traffic, but I rode slowly in any case, as dogs and children have a way of suddenly appearing in a place like Garrow. Indeed, even as I passed, a tiny Jack Russell terrier shot across the road in pursuit of an imaginary cat, he, in his turn, pursued by a woman in a loose coat of bright-red tweed. She made an elegant, unexpectedly gay figure, hurrying after her dog.

It occurred to me that I ought to hurry myself. While I had stayed talking to Jaimie the weather had deteriorated. Snow had started to fall. I was already thinking uneasily of the road ahead. The cobbled path toward the causeway was deceptively gentle in its slope at first, but before you knew where you were, you were roaring down a slippery incline. The sharp bend came at about halfway down, and, if you were not prepared for it, it could be awkward. I was looking toward the island as I rode along. The sea, now visible on my left, was gray with white waves. The mysterious, beautiful quality it had possessed the day before had gone and it looked unmistakably menacing, a killer sea if I ever saw one. The snow was falling fast. The causeway was clear; water was splashing over it, but it should be possible to ride straight across and up the other side.

Unconsciously I had let my speed rise in the straight stretch of road after the village. Now I slowed in preparation for descent. Snow dashed itself into my face and eyes, and I tried to slow down. The machine did not respond. I pressed harder on the brakes, but the bike gained speed. With every second, every foot, I was going faster. My mind automatically registered that the brakes had failed. If my mind was cold, my spirits were not; I felt incredulous and frightened at the same time. How could this be happening to me? Almost at once I stopped thinking about that and concentrated on what I was doing. I was rushing toward the bend in the road. If I didn't steer accurately, I would be over the edge and into the rocky sea below. Once in that sea, hampered by the bike, injured perhaps by the fall, I would probably drown. Would *certainly* drown, I corrected.

The air rushed against my ears as I went down, the snow blinding me. The bend loomed a mere two hundred yards ahead. With the acute sensitivity born of fear, I pictured in vivid detail the nasty jagged edge of rock that lined the bend like teeth. The bend sharpened itself almost to a right angle before my terrified eyes as I tore toward it. It seemed impossible to me that I should negotiate the bend accurately and safely. Then the miracle happened. I was still cold, but was suddenly frozen into a state above fear. Even while I traveled fast the air about me stilled, the snow seemed to suspend itself motionless; the distance prolonged itself magically. Time was slowing down. Eyes, ears, muscles coordinated, I reached the bend—and—swung around it, at great speed, but with delicate precision. In one moment of preternatural perception, I thought I saw a human figure waiting for me below. A dark, hooded figure.

Almost immediately time speeded up again and I was hurtling toward the sea. Right ahead was the causeway. If I could get straight across, maintaining my balance on the slippery cobbles, then the rising ground ahead would slow me down and eventually stop me. Or allow me to jump off. But if I couldn't steer a straight course across the causeway then I would go riding off into deeper water. I knew that on either side of the path the sand fell away sharply.

I hadn't much time. The clock, having run itself down, was now catching up again. My body made the decision for me. As soon as I approached the bottom of the road where it came near the edge of the sea, I swung the bike around so that it ran with me straight into the sea.

The bike slid forward, wobbling; I splashed into the water, traveled for a second, then gave up as the sand and sea and snow seemed to engulf me.

The bike sank sideways and I rolled with it. Water rose past my waist, a salty wave splashed into my eyes, I choked and coughed. My knees scraped against rock. I tried to stand up, but it was an impossible effort. The water assaulted my mouth and eyes. I was still coughing and choking. The pressure on my shoulders increased. I thrashed around, but it could have been human hands pressing me down into darkness, so persistent and terrible was the force of the water. My throat was constricted, the scarf around it was being drawn tight. The wild idea flashed into my mind that the Angel of Death had arrived and was there in the cold salt sea with me.

Finally blackness descended.

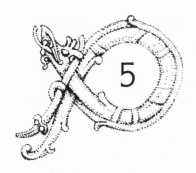

5

I was lying in water. I could feel the water drifting through my hair and the pulse of the waves against my body, touching me softly and then moving again. Someone lifted me up and held me. I opened my eyes briefly, then let the lids drop again. An enormous fatigue weighed them down.

"Come on, now, that's better. Wake up." A gentle slap on my cheek. Another slap. "Eyes open."

With all my will, I forced my eyes open again, this time to find myself staring straight up into a man's face. A young tanned face with black curly hair, dark eyes gazing intently into mine. "Well, that's more like it. You're with us again."

"You were trying to kill me." Speech was difficult, my throat was bruised and aching, my lips sore.

"What's that? Can you lean against me? I'll lift you." Without waiting for an answer, he picked me up easily and waded with me to the cobbles. "No one tried to kill you that I know of."

"I know you: I've seen you in Garrow. You're a fisherman."

"Am I? I guess I fished you out of the sea." He set me

down on the stones and sat down beside me. "I found you lying on your face in the water."

It was still painful for me to talk, but breathing was becoming easier. Reality was, however, harder to master. It seemed to keep coming and going. Now it was here, now it wasn't.

"Put your head down on your knees," he said sharply.

Obediently, I did so. I was lost in my nightmare of smothering sea and snow. I hardly knew where I was, what had happened, or what part this man had played in it. Gradually things began to settle down and I remembered my headlong rush, the cold, cold sea, and the tightening scarf around my throat. I reached up to touch my throat—the scarf was gone. I tried to stand up. "I'm all right now. I'll go over to the house. I live there."

"I know who you are."

Another voice broke in. "Are you all right, miss?" It was Kenny, who had come rushing and slithering through the snow and the water across the cobbles. He carried a torch in one hand. "I was out with Mum on the shore when I saw you lying in the water and Charlie trying to get you out."

Helping me out or pushing me in, I thought. "Charlie?" I said.

"Charlie Guise," said the fisherman impatiently. "Come on, Kenny, give me a hand with her and we'll get her up to the house before she catches pneumonia."

"I can manage."

"Yes, yes, I know you can, but we'll help you."

Kenny came up closer. "You help her, and I'll carry her things."

"The bike," I said. "It's in the water. I crashed. I might have been killed."

"I shouted, miss, when I saw you lying there. Didn't I, Charlie? You heard me, you looked up."

"Yes," said Charlie Guise. "I heard you."

"Then I came over here as fast as I could. But Charlie had you out. How did it happen?"

"The brakes went." In spite of my brave words, my legs began to feel strangely weak, and they were not quite there. Charlie gave me one look, picked me up, and carried me across the causeway and up to the house.

"Go and get your mother, Kenny." And against my muffled protest, he said: "I can't undress you and give you a hot bath, and that's what you need."

"Yes, I'll go," I heard Kenny saying eagerly. "Mum's gathering seaweed." He pattered off.

"Gathering seaweed," Charlie muttered under his breath. "That old witch!"

I was not anxious to meet Mrs. Beanley's gaze when, with incredible and happy speed, she arrived. Her expression was both predictable and only too easily readable. Charlie Guise had once again proved his way with the girls. "Whatever happened? You're soaking wet. Best get her to bed, eh, Charlie?" She gave a deep chuckle.

He ignored the question—and its implication. I thought he didn't seem any better pleased with her little pleasantry than I did.

She bustled forward. "What a mercy you had a good fire lit. You can't beat that old kitchen range for giving out a good heat. And the kettle'll be on the boil in a moment. I'll give you a hot drink. And there's a nice, hot bath. You go and get those wet clothes off. I'll keep Charlie here, never fear." Again that cheerful laugh.

I was too wet and physically uncomfortable to give her the sharp retort she undoubtedly merited, but I considered it crossly as I changed, and wished I had spoken. The leather coat was sopping wet and seaweed was stuck to it, but I thought it could be saved. My boots, however, were a mess. I threw them into a corner of the room.

"Bath's ready, m'dear," called Grace's cheerful voice. "Real scalding it is and I've thrown a nice handful of sea salt in, I have. You lie there and soak yourself."

I poured in lots of my favorite bath oil, hoping that it would exorcise the sea salt, and climbed in. I had to hand it to Grace, it was a delicious bath.

When I got back to the kitchen, Mrs. Beanley was drinking tea, and Charlie Guise was standing by the kitchen fire smoking a cigarette. Mrs. Beanley handed me a steaming mug. "Here, drink that. I've put some rum in it."

"I know. I can taste it." The flavor of the sweet tea, thick with rum, was atrocious. I wondered where the rum had come from. "Shifted" from somewhere, no doubt.

"You'll be none the worse for having that inside you," she said with satisfaction. There was more than a little bit inside her, I thought, judging from the rosiness spreading over her face and her comfortable, expansive manner. "Now come on, Charlie, drink you up."

"Thanks," said Charlie, but he continued to smoke and not drink.

Kenny was not in the room, but he soon appeared, reporting that he had hauled my cycle out of the sea, dried it, and put it away in the shed. His face was rather white, and he went quietly to sit by the fire.

"Did you find a scarf?" I said to Kenny. He shook his head silently.

"Here." Charlie Guise drew out of his pocket two pieces of yellow and white silk. "I took it off you. It had caught on the bike and was in the way. Sorry I had to tear it."

I looked down at the two tattered pieces of silk. I could remember vividly the way they had cut into my throat.

"How did it happen, then?" Mrs. Beanley was all ready for happy conversation.

"The brakes went," I said shortly. "I didn't manage the last bend."

Her eyes widened. "And how did the brakes let you down like that, then?"

"I wish I knew. I'll have to speak to them in the garage."

"You'll get no joy out of them," said Grace Beanley, shaking her head before taking a deep swig from her mug: neat rum, it must have been. "Never was a time that man would admit he was in the wrong, and his work don't get no better as time goes on." She took a good long drink. "Lucky you passed by when you did, Charlie. Reckon you must have knocked yourself out, miss, when you went down."

"No," I replied, recalling all too well the feeling of pressure on my shoulders, the tightening of the scarf around my throat. Calmer now and safe, I had to admit the likelihood that the idea that there had been someone there, pressing on me, strangling me, was the result of hysteria. My scarf had caught in the bike wheel: that would explain the struggle. The man's words were only now registering.

"What were you doing this way, Charlie?" inquired Grace Beanley.

"I came around to see about the boat."

"Funny time to come." She was down to a pretty little giggle—she must have been a ravishingly lovely girl before flesh thickened over delicate bone. The same thought had occurred to me, only I didn't say it aloud; I suppose my eyes spoke for me, though, because he reacted to my doubt.

He put out his cigarette. "Yes, well, that's how it was." He wasn't offering any explanations.

Grace giggled happily; Charlie was her darling. He looked at me. "You all right?"

I nodded stiffly. I said, "Thank you." I licked my lips. "Did you see anyone? Was anyone else down there on the sea? Or on the path?" I shouldn't have piled the questions up so desperately; they were all looking at me.

"No." He shook his head. "I didn't see anyone." There was not much expression on his face at all, yet he managed to convey something to me. Disapproval, it looked like, as if I didn't have what he found attractive in a woman. It annoyed me. "But then I wasn't looking. Even you were a surprise." He turned away. " 'Bye, Grace. I'll be back to talk about the boat, Miss Melrose."

I gritted my teeth; it would not take much to make me very angry indeed with Charlie Guise. "I haven't asked you yet," I said.

He walked toward the door, buttoning his coat, and timing his delivery nicely. "No, but you will. Glad to get me."

I went to bed shortly afterward, attended by a flushed and happy Grace Beanley, who carried a hot-water bottle in one hand and my caged parrot in the other.

"Brought the bird to keep you company." She planted the cage firmly on the bed table. Cromwell was awake, but silent.

"I don't want the bird."

"Don't you worry. He'll be company." She put the hot-water bottle in beside me and fussed around the room. It was odd but, as I had already noticed in her own cottage, she did have a knack of creating comfort in her own way. The bottle was soothing, the minor adjustments to the room somehow settling.

"I'm off." She paused at the door, rosy and tipsy. "Tell you something; I ain't really a witch."

I raised my head from my pillow in surprise. "I never thought you were."

"Just in case they tells you I am. Odd little spells or two, I *may* have cast, but 'tis all white magic, not black." She nodded comfortably. "And I can tell the future. Just a swirl of the tea leaves." Then she really gave me a jolt. "The sea and a journey and your own true love are written into your future. I see it there." She must have seen more alarm than pleasure in my face, for she giggled. "Take no notice. 'Tis what I tell all my ladies. But, take it this way and that, sometimes it works out true."

In her own way she *was* a witch, I thought.

I lay there brooding, not so much on what she'd said (once she'd gone, I didn't take her too seriously) but on the whole episode.

I had come near death. Lying there looking up at the ceiling, the fact seemed inescapable to me. I assembled the evidence: my brakes had been rendered defective, possibly at the garage, and whether by accident or design I could only guess. But my guess was that it had been done deliberately. The very punctured tire which had led me to the nearest garage now looked like a device to get me there just in order to have my cycle turned into a lethal weapon. Fantasy? I swear it did not seem like fantasy to me then.

I had gone into the sea. I had not knocked myself unconscious and rested helplessly there in the water to drown. But that eventuality had been provided for. Someone *had* been waiting for me. I could still feel that steady pressure on my shoulders, and then the tightening silk around my throat.

Had I been saved by the timely arrival of Charlie Guise? Heaven knew. I didn't know what to make of him. I had to ask myself if he had indeed saved me, or if, on the contrary, he had been stopped from finishing his plan by the shout from Kenny.

But why should Charlie Guise want to kill me? Why should anyone, for that matter? I knew that the island and the house were the key.

I tossed and turned, fantasy and reality jostling for a place in my mind. It was horrible. No preparation for the work I was trying to do for Bert, either. But I was not going to leave the island. All my obstinacy asserted itself.

The door opened and Kenny came in, bearing a mug. "Here, you're to drink this. It'll stop you getting a chill or having nightmares."

I stared into the foaming beaker of pale, amber-colored liquid. "What is it?"

"I dunno," he said indifferently. "Something brewed up out of herbs. A simple, she calls it, but it won't kill you. She knows how to do it."

I sat up in bed, taking the hot liquid from him. "Thank you for helping me, Kenny. I owe you a lot."

"Oh, it was Charlie."

"Maybe." I studied his face; there was something he wanted to tell me. He wore the expression of someone who needs to share a burden. "What is it, Kenny?" He did not answer. "Come on, now, tell."

He hesitated a moment more, then he said, "You know, you asked Charlie if he saw anyone else down there? Where you had your accident, you know?"

"Yes, and he said he saw no one."

Kenny turned away, so that I could not see his face, only a tense profile. "I saw something, though. I thought so, anyway."

I waited; he continued reluctantly: "Snowing it was and getting dark. Just for a second, I saw—"

I waited. "Go on," I said.

"Thought I saw something in the water; something floating there, and then it moved away. A shadow, but it moved like a big fish." His eyes were round and tense.

"Probably was a fish," I said, uncertainly. "But you were right to mention it."

He gave himself a shake, as if he had unloaded a nasty burden. I drained the mug of its warm, bitter tisane and handed it back, emptied. The flavor lingered on my tongue, but not distastefully.

Then the strangest, sweetest sleep descended on me.

I was still happy when I woke up. The snow had ceased to fall and the sky was clear. Indeed it was a hard, bright blue with a freezing wind skidding across the top of the water and raising waves. I was getting used to the sudden changes in the climate. In a city, although one complains enough about the weather, it doesn't have as sweeping an impact as it does on an exposed coast. The weather here was real, a force to be considered constantly and reckoned with. How much worse it must have been centuries ago for all those earlier settlers here, Norman, Anglo-Saxon, Norse. A cold welcome the Vikings had encountered when they arrived, and a cold welcome they expected, no doubt, feared and hated as they were. Yet, judging by what I had seen in the museum at Berwick, some of them had liked it well enough to settle here until they died.

As soon as I could get across to the village, I went to visit Grace Beanley.

"What a night of comfort you gave me," I told her.

"Oh ay, sorrel is comforting. And did you dream? You should dream of your laddie, or him that will be. A sorrel simple brings good dreams."

"I have no laddie," I said, sadly, I believe.

"Then you would not have dreamed." She stared into my face. "And I think you did dream."

"But I've forgotten the dreams. They faded."

"You'll remember them one day, and find out old Grace did you a good turn."

I don't know if she really believed her own words, but she managed to instill a cheerful conviction in them. No sting of a hangover from last night, either. I thanked Grace and returned to Markaby, eager to make up the lost day. I fed the parrot, who had managed to make it unmistakably clear that he ate the same as I did, thank you, and none of this stuff put up in packets and marked "birdseed"; he'd have egg and bacon when I did, and fruit when I did, and anything else that was being served. As I was hungry that morning, we both ate well.

After eating I worked, which, for me, meant taking myself into the sunny room overlooking the sea I had made my own and studying my script. Although it was so interesting and exciting, I found it difficult to get a grip on my part. I still couldn't really see the woman physically. It suddenly occurred to me that she was a woman living on her own, she was unhappy, she liked to dance, yet there were hints she was worried about her weight. For instance, she was always saying she was "in a heavy mood" or "the situation is very tight" or "there is a weight on my shoulders," and I saw now that these could all be taken as puns upon her physical state. Immediately my body sagged, my legs felt heavier, and I started to move across the room, as I felt that woman would have moved. My conception of the part had begun to solidify.

Later in the day, just as the golden light of evening was filling the room, I thought that it was about time to contact Bert. It would never do to get my interpretation settled into too firm a mold without discussing it with him. After all, I had to work with him and the other players; we were a team. Nevertheless, it sang in my blood that what I was doing now was right and would develop successfully. One thing I suddenly knew without reason but with absolute clarity was that I hadn't dreamed of Bert last night.

I called his office and at once spoke to his secretary and Bert was almost immediately on the line. In the old days of my loving him, I would have had difficulty in getting the telephone answered, and when I did, Bert would have been on another continent. I didn't mind. I didn't make little jokes about irony to myself. It seemed to me that this was the way life should be—there should be resistance, life should not bend to one's will. It was reasonable that the things one wanted should be slightly withheld. It made the struggle enjoyable. This was the extent of my self-confidence that midwinter's day.

Bert listened to me attentively, asked a few questions, then gave me some hints about the production plans, and the roles that had already been cast to help me direct my reading preparation. I could tell that my confidence had transmitted itself to him—and I knew that he wanted me to get the part. He would be sending me some drawings and diagrams of the production for me to study. I was to remember please that although I was tall not everyone was, and that the actor who would be playing opposite me was rather short. I was also to remember that *color* was going to be very important in this production: we would play to red. I couldn't quite make this out, but red is the color of joy, and so it sounded good. I did have one vain misgiving, however.

"I shan't have to wear red?" I questioned. "You know how I look in red. Not my color."

"No, just think red."

"I'll try." No doubt I would find out more of what was in his mind as time went by. Bert usually explained himself lucidly in the end if you showed patience and waited. The mystification was part of the process of discipline he imposed on his cast.

"I am getting some rewriting done on the script. I'll be sending it to you," said Bert. "I think you'll find your part is expanded."

"Oh, great!" I exclaimed.

He grunted. "Just an experiment. Don't know yet if you can carry the play. It would mean your carrying it if you get the part."

"I'll knock myself to bits trying, Bert," I hastened to assure him. "Is there anything more you want to say? Any advice to give?"

"What you've been doing sounds great. Now remember to keep the middle of the next month *free*. I shall want you down here then. What are you doing up in the wilds, anyway?"

"Just working," I said.

He caught something in my tone, some stress or anxiety I had not meant to show.

"And *what*?" he demanded.

"Oh, nothing really," I said. "It's a strange place up here, and just occasionally the unexpected happens."

"Atmosphere, is there?"

"Yes," I admitted.

"Lonely, isolated, hostile countryfolk? Peasants, if you like to call them that?"

"Mm, yes."

"And is there a witch, and a monster, and someone who seems able to disappear at will?"

"Well, yes, in a way."

He laughed. "Know what it is, don't you? It's that horror film you made. The genre has got into your blood and you're seeing everything in its bloody light!"

"Oh, I do hope not." I was aghast at the thought.

"Shall I come up there and make it better?" he inquired with a great gusty laugh.

He didn't wait for an answer, though, he wasn't really interested. Reality for Bert ceased at a radius of a hundred yards or so from himself.

As soon as we hung up, I went for a walk on the island. The snow had melted, the sun was low in the sky, the shadows long.

I was grateful to be outside. While working, and perhaps under the influence still of Grace Beanley's herbal remedies, I had put aside all thoughts of yesterday, all fears and apprehension. But with the first breath of cold air they all came rushing back.

What was there on Dragon's Eye to inspire violence? As far as I could see on my solitary stroll, it was a bare, quiet island with one house, a few trees, some sheep, and a hill. And yet, as I walked—this time with eyes alert for signs—it seemed to me that I *did* see indications that the island had received visitors. Regular visitors.

The tiny trackways crossing the island, going somewhere but I hardly knew where, had been used. They were too well and too recently trodden down for a deserted island.

I paced them thoughtfully, observing here brown and broken bracken, here muddy puddles of melting snow, marking areas where the ground had been walked into hollows. It could be the Beanley family, but they, or most of them, had been ill. Perhaps it was Billy English's forgotten sheep. Every so often I caught sight of the animals sedately pacing the island paths. Someone had been smoking a cigarette, too, and had been careless with the stub. I could see it in a patch of grass in front of me. The snow had soaked it so that it was a sodden little bundle, but still recognizable for what it had been. Sherlock Holmes would have known the brand. I couldn't achieve that feat. But moved by the spirit of the thing I bent down, carefully edged the little object onto a dead leaf fallen from a bush, and folded the whole thing up in my handkerchief before putting it in my pocket. I'm still not sure why I did it, except that it was evidence of a sort.

I walked on. My circuit of the tiny island was over. I was back to where the front of Markaby faced the causeway. Last night Kenny had put my Honda away, but I myself, wet and shaken, had not inspected it. Now was the time to do so. I went into the shed and saw that he had placed it tidily against a wall and covered it with an old sack. By the look of it the sack had first been used to dry the cycle. I removed the sacking and knelt down to take a good look. My cherished vehicle had lost its glossy, privileged air. Scratched and dented, it had a battered, crippled look. It clearly wasn't the virgin soul that had been wheeled from the factory floor. Nor was it in a state to be used, even if I had wanted to. I closed the door behind me, locked it, and pocketed the key.

Then I went back to the house and telephoned Jackson at the garage in Berwick. "I want to hire a car, not the one I had before, but a smaller one. Can you let me have one?"

"Yes, I reckon I can. Got a little Fiat you could have. That do you?"

"Yes." We settled about payment, then I said, "One more thing: I want to garage it somewhere in Garrow. Can you fix that for me?"

I could almost hear the surprise register at the other end of the line, but I guessed he wouldn't want to lose a good customer. "I reckon I could get it into the Percy Arms. My cousin works there."

"Splendid," I said. I was thinking that there would be a bonus here. I might find out from a local person who in the area had a motorboat, thus narrowing down who might be behind all that was happening. It was like the house that Jack built. "When can I have the car?"

"When you like." He was laconic.

"As soon as possible, then. Today."

"You'll come and collect it?"

"No," I said. "I have no means of getting over. You bring it."

More thought at the end of the telephone. Finally he muttered he would get the boy to bring it over, and the boy could cycle back. I could expect it within the hour at the Percy Arms.

I set out to walk to Garrow. I calculated that the car and I would arrive there at about the same time. The tide was ebbing, but a few waves still slapped across the causeway, making it necessary to tread cautiously. Soon I approached the scene of my crash.

I felt as though the site ought to be marked with my blood, but there was not much sign of anything untoward having taken place. The snow and the sea between them had seen to that, cleaning away any marks of disturbance. I looked at it for a minute, then left it gratefully behind. I had survived.

I had plenty to think about as I walked. It seemed to me that I was surrounded by two concentric but not touching circles of puzzle and alarm. The inner circle, the one closest to me, involved my ownership of Markaby and Jaimie, Angel, and Robert Berwick. On the outside, but much more menacing, was a circle in which swung Charlie Guise, the stranger in the motorboat, and the unwelcoming villagers of Garrow.

Head down against the wind, I trudged on. Apart from Grace this morning, I had seen nothing of the Beanleys today. Kenny, having unloaded his worry about the "thing" he had seen in the water, was no doubt having a happy day.

The first person I spotted when I finally arrived in Garrow was Charlie Guise, who was just coming out of the fruit and vegetable shop, laughing and throwing remarks over his shoulder to the woman inside. She liked him, of course. He was one of them. I turned away, meaning to avoid him.

No good, though. He caught me up with a few easy strides. "You all right?" he said, still sounding good-humored.

"Oh, fine."

The good humor faded a little from his face. I dare say my tone was daunting enough. "Oh, I forgot. You don't like questions."

"I don't know what you mean." I was discomfited.

"I got that distinct impression yesterday." The good humor was back again. "But you'll have to be better with me."

"Why you?"

"Because I'm your boat man." He made two words of it. He smiled. "That means there's a special relationship between us. That's how it works."

I frowned. "Oh, yes. You take my turn in the lifeboat if it goes out. You must let me know what I owe you."

He dealt with that easily. "You don't pay me. Not in money, anyway."

"How then?"

"It's the relationship." He grinned. "Like I explained."

I could have hit him then. I should have.

"If you're feeling better, I'll take you and show you the boat." His offer somehow managed to convey a commanding tone.

I'm afraid the surprise and probably also the hostility crept into my voice. "Is that necessary?"

"It's usual," he explained, formally. "It's the custom."

"I'm just about to collect a car," I said.

"To replace your motorcycle?"

"Yes, I shan't get it repaired immediately." I turned my head away and looked toward the Percy Arms, where a car was just arriving.

He gave me a sharp look, as if what I had said was unexpected, but entirely comprehensible. Then he followed my gaze. "Is that the car? Useful-looking vehicle."

"It'll do." The driver was a thin-faced boy with a fuzz of hair that looked bleached on top and dark underneath.

"Then we'll collect the car and drive to the boathouse. Naturally it's nearer the sea than the village."

I let the boy see my driving license. I gave him a check,

accepted the car keys, and watched while he got a small collapsible bike out of the back of the car, put it together, and then slowly pedaled off. I wasn't sure I wanted to see the boat, but it looked as though I was going to have to. One look and I need never see it again. I didn't believe then that there would be a storm so bad that Charlie Guise would have to go out in the boat in my place.

I did the driving, although Charlie Guise made a tentative effort, easily repelled, to take the wheel. I had only driven a short way when Charlie gestured with his hand. "That low building ahead is the boathouse."

The road ended here, dwindling into a track leading toward the sand and sea. A simple wooden building stood close by.

"We open the doors, drag out the boat and we're off. No messing about. Everything brisk and ready to hand in a crisis."

"So I see." I made no move to get out of the car. "Do I have to go in?"

"It's usual," he said seriously. "One look, that'll be enough. One look and put your hand on an oar and say, 'This is my oar, and Charlie Guise will take it for me.'" I looked at him suspiciously, but his face was quietly serious. "We have an engine, too, of course, but it's traditional to have oars as well. Markaby's oar has its name on it."

It was as he said. When I put my hand on it, I saw that the name had been burned into the oar in an old-fashioned, flowing script, as if someone had written the name there with a hot poker. The boat itself was newish and efficient-looking; the oar was old, old, old.

He saw my expression and smiled. "Yes, the oars get handed down from generation to generation. Just a tradition. Call it a superstition, if you like, but that's the way of the sea."

There was a claustrophobic feeling to the boathouse. The roof was low, the sides came close up to the timbers of the vessel it contained and a very pungent smell of diesel oil and sand and seawater permeated the building. I admitted to myself, if a little uneasily, that this place had a very strong character. It belonged to the boat and the boat belonged to the sea. Probably there had been a boathouse on this site for generations. The coast itself was all but unchanged since the days when the Viking ships had crept quietly out of the night to berth on the coast, while their crews hacked and burned and fought their way across the countryside in search of booty. Ravagers at first, they had become settlers. The original Markaby itself owed its existence to them. But their deep feeling for their boats had lived on and on. Superstition, he had called it, but in those early days it had had the force of religion. The story Jaimie had told me in the museum—the tale of the old Vikings being buried in their boats, with women slaves sacrificed beside them—practically came to life in these surroundings.

I put my hand gently on the oar and said my little piece. I had no wish to offend the old gods.

"Now you must take my hand," said Charlie Guise, "and I take yours and we hold together for a moment."

His hand was warm and firm and gentle, I thought with a shock. We stood together for a second and then I drew away. I thought I saw a faint, remote look of triumph on his face. I never trusted him for a moment.

Later, when I told Grace Beanley about it, she listened intently and I heard her murmur under her breath: "The bugger."

"Isn't there such a tradition?" I pressed worriedly.

"Oh yes, there is a tradition," she answered, but she wouldn't tell me more.

"I don't like the boathouse," I said to Charlie, as we walked away. He was genuinely surprised.

"Ah, it's a lovely place."

"For you," I said. "Not for me. It smells of death."

A look combining all sorts of things—worry, skepticism, and amusement—passed across his face. "It smells of the sea," he said.

"Yes, that *is* the smell," I said irritably. "And for some reason, I don't like it."

"There's always death in the sea," he said, laughter fading from his face. "You don't take liberties with the sea."

We got back into the car. "You're a strange fisherman," I said as I started it.

"How do you know I'm a fisherman?"

"I heard the man in the shop ask you about the fish at Seahouses, remember?" I said. "The first time I saw you."

"Oh yes, Ned Ogle did ask." Inexplicably the amusement was back. He was so hard for me to read.

So I decided not to try. Having resisted all his attempts to talk, I let him out of the car in the village and drove away fast, not looking back. The expression of surprise and disappointment on his face as I left him behind was not lost on me. I won't deny that it gave me a flash of satisfaction.

Satisfaction quickly gave way to self-criticism as I parked the car in the courtyard behind the Percy Arms and headed back to Markaby on foot. After all, the man appeared to have saved my life, and had since treated me with pleasant good humor. Unluckily, my own suspicions could be neither verified nor denied. The magnetism and charm of Charlie Guise, however, were evidently beginning to break through even *my* wall of distrust; that power of his personality frightened me in its seductiveness. It was hard not to like him, but I vowed to be doubly careful wherever Charlie Guise was concerned.

My musings had kept me company all the way home. Exhausted, I went to bed early and slept well.

6

By the time I woke up Sunday, the sun was high in the sky and brilliant. I believe that, as tired as I had been, I might have slept the day away, but Cromwell was starving and registered his complaint by shrieking me awake.

As I gradually came to understand the parrot's sophisticated palate and he to appreciate mine, we got along increasingly well. Once we had established that we both preferred Stilton cheese to Roquefort, and liked our butter salt, we became good friends. I had abandoned my notion that he was a ship's parrot and decided that he had been kept as a pet in a Soho restaurant, where he had learned to eat and drink well, and to enjoy garlic. He certainly liked garlic. Grace Beanley left a string of garlic bulbs hanging in the kitchen, as a specific against the wrong sort of witch, and Cromwell had pecked into each one.

To me he was invaluable as a kind of living diary and aide-memoire. I said things to him like "Order milk tomorrow" or "More bread needed" or "Lunch with Stephanie Lyon on Sunday," and he chanted the phrases at me at intervals, perfectly uncomprehending, no doubt, but very conveniently.

I don't think I would have forgotten about the Sunday arrangement, in any case, because I found, as I dressed for it, that I was excited. Lydia had not telephoned that day or for days before it, nor got in touch with me in any way. And my attempts to telephone her had ended in failure. There were many possible explanations for this, and I hoped soon to light on the right one. She was deliberately leaving me on my own, I knew that. She had given me my freedom, but I also knew she wasn't punishing me for taking it. So there had to be another reason why she remained elusive.

There were three people standing in the room at Stephanie Lyon's when I arrived: Angel and Jaimie Berwick and my hostess. They all turned to meet me wearing identical expressions, so it was easy to conclude that they'd been talking about me. Stephanie came forward, hand held out in greeting.

"My dear child, how nice of you to come. You found the way?"

"Oh, easily," I answered. My gaze fell on Angel. She was looking even more beautiful than I remembered. I tried to see traces of the bruises on her face from the attack Jaimie had made, but her skin was clear and shining.

When you walk in upon a group of people who have known each other a long time, you become aware, if you are at all sensitive, of undertones in the conversation, and of links and relationships between the characters of whose nature the speakers may be perfectly unaware.

Now, for instance, I saw at once that Stephanie was very fond of Jaimie and Angel, but did not like Angel's dominating part in the duo. I saw that Jaimie responded to Stephanie easily and that Angel, on the other hand, did not. Jaimie came forward and took my hand, then let it fall—a gentle, affectionate gesture which did not go unnoticed by Angel.

And in Stephanie herself I recognized the woman in the bright-red tweed coat I had seen in Garrow the other day, the day of my crash. As if to drive the reminder home, the little Jack Russell terrier came from behind a curtain and crouched near his mistress's feet. With a smile Stephanie introduced me to the animal. "And this is Lord Percy of Elsdon: that's his kennel name. We call him Don for short."

It was odd seeing Jaimie and Angel together and knowing so much more about them than when I had seen them at the railway station. Jaimie was smoking nervously, but he soon left Angel's side and came over to me. She smiled faintly as if she could see right through Jaimie's maneuver and clear to the other side.

"I want to see you later," he said. "We can't talk here. I'll see you home."

I nodded, bending down to stroke the little dog, which, like all of his breed, had a cheerful, impetuous friendliness. He ran from me to his mistress.

"I believe I've met your guardian, Lydia Shelley," said Stephanie. "I think we met once, years and years ago. She was only a girl really. I remember thinking she was going to have a great career." She gave a faint sigh.

"She's having it," I said.

"And she regrets nothing? All the sacrifices she must have made?"

I shook my head. "I don't think so." Had they been sacrifices when made? Was it not only recently that Lydia had begun to feel the loss of what she had never had? Prompted by this train of thought, I said, "I think Lydia has a friend who lives near here. She mentioned him to me. Michael Sars, a Norwegian."

"Michael has gone back to Norway now," said Stephanie. "I hardly knew him, though." She turned to Jaimie, who had been listening. "You know him, don't you? You are friends, surely? Isn't he the only person who knows as much about the Vikings in Northumberland as you?"

"Oh more, much more. Michael's a real scholar," said Jaimie modestly. "Yes, he taught me a lot. But we were hardly friends."

"Say pupil and master," said Angel, strolling up.

"Yes, call it that if you like," said Jaimie, with a spark of irritation.

Other people had arrived by now, and out of the corner of my eye I could see an older man and a woman talking. Stephanie was pouring sherry, carefully and with an unsteady hand, into delicate Victorian glasses. She had a gentle smile fixed on her face, but it barely concealed an air of remoteness and other-worldliness, as if her feet were not quite on the ground.

Angel, Jaimie and I were left standing together. My instinct was to turn away and find another group of people to talk to. But Angel would not let me. She kept me there as she sipped her sherry and talked, idle, party conversation, her great, luminous eyes never leaving my face. She was a tall girl, and although slender, muscular.

"You're not frightened of me, are you?" she asked suddenly, leaning forward. I realized then that those huge blue eyes were nearsighted; she was too vain to wear spectacles. To an actress it was an essential clue to character.

"No."

153

"Jaimie is." She was taunting him.

"Oh, shut up, Angel," he snapped.

We were interrupted in the nick of time by Stephanie, who introduced two new arrivals to us as Lord and Lady Ranelagh: I believe there was once a famous set of London pleasure gardens in the eighteenth century at Ranelagh, rivaling even the more celebrated gardens at Vauxhall near the river. Lord and Lady Ranelagh had a distinctly eighteenth-century flavor themselves: pink-cheeked and bright of eye, they might have stepped out of a painting by Gainsborough.

I don't remember much of the lunch because of what came after; but I believe we ate some delicious hot chicken dish, because I remember thinking that Stephanie, in spite of her air of being out of touch with the world, must either have had a very good cook or be a very good one herself. She didn't look rich, so she must have been more practical than she looked, after all.

The Ranelaghs departed soon after lunch, murmuring that they had either to open or to attend some county function. This explained the watery glitter of the diamonds on the brooch on her ladyship's jacket and the fresh white gloves that presently appeared from her handbag.

We walked outside as soon as they had gone and strolled in Stephanie's garden, where she wanted to show us her snowdrops. A few pale-violet crocuses were appearing, with a yellow one here and there. Spring was truly on the way.

"The birds always eat the yellow crocuses, have you noticed?" said Stephanie. "But they leave the purple."

"I suppose they don't taste as good," I said. Angel bent down and picked a snowdrop and tucked it into her buttonhole.

Stephanie's garden opened straight onto the cliff edge, the sea far below. Her house commanded a splendid view. I looked across and saw Markaby and Dragon's Eye, just as she had told me I would do. It seemed very close in the clear air and I even fancied I could make out the sheep grazing shyly in the northwest corner of the little property and could see one of the Beanley children playing near the causeway.

"Billy English's sheep," said Angel. "Funny, the way he left them there. Still, they've survived."

"Be a few lambs there soon," said Jaimie, with a smile. "You'll have to watch or you'll be overpopulated." It was the first time he had spoken directly to me since before the luncheon, but we had been extremely conscious of each other throughout.

Out on the cliff edge, where we had wandered, Stephanie drew my attention to the wheeling, screaming creatures overhead. I noticed that she moved her hands slightly at her side as she watched, giving me the uneasy feeling that she was mimicking flight. I still hate the sound of seagulls. Passionately, I hate the sound of seagulls.

Seen from this distance my island looked not like a dragon, as I had thought it might, but like some small, couchant animal with Markaby and Dragon's Hill as its twin humps. Surprisingly, a small boat was creeping across the glittering surface of the sea toward Markaby. I watched Charlie Guise get closer and closer to the island. Yes, I had no doubt that it was he, and he was certainly going visiting. Stephanie and Jaimie watched him too. So enchanting was my reverie about the island itself, however, that the boat and its pilot did little more than distract me for a moment.

"Did you know that there is a monster on the Dragon's

island?" I asked idly. "Or more likely just in the sea near-by? I've seen a map which says so. It was an old map, but then I wouldn't be surprised if there were some new monsters. I wonder what sort of monsters exist, and where they come from? Monsters can hardly be born in the normal kind of way, can they?"

Stephanie turned away quickly, as if the view no longer pleased. I knew, at that moment, that there was something very wrong with her, and that behind that bright charm was darkness. I wondered if I had said anything to disturb her.

I also knew something else even more important: I had to save Jaimie from Angel. Stephanie's party had clarified why Robert Berwick had not told me any more than he did. Angel Berwick radiated trouble.

Jaimie took me home. "You ought to know something about Stephanie," he said abruptly. "She's been ill. Mentally ill. She's only just come back home."

"Yes, I see." It explained her remote and dreamy air, as if she were twenty years removed from the world, and perhaps I was not so very surprised to hear it. I wondered how completely Stephanie had recovered.

"My grandfather was one of her oldest and dearest friends. He asked us to look after her, Angel and I."

"And you always have?" I asked.

"We always have. That is, since he died. Before that he did so himself."

"What a sad person she is."

"She feels a link with you. She lived at Markaby. Yes, she lived there as a girl."

"It belonged to her?"

"No, to a distant cousin who let Stephanie and her

mother live there. Later, he sold it to the man Stephanie married, and they lived there after their wedding. I suppose Stephanie was very young then. She's not old now. When her husband was drowned, my grandfather bought it. Stephanie was already ill, and had been for years."

He said nothing about the bequest of Markaby to me; we had buried this subject, but it was part and parcel of the enigma of Robert Berwick. Why me? The funny thing about this question was that it seemed to get bigger and more crucial the longer I lived with it. When I first received the letter from Robert Berwick's solicitors, I took the bequest in my stride. Now it was becoming something I puzzled over constantly. "I like Stephanie very much," I said truthfully.

"Yes, everyone must."

We were standing by the causeway. The afternoon sun had summoned up a light mist which hung over Dragon's Eye and Markaby, endowing them with a remote, mysterious quality.

"How lovely it looks," I said. "I don't think I can ever bear to leave here."

"Yes, you belong. You will stay, Kate? Forever?"

"I have to work, you know. I'm not rich. Besides, I'm ambitious." I was struggling very hard to retain my emotional balance. Jaimie and Markaby together made a powerful magic.

"You're just putting me off, Kate. You know what I want to say. What I *am* saying: Kate, will you marry me?"

"Yes, it would keep Angel out of Markaby, wouldn't it?"

He said sharply: "You know that's not the reason. Say you know it, Kate?"

"I do know it," I said slowly. Everything seemed to be pushing me toward him. I meant to say something soothing in dismissal; instead I heard myself say: "Yes. Yes, Jaimie."

"I'm glad you said yes more than once," he said solemnly. "That shows you mean it. Only one yes would never have done."

Markaby and Dragon's Eye seemed the perfect backdrop for the wonder of our drama.

"Here's one kiss on your mouth for one yes, here's another on your eyes for another yes. And another . . ."

Words melted away into silence.

When I drew away breathlessly, I said: "I bet the Beanleys are watching. They see everything."

He ignored the thought of the Beanleys. "It'll have to be a civil wedding. Well, you see that, Kate? But soon? No need to wait. There's nothing much to arrange. You won't need to go back to London?"

I thought for a moment. "No. But there'll be things to do. Clothes, for instance. I don't mean white satin, that sort of thing." I was actress enough, and feminine enough, to feel a momentary pang. What girl hasn't dreamed of white lace and tulle and lilies of the valley? We all have our weak moments. "But I do want something special." And I was rich enough to afford it, I thought. "I expect I can find something, but I'll need a little time to prepare, please, Jaimie. And we won't say anything. Not yet. Let it be our secret."

He agreed to keeping the secret, but reluctantly.

"Goodbye, Jaimie. No, we must say goodbye now." I did not let him come across the causeway. He stood there watching me cross. I waved and walked into the mists around Markaby. I felt as though I was walking into a dream.

The nightmare began later.

Needless to say, I did not sleep much that night. I worked on the script, excited and happy. I fell asleep in a chair at last, and finally stumbled up to bed, still in my waking dream.

In the morning the sea was still and misty, so that I could imagine a Viking fleet silently gliding out of the fog to land on Dragon's Eye. "To go Viking" meant, to the Norse people, "to go adventuring." So I suppose it was a sort of eighth-century equivalent of "Go west, young man."

I was standing at the window, considering all this, when the parrot broke in.

"Remember Mr. Naseby," said Cromwell from his cage on the table behind me.

His words gave me a jolt. "Thanks, Cromwell," I said gratefully. "I had forgotten. And I think the time has come for me to put one or two questions to young Mr. Naseby myself, if I can. Thanks for reminding me, bird, I'll be off."

"Mind your step and drink only water," said the old bird, with horrid pertinence, making one forget that he didn't, couldn't understand what he said. He had an uncanny knack for making appropriate statements though, I'd noticed.

I crossed the causeway, the tide being low, lower than I had ever seen it, so that Dragon's Eye stood up out of the sea more exposed and more nearly ugly than I had ever imagined possible. The bare rock which was usually covered by sea was cracked and broken into numerous fissures, some cutting quite deep. Seaweeds and lichens and blotchlike mosses covered this area. It was upsetting to me to see that my beautiful Markaby rested on such an unlovely foundation.

Fetching the car from the old stable yard at the back

of the Percy Arms, I set off. I hadn't so far managed to have any conversation with the staff at the inn. They didn't seem a very talkative bunch. There were an older man and woman who appeared to be the joint owners, a dark-faced man who could be seen washing glasses in the back kitchen overlooking the stable yard, and a couple of very young women. However, I didn't give up hope and I smiled politely at each and every one as I met them in turn.

I drove quietly to Berwick with no mishaps and no fog. I had got so used to excitement lately, I thought wryly, that a quiet day with nothing untoward happening seemed almost boring. Actually, I was glad to be tranquil and happy as I drove along.

I parked in the main street of Berwick, which was wide and empty and had that newly washed look some towns have on a Monday morning. Once again a group of school-girls in green-and-white tweed uniforms was being ushered through the town. They were in the charge of two nuns: one young and pink-cheeked, the other the frail tiny creature I had seen with Angel. They tripped past me—the young one, whose femininity was not in the least suppressed by her habit, with eyes averted; but to my surprise a wide and cheeky grin spread across her companion's face, and she gave me a little bow. Somehow or other she knew who I was, and liked me. I was surprisingly heartened and cheered by this encounter and I returned the greeting with a smile of my own.

I believe I was still smiling when I entered the offices of Naseby and Son, because the elderly clerk said:

"It *is* a nice morning, miss, isn't it?" He was a gentle, quiet old man, whom I remembered from my earlier visit. "Quite a pleasure to be alive on it."

His own skin had an alabaster whiteness that suggested

he never stirred far from the dark, inner office. The law offices were in an old house which appeared to be built into part of the fortifications of the town. Bastion Walk, it was called. Each room was paneled in oak dark with age. The brass plate on the door outside with the legend "Naseby and Son" engraved on it looked of almost equal age, its lettering worn shallow and faint. The lawyers had been here a long time and their clerk seemed to be part of their more ancient history. I wondered how many Nasebys and how many sons he had known.

He showed me into Phillip Naseby's room and turned an indulgent eye on his young master, caught attempting a golf shot from floor to armchair. Pip Naseby pinkened and sat down hastily but with dignity behind his desk.

He met my eyes, and in spite of his dignity, smiled. "Nice morning," he said. "The truth is I'm not very good at golf and my game's *got* to improve. I'm off to St. Andrews next week to tread the sacred turf of the Old Course. Can't let myself down in front of all those canny Scots."

"Some of them must be less than superior players," I sympathized.

"Not as many as I'd like, and certainly not my godfather, who is taking me around as his guest."

"Oh well, if he *lives* there," I said consolingly. I couldn't help liking the serious-faced young man. "I mean, he must play all the time."

"Not he," he said. "He lives in one of those tiny little oil sheikdoms and runs the sheik's army and his civil service and his health service and everything else that is the sheik's. Never let it be said that the spirit of the British Empire is dead. He only comes back for a fortnight's golf every year. The sheik can't bear to let him be away longer than that. Says he doesn't feel safe. Quite right, too, no doubt. They fly him into Prestwick specially in the sheik's own jet, and it waits there till he's ready to go back again. He won a cup last year. A fluke, he said, but don't you believe it." Pip Naseby shook his head dolefully, then remembered where he was and who I was and why I was there, and dragged some papers out in front of him and coughed. "Now, I have these documents here for you to sign, if you will, Miss Melrose. We'll have to have witnesses, of course." He pressed a bell and my old friend from the outer office appeared, as if he had been awaiting such a signal. "Ah, Mr. Monk." Behind Mr. Monk was a pretty blond girl, whom I took to be the other witness.

"All ready then, Mr. Phillip, eh?" Mr. Monk put on a huge pair of spectacles and produced a pen. I would not have been a bit surprised if it had been a quill, so old-fashioned and Dickensian was the atmosphere of this office; but in fact he used a neat if unexpectedly opulent silver fountain pen. He noticed my interest.

"A present, after twenty-five years' service with Mr. James Naseby, Mr. Pip's father," he said. "And that wasn't yesterday. Before you were born, Mr. Pip."

"Only just," said Phillip Naseby defensively. "I was almost there." He too put on a pair of spectacles, dark tortoiseshell, in what I recognized at once was an attempt to look adult and professional. It was a gallant attempt, but it only underlined his youth. He pointed to where I should put my signature. I signed, and so did Mr. Monk. The girl followed suit, she and Pip Naseby giving each other appreciative looks over the desk. And that was that: it was over.

When Mr. Monk had gone out again, his employer shook his head. "I sometimes wonder what it would be like to practice law in a town where not everyone had seen me sitting up in my pram and waving a rattle." He said this with some bitterness, as of one who had suffered. "They never forget, you see. How can they trust me?"

He hadn't changed much, I guessed. He must have waved his rattle with just that same red-faced determination I'd seen as he wielded his golf club.

"You'd miss it all," I said. "Having no one close, living in a big city, being anonymous, it's not much fun." I suppose I envied him his safe, sure world, which he possessed so securely, unaware of what it gave to him.

"I don't know if it's always wise to stay in one place," he said soberly. "I daresay you're right about it suiting *me*. But it's not good for everyone."

"The Berwicks are an interesting family," I said, sensing that what he had said somehow related to them. "It puzzles me, though, that Robert Berwick left *me* Markaby. Have you any idea why?" I looked at him.

"I have wondered, of course," he admitted. "I haven't come up with any answer. He didn't tell me, I can assure you of that, in all truth. He never did give reasons. He did what he wanted, in the way he wanted. Or so far as he could. Circumstances defeated Robert Berwick occasionally." He smiled at me. "He wanted you to have it, though. Be sure of that."

"Well, thank you."

He got up politely to see me to my car.

"What would happen if I married?" I asked.

"Nothing." He sounded surprised. "Your possession would be unaffected. You'd have to make a new will. Marriage cancels all former testaments."

He clucked in a deprecating way at this confession.

"You ought. We can't have you dying intestate; it would make for no end of legal confusion. Shall I draw one up for you?"

"I'll leave it for a few weeks," I said thoughtfully, reflecting that marriage to Jaimie would change the situation.

"As you wish." He was polite. On the stairs, he commented, "I'm glad you've met Mrs. Lyon." I turned to him in surprise. "Oh yes, she's one of our oldest clients. Friend, too. Jaimie Berwick rang up and told me."

"He told me a little about her," I said soberly.

He gave me a sharp, penetrating look. *Not* so young and ingenuous, after all, I thought. "She's had a sad life," he said. "Tragic, really. She and her husband had a child that was born dead, and Stephanie never seemed able to recover or even to accept it. She was in a private clinic for years and years, simply withdrawn from the world. So my mother says; she tried to visit her once or twice. But gradually she's recovered. Only by then her husband was dead—drowned. My mother says—" He stopped short. I waited. "She says that Stephanie only seemed to start to recover when he died, but I don't mean what that seems to imply. He adored her. No, it was like some sort of Greek tragedy."

"He was drowned at sea, wasn't he?" I asked, more to fill in the awkwardness of the moment than anything else.

"Yes. Markaby certainly isn't a lucky place." Then he remembered what he'd said and who I was. I thought Pip Naseby wouldn't make a real success of the law till he learned not to gossip so much. "Sorry," he said. "I wasn't thinking." But his tongue still ran away with him. "And then there was Billy English. Had a little smallholding.

Got permission out of me to fold his sheep on Markaby, and then went off and left them. Had a row with a girl, and cleared out."

"Is that what happened?"

"So they say. Leaves you holding the sheep, I'm afraid."

A sudden light dawned. "I suppose you shoot around these parts?"

He nodded. "I take a gun out there every so often. Bought the rights from Robert Berwick. Billy English used to come out with me sometimes for a bit of the rough. Marvelous shot. Got a bit of that tinker blood in him, I think. Not pure, though—too much red hair on him for that."

"Do you know someone called Charlie Guise?"

"Yes, I know him, the devil. Everyone knows Charlie. The same as they knew his father. Broke his neck taking a fence, and Charlie'll do the same one day, that great black brute he rides."

"I think he knows how to look after himself," I said.

"Yes, and so he should," he said with a scowl, and somehow this seemed to move him even more than the hope of Charlie breaking his neck on a horse. "Well, goodbye. There will be a little more legal fuss and fiddle, before we're through. I'll telephone." And he waved me off.

I found something oddly comforting and very English in Pip Naseby's offhand attitude to his chosen profession. Legal fuss and fiddle, yes, that was how one ought to ride to life, light and easy in the saddle. I didn't do it myself, and it was a fault in me that I didn't.

All the same, I knew without thinking about it that Pip was probably not a very good rider himself, although kind and considerate to his horse, and that Charlie Guise could ride anything, and probably never thought about his mount at all. And then there was Jaimie, I reflected, as I started the car, who would certainly get off his horse and walk home rather than overload the beast.

Before I left Berwick I made one more call. Stopping into the shop where I had bought fruit for my picnic on my first visit, I chose a bunch of white lilac and mimosa, out-of-season and expensive, but fragrant and lovely, and drove over with them to Stephanie Lyon's.

"Thank you for the luncheon party," I said.

She buried her nose in the flowers. "How beautiful they are! It's almost like a wedding posy."

"Yes." I was startled. Had I, unconsciously, selected my own wedding flowers? "I chose them without thinking. Partly because of their smell."

"Which is delicious," she said, with a smile. She took the flowers to a table. "To bring flowers to your hostess is a charmingly polite and old-fashioned gesture."

I explained, "I felt I'd been clumsy yesterday. Perhaps said something that distressed you." Stephanie did not look at me, but started to arrange the flowers in a crystal vase. "I know how much you must love Markaby. And we were talking about it. I was making silly jokes. I felt I must have said something. You lived there, I know. It must be dear to you. You *do* like it?" I ended doubtfully, feeling that with every word I was somehow falling into deeper and deeper water.

"Let's say I have mixed feelings." She picked up the flowers and sniffed the mimosa and then the lilac. "Lovely, lovely flowers." A little happy flush of color flooded her cheeks and for a moment she looked what she must once have been—a loved and cherished young woman. I supposed she was now in her mid-forties, but in some ways her years out of the world had kept her youthful. "Yes, mixed feelings, my dear, about the place. I did love it once, and then later—not so much." She seemed to have difficulty in finding the words to express what she wanted. I listened, because I thought I was being told something important, to her, at the very least. "I've never wanted to go back. I think I'm happier in this house where I can see Markaby than I would be living in it." She looked across the sea. "How beautiful it is. I used to swim in the water around Markaby, but it's never been really safe."

"Why not?"

"Oh, the northerly current of the water. It pulls you away. And then, the temperature—it varies surprisingly from warm pools to ice-cold patches. It's very rocky, too, you know."

"And the fish?" I asked.

"I don't think there are many fish around Dragon's Eye," she said. "They seem to keep clear."

"I thought there might be a big fish or two that swam in its waters."

"When I was little I used to imagine there *was* a big fish, living close by. A childish pretense, I suppose."

"Perhaps you *did* see something."

"The local people used to say there was a big old fish to be found if you looked hard. Old Bluetooth, they called him. I haven't heard much talk about him lately." She smiled. "Funny world. You won't go swimming, will you?"

I didn't answer that question; I didn't want to talk about it, and what worried me was why I didn't want to talk about it. I felt I believed her.

The color had faded from her face, but the air of beauty

still persisted. I saw that her dress, although simple, fitted perfectly and was carefully cut to hide her extreme thinness. Its dark red suited her.

"I want to buy a new dress, Stephanie. Can you tell me where to go? What you are wearing is lovely."

She looked down at it. "I love this blood color. I feel as if I've had a transfusion whenever I wear it. But I've had it a long, long while. Since before I became ill."

"Yes, I know about your illness. Jaimie told me."

"Did he?" Disconcertingly, her eyes, fixed on my face, seemed to comprehend a great deal. "I expect he thought you ought to know. So you should. You'll understand that the dress is probably older than you, which says something about fashion, doesn't it? I think the shop, in Newcastle, still exists, though. I fancy I've heard someone talk of it lately. Wait a minute, I'll find out." She called over her shoulder, "Do you really want to know?"

"I really want to know." I sat there, waiting.

Presently she returned. "Yes, still there. It's called Mrs. Pink's, just as it always was, in Priorgate, Newcastle. You'll easily find it." She smiled. "When I first shopped there, it was still called a 'Court Dressmaker,' but I don't think that term is ever used now. I suppose they say 'Couture.' It's expensive, by the way."

As I left, surprisingly she kissed my cheek, stroking it softly as I drew away. "Goodbye, my dear. Come and see me again."

No one had ever embraced me quite like that before. Certainly not Lydia.

The mist had vanished from Markaby for the day when I got back, and everything was surprisingly matter-of-fact and normal, which suited me. Even the sheep grazing on the small hill seemed prosaic and comfortable. Cromwell was asleep, and that suited me too.

Jaimie did not telephone or call, but I was content to work on. Indeed, I was glad to be on my own. Even when we are married, I thought, I must be on my own a lot. The days passed quietly.

Without trouble I plunged back into the world of the script Bert had sent me, where I was a young married woman, I had a child, I was witty, biting and amusing, all the things I am not naturally. I was getting used to the very individual, jerky dialogue. The tempo was important, I thought. Without self-consciousness I was speaking the dialogue aloud, listening to my own voice come back at me. I listened critically, with detachment. It was coming along well. So when my peace was shattered by the telephone I was startled and sat for a moment without moving.

"Hello."

I was surprised. "Lydia, is it really you?"

"Well, sound pleased," she said tartly.

"I *am* pleased, madly pleased. Just surprised." It seemed

necessary to add a bit more. "I thought you'd more or less crossed me off your list of responsibilities, since I hadn't heard from you."

"Am I usually like that?" said her familiar voice. Behind her I could hear strange noises, like people walking about on a hard floor, calling to each other. Metal objects clanged. A bell rang.

"No. Where are you? At a railroad station?"

She laughed. "No. In a hospital."

"What? Lydia, wait, I'm coming down to see you."

"Hold your horses, dear!" she laughed. "Can't you tell from my voice that I'm fine? Kate, when you left London I did have a secret worry about my health. No, don't interrupt, let me go on. As soon as I was on my own I made arrangements to have it looked into. It's all over now, my darling girl, and there's nothing to it."

"Do you swear that, Lydia?"

"Solemnly, truly," she said. "I had cause to be alarmed, and I'm going to be treated, but it's a relatively minor gynecological condition."

"Thank goodness for that. Lydia, you make me feel so selfish, living my life up here and leaving you to face it alone."

Her deep voice said: "It's what I wanted. And I wanted to think of you at Markaby. That part of the coast has always had a special meaning for me. And as for facing things alone—you know, in the end we face everything alone."

Across the telephone wire the room at Markaby caught the echo of a bell ringing in that hospital in London and vibrated with it. Strange how close some distant things are.

"But that isn't why I rang."

"No?"

"Kate, there's something I want to tell you." Her tone was urgent.

I tried to be soothing. "Later will do."

She was not above showing the irritability of the invalid. "I want to talk *now.*"

"Take it slowly, then."

She ignored this advice. "I want to talk. There's something I've kept from you. It seemed kinder, wiser to do so. But when I realized that I might not have been so lucky, that I could have been dying, it weighed on me; when I thought I might die without telling you, I couldn't bear it. It worried me out of all proportion to what it probably means."

"Well, come on then!" I couldn't imagine what could be so earthshaking, and the talk of death upset me.

Her voice sounded weak and lucid. "Robert Berwick was looking for his daughter." I suppose I made some noise, skeptical, even alarmed. "Yes, his daughter. He thought he had one."

"How could he?" I asked. I wondered if her illness had produced some hallucination which still seemed real to her. "How could he have one?"

"The usual way," she said tartly. "It's not impossible, or even unlikely."

I was silent, while memories of Jaimie's words about his grandfather's succession of "girls" raced through my mind. Perhaps these girls had not been objects of sexual interest to him, but girls who might have been his daughter. A strange thought, still incomprehensible to me.

"He was looking for his daughter," repeated Lydia. "Perhaps he thought he'd found her in you." Her voice was tiring and I made an anxious sound, but she pressed on. "When you were in Spain, I met Robert Berwick in

London. No, it wasn't quite by chance, although I thought it was at the time. I believe now he sought me out. I remembered who he was; he hadn't changed much. He asked a lot of questions about you. He said he remembered you from that day at the auction."

"Probably true," I said, more to interrupt the flow, which I thought was exhausting her, than because I believed what I said.

"Yes, it was true. I believed it then, but I realize now he knew more about you than a mere memory had provided. He knew you were an actress, where you were working, perhaps had even seen you."

"I think he had," I said, remembering the theater program I had found with his letter to me.

"I would guess he'd had a private investigator checking on you." She paused. "He more or less said so."

"Oh, don't go on, Lydia." I was embarrassed by the thought, in case she was, too.

"No, it's not painful, and I must. He told me that he had had a love affair, that a child had been born, a daughter. The baby was sent away for adoption before he could claim her. The affair had been clandestine; he had no legal right."

"You mean they weren't married?" I inquired bluntly.
"No."

"I wonder why not? His own wife was dead. I suppose the lady may have had a husband."

"He didn't say," said Lydia. "I suppose so."

"It wasn't, no, it couldn't have been. Lydia?" I said, my voice rising into a question.

"No, it wasn't me," said Lydia drily. "I was not Robert Berwick's love. And may I say that had you been my natural child I should have been delighted to claim you.

I have never told you any lies, nor am I telling you any now."

"I know that really, Lydia. Sorry."

"But Robert Berwick had a daughter, or he thought he had, and he had spent some years trying to find her. Peculiar, you and I may think, but human nature is strange. Anyway, the Berwicks have always been a law unto themselves."

"I wonder where the mother was?"

"Dead, perhaps," said Lydia. "He told me he'd found and investigated several likely girls. Finally, he had come back to you. He was going to get in touch with you later. What actually happened was that he went back to Northumberland and I never heard from him again. He died. When I knew this, I decided not to say anything to you about his belief. Let sleeping dogs lie, I thought." She sighed. "But I think now I was wrong. I should have told you," she murmured.

"You've told me now," I said, and I sat for a while in silence. I was thinking that if there was anything in this story of Robert Berwick's and it wasn't just some private fantasy of his own, then there was something very odd surrounding the circumstances of his daughter's birth.

Aside from that, something inside me was not at all convinced that I was the girl in question. I was not sure that I was Robert Berwick's daughter. It did explain one fact, however—the bequest to me of Markaby.

But I too had something of a confession to make and a story to tell Lydia.

"I've got something to tell you too, Lydia. Are you listening?" I plunged into it without waiting for her to reply. "Whether Robert Berwick finally came to believe I was his daughter or not, I don't know. I think he may have had some lingering doubts. He wrote me a letter, Lydia, when he knew he might die and left it behind for me to read. He doesn't mention the daughter bit, but he asked me to do something for him. It was what you might call a direct request from friend to friend. I *did* think of him as a friend, Lydia, after all these years."

"What could you do for Robert Berwick?" she asked wonderingly.

"He asked me to save Jaimie. At first I didn't know what was threatening him, what to save him *from*. Now I think it was from his relationship with Angel. She's very dominating. Not good for Jaimie. He asked me to rescue him."

"If you can," said Lydia, dreamily. It was obvious that the reality of Jaimie Berwick and whatever fate endangered him was not very vivid to her.

Now was my chance to tell her of our marriage plans, but I hesitated. And while I did so, she swept on, to make a fresh revelation.

"Do you remember I spoke about a man called Michael Sars?"

"Yes," I said promptly. "He's no longer in Northumberland. I asked if he was."

"No, he wouldn't be. He was one of my worries."

"Are you fond of him, Lydia? I had wondered."

"I think I was beginning to be, Kate." She sounded far away from me. "It's funny, you go through years and years, most of your adult life, in fact, without finding any man who interests or touches you. So much so that you decide it's not for you, and then, bang, someone gets under your skin and into your mind."

"And that happened with you and Michael Sars?"

She sighed. "When I came here I was full of thoughts of him, wondering how it would go, and what the future would be. But while I was here . . ." She hesitated. "I won't go into the details of how I discovered it—through gossip of mutual friends really—but I found out Michael Sars was living with a woman in Northumberland. She's been in his life a long time." She added awkwardly, "I believe he has also a wife, long estranged, in Bergen. So I have been very stupid."

"Oh, my poor Lydia."

"I think my pride was more hurt than anything else," she said reasonably. "Dear Kate, at my age, one should know how to weigh up what a relationship is worth, what it means, and what sort a man is. But, after all, I suppose in these things I am inexperienced, and inclined to read more into what was offered than what was really there. I blame myself. So there, you see, now you know."

"Thank you for telling me, Lydia." I felt awkward at receiving the confidences from my reserved guardian. "You didn't need to tell."

"Ah, but I had a reason. I owe a lot to Michael Sars. He taught me, for one thing, to admire the Vikings. He's a great Norse specialist, always seeking out sites of Viking settlements and investigating them. I went to Oslo with with him once, did you know, and he showed me a Viking longboat. They're clinker-built, with a side rudder, but so spare and elegant."

"Oh, Lydia, don't." I thought she was talking far too much.

"Well, he gave me that glimpse into another world and I'm grateful. That's what I want to say, Kate: take your happiness when you meet it. Do you understand what I mean?"

I said: "I think so. I believe there *is* someone here, Lydia."

"I'm so glad, so glad. I was beginning to think you were like the Snow Queen, with a splinter in your heart. Who is it? Someone I know?"

"Jaimie Berwick," I said.

There was silence from her, broken only by the rattles and thumps from the hospital corridor.

There were no more telephone calls that day, and I was protected from other visitors by the tide which had covered the causeway. I was well into my part and had decided from textual implications that my heroine had yet another trait: she smoked excessively. My picture of her was building itself up, when I heard Kenny's voice, calling my name. He had splashed across the causeway with a message.

"I bin come to tell you that there's a little parcel for you at the post office."

I got up. "I'll come and collect it." I was putting on a coat. "Did Mrs. Ogle send you?"

"No. Charlie. He said better cut off and tell you."

"Charlie Guise? How did he know I was home?"

Kenny shrugged. "Didn't say."

"Clever Charlie. Come on, Kenny, let's go and get this box."

Unexpectedly he slid his hand into mine. I looked down at him, but he was staring straight ahead.

"Brave of you to come, Kenny," I said. "You don't like it here on Dragon's Eye, do you?"

He shook his head silently. "Not since the night you went into the water, miss."

"And you saw something that frightened you in the water?" But I spoke gently.

"Let's not talk about it, miss. See, we're off the island now," and he hurried me forward.

In the post office Mrs. Ogle handed over my parcel. Her husband and Charlie Guise were standing together, gossiping and smoking. For a moment I thought of taking it back to Markaby to open, but a brief glance at Kenny's eager face changed my mind. "All right, Kenny."

Inside was a small cardboard box. I opened it. On a nest of crumpled tissue paper rested a thick band of dull gold, big enough to encircle my wrist. It was decorated with an elaborate pattern pinched out in dots. In the middle was a small figure with large hands and a smiling mouth.

A card said: "This is a Viking princess's armband. Wear it for me." The note was unsigned, but I assumed it was from Jaimie.

"What's the figure?" asked Kenny.

"I don't know." I was studying the ugly, lively little face. Was it a man or a ram?

Charlie Guise leaned forward. "That's the Gripping Beast," he said.

"Oh." It didn't seem an attractive name.

"Some people think that's another name for Frey."

"Who's Frey?"

"The god of love. There was also his sister Freya. She was his feminine counterpart."

"Friday," called Mrs. Ogle from behind her counter. "That's Frey's day. Maybe we ought to call it love day."

"It's Friday tomorrow," volunteered Kenny.

"So it is," I said. I put the bracelet on. Charlie Guise watched me and he smiled. Mrs. Ogle, not noticeably a very religious woman, crossed herself.

Enough is enough for one day, I thought. So with as much dignity as I could muster, I pocketed the box and turned for the door. "Good night, everyone," I said.

But I wore the bracelet all that day and slept in it at night. And I didn't forget Charlie Guise's smile.

On Friday I drove myself to Newcastle, parked the car near the city center, and took a taxi cab to "Mrs. Pink's, Couture." As Stephanie had promised, the establishment was easy to find. Outside, a modest shopfront painted dark green. Inside, floors thickly carpeted in a moss green. One large room led through arched doorways to a series of small rooms. Across a velvet-covered sofa lay a confusion of dresses which looked as if they had been casually tossed there, but which I guessed had really been placed with some art. Whoever Mrs. Pink, Couture (lately a Court Dressmaker) was, she had learned the tricks of modern retailing.

A young girl, wearing a closely fitted black-and-white dress, stood in the middle of the room. She did not speak, but let me pick up a scarlet-and-black creation, frilled from neck to hem with tiny, tiny frills.

"Pretty," I said, with deep appreciation. "But—"

"No. Not for you, is it?" Purposefully, she moved into an inner room and came out with a couple of dresses over her arm.

"Are you Mrs. Pink?" I asked, studying one cream chiffon dress.

She smiled slightly. "No. That was my grandmother. Gran was Mrs. Pink. I'm Anna Melinda Pink."

She held up a dark-green jersey dress. "Looks nothing off, but try it on."

She was right. "Lovely," I said. "How do you do it?"

She shrugged. "It's in the blood. I'm the fourth-generation Pink in the business." She was kneeling, making a minute adjustment to the hem. "I've been sewing since I was five. Then the London School of Design. Then I went to Paris to work in the St. Laurent workrooms, then on to Mila Schön in Rome. You *learn* that way."

"You're wasted here. What about London?"

"No. I'll stay in the north," she said, in a decided voice. "I'm opening in Edinburgh, Prince's Street, next month. Next year it'll be Aberdeen." She knew where she was going.

Together we sorted through the dresses she produced. I did not tell her the purpose I had in mind for the high-necked, white corded-silk coat, buttoned from collar to hem, that I chose, but I think she may have guessed.

"You could wear your bracelet over the sleeve," she said tactfully. "It's a beautiful thing. Unusual."

"Yes," I said briefly. During all this time a sense of unease had been growing in me. I couldn't explain it. But then, as we moved into an inner room where I signed a check and she packed up the clothes, the feeling became stronger.

"What's that lemony scent, something like verbena?" I said. "I think I smelled it in the other room. It's even stronger here."

It was the scent I had detected first in the motorboat that had brought a prowler to Dragon's Eye, and later in the bookshop. I was quite sure it was the same smell.

"It's lovely, isn't it? I wish I could afford to use it myself. I get it from London, from Le Jardin. They make it up specially for a client of mine. She chose the essences herself. It's very dry, isn't it, and yet with that sharp verbena note? We just got her a new supply and she came to collect it. She's here now, as a matter of fact." The girl nodded to an inner room, curtained off by velvet curtains, beyond which I heard low voices.

There came a laugh and a tall figure appeared at the arch, holding back the curtains for a moment to call goodbye, and then letting them fall. It was Angel Berwick.

A gust of the scent came with her. Angel, I thought—it was Angel who came to Dragon's Eye, Angel who threatened me.

"Kate!" She gave me a radiant smile. "What are you doing here?"

I was stung into a truthful answer. "Choosing wedding clothes."

"How amazing. So am I." There was a strange note in her voice. "But mine are very plain."

I thought she was joking. On the other hand, she was speaking with apparent seriousness.

"So you really are going to marry Jaimie. What Jaimie said was true. I thought it must be true when Stephanie telephoned to ask me about clothes: she said it was on your behalf."

"You knew I'd be here today."

"Guessed it. I never thought you'd be so rash, Kate."

I was angry. "Hasty, perhaps. Rash, no. It doesn't seem unwise to me."

"You know so little about Jaimie and me."

"I feel as if I'd known Jaimie all my life," I said. And then I added deliberately, "And I think you are a jealous and possessive woman."

"Yes, I am. A jealous and possessive woman. I admit it."

I was still angry. "You seem to enjoy admitting it," I said.

For a moment I had punctured her self-assurance. A strange look crossed her face. "Yes, I must admit that, too," she said, not to me, but as if she was talking to someone else.

For some reason this angered me more. I couldn't control myself—I had to confront her now. "I know it was you who has been trying to frighten me off Dragon's Eye," I said. "Perhaps you've even tried to kill me. I recognize your scent. I smelled it today and I've smelled it in a boat that came by night to Dragon's Eye."

A startled noise from Anna Melinda Pink reminded me that she was listening. I grabbed my package.

With my movement, Angel saw my bracelet. "So you're wearing that? It was mine once. Don't go back to Dragon's Eye, Kate. Go back to London, and leave us alone."

"You're very clever, Angel," I said. "You sound as if you really mean that. Jaimie understands you very well. He told me, 'What Angel doesn't get one way, she'll get another!' Well, I'm tough and clever, too. Goodbye, Angel. I'm off to Markaby."

As I left, passing rapidly through the inner rooms, I heard Angel behind me. "Come to my birthday party, Kate, if you're still with us."

I had left Cromwell with the Beanleys for the day. I didn't think Kenny seemed very keen; he and the parrot had an uneasy relationship.

I parked the car by the causeway and walked across. Dragon's Eye was outlined against a pale-blue sky so clear that it looked white toward the horizon. The house itself looked reassuringly solid and earthy.

Jaimie rose from a crouching position by the front door.

"Been waiting for you." He put his arms around me. "I've been here ages, just waiting for you. Where have you been?"

"Buying clothes." Still upset by my encounter with Angel, I was grateful for his strong, reassuring embrace.

He laughed triumphantly. "So you have done it? So have I. The date is fixed. Ten days' time in Berwick." He held my wrist up. "So you're wearing my bracelet."

"Angel says it was hers once."

"No, never. Not to own," he said promptly.

"I didn't believe her," I said. "But she frightened me."

"She frightens me," he said with feeling.

I unlocked the door and we walked inside. A fragrant warm breath of well-polished furniture and wood smoke drifted toward us. Markaby sometimes seemed to breathe an air of its own.

"She came to this island," I said. "I'm sure she tried to kill me. I smelled her scent."

He put his hand gently over my mouth. "No more. Let's forget all about Angel. This is *our* day. Not a day for remaining inside. Walk around the island with me, Kate."

Together we followed the path that circled the island. The sheep that grazed here moved quietly away at our approach. One or two were in lamb, but not as many as I might have guessed. I suppose fertility was not high among these sparsely fed animals.

Jaimie led me to where a little tongue of rocky land looked out at the sea. There was just room for two people to stand if they stood close together. He put an arm around me and held me tight.

"I feel very close to the old people who first built a homestead at Markaby, don't you?"

I responded readily. "I find myself thinking about them

a lot. Not in any ghostlike way, I don't mean that, but as real, living people." I looked about me. "I don't suppose the island has changed all that much."

"I brought you to this spot on purpose," he said.

"Did you?"

"Yes. In the earth here, digging about—I was only a boy, I'd be about ten, I suppose—I found a stick of old, carved wood once. I knew it was Viking stuff, boy as I was."

"But that's exciting." I turned to study his face; he was gazing dreamily forward, out to sea.

"I think from then onward I realized what an immensely valuable Viking site this Dragon's Eye must be. That stick is in a museum now, but before they stuck it in a glass case an expert read the carved characters. Runic writing, it was. I wish I'd left it where it was now. Objects like that ought to stay where the old hands left them. It seems a sacred trust to tend them where they were left."

"What did the runes say?" I was curious about this piece of old wood he'd found so long ago—its detail remembered so vividly and its parting with regretted so much.

"The meaning is one of the reasons I wish I'd left it undisturbed. When they made it out it said: 'Here lies the woman Mai who was cast overboard in the northern sea.'

"It was a memorial, you see, to a dead woman. But you notice it is so worded that the stick *is* her, it embodies her even though her actual body is in the sea."

"She died on a voyage, and was buried at sea?" I questioned.

"Died or was sacrificed. I think the latter myself." He drew me back from the cliff edge and we turned to walk toward the house. "It was their practice to sacrifice when it seemed expedient to them. She might have gone joyfully."

"I doubt it," I said with a shiver. "And more fool her if she did. I'd have put up a fight."

"Yes, you were made for other things, my darling. For the Freya thing." He stroked my wrist.

"What's that?"

"Freya was a goddess, sister to Frey, whose symbol you wear. Tacitus describes her as living on an island where only the priest may visit her. For lovemaking, we are led to understand. After which she is ritually purified in the water, and all the slaves who attended upon her are drowned."

I said thoughtfully, "We don't have any slaves."

"Just as well." There was silence. We stood still, facing each other. "What do you think, Kate? This is Freya's day."

"Yes." I barely breathed the syllable, but he heard.

"From the moment I saw you wearing my bracelet, I knew you'd say yes."

As we walked toward the house, I said nervously, "I suppose if we were really Vikings, there would be boats drawn up on the beach opposite, a bonfire blazing, and a crowd waiting."

"Yes. Very like that, I should think."

"Rather public really. I'm glad we're us. I'm rather a private person."

They were my last rational words. All the rest that followed were wild, fragmented, broken—belonging more to Freya, goddess of love, than to cool Kate Melrose.

Jaimie fell into an exhausted sleep. I found myself enchanted with the memory of his story of the Viking goddess and of her ceremonial immersion. A lustral dip might be a bit cold, but suddenly I wanted to swim. I felt alive and alert and very happy.

For some days now I had been walking around the surface of Dragon's Eye, searching it and studying it. Now I wanted to learn what lay beneath the water. The thought had been growing quietly in my mind that what lay below the water might be as interesting as what was above it.

It would be bitterly cold in the water. After a moment's hesitation, I ran back to the house to change. When I returned in my special protective suit, which covered me all over and helped maintain the body warmth, I was wearing a waterproof watch, and carrying a flashlight. I would allow myself ten minutes. I thought that was probably long enough in the North Sea in the winter. I was going swimming. Swimming was always discovering, I had discovered in Spain.

Underneath the water the peace was absolute. I swam gently along one rock passage. Even seen close up, it looked as though the rocks had been worked by man. The area where I was swimming lay between the island and the mainland. I wondered if there had ever been some sort of harbor here and what ships could possibly have used it. A long while ago, that was sure, if it had ever been used at all.

I paddled about inquisitively. Seaweeds waved softly before me. I avoided them. From experience I knew they were more clinging and uncomfortable than their languid air suggested. Fewer fish were to be seen than I would have expected, but the water was relatively shallow here and perhaps, in other ways, unsuitable to support much animal life. The bright torch beam probed the dark.

I noticed movement in the sea to my left, a strong

stirring of the water which attracted the eye. The water swirled darkly, as if something was moving about. The upward flight of this water struck very cold. Instinctively I moved away, but I looked down again. It seemed I could see a dark, moving creature below me. Then it was gone.

My own movement brought me close to an area of the rock face. It was amazing how beautiful the formation was here. Shelves of rock fell away beneath me, while at my eye level the rock was cut into alcoves like the wall of a building with small recesses and hollows. Unlike what I had seen before, I was sure these rock formations were quite natural. They had that rugged, improvised air which nature so often uses.

I was beginning to feel chilled. It was time to leave the water. Ahead of me one of the rock niches seemed to be darker than the others. One long strand of reddish brown seaweed floated softly toward me. I swam closer.

Before me, stiffly erect like an archaic statue, supported between projections of stone, was a figure out of a nightmare, propped against the rock behind so that there was a strange semblance of life. The flesh of the limbs had become swollen and blackened, fish had eaten at it, the face was falling apart, the mouth grinned, but I knew it by the red hair.

I had found Billy English.

For a moment I was frozen in the spot and then my whole body revolted, instinctively jerked, propelling me backward. But I forced myself to return. Incredulity and doubt made me look again. But a second, closer look showed me I was right. "I can't think, I can't think," I was muttering feverishly. "Take something back with you.

Take something concrete, real, from here, to convince you when you surface."

Without taking my eyes from where his face had been I groped, felt a solid piece of stone, slid it in my pocket, and rose to the surface of the water.

I hadn't even been looking for Billy English, but I had found him; once found, something had to be done about him. He couldn't be left there. However he had got into that rocky tomb, he could not be allowed to stay. He must be moved, and now it was up to me to see it was done.

I got out of my wet suit and hung it up to dry, in the correct way one should after each use, and was getting into trousers and a warm sweater. All the time I was trying to put an interval between my own life and what I had just found. I wanted to separate my own happiness from the death under the water.

Jaimie was stirring. I watched him with love and sympathy.

"Are you awake?"

"Yes, of course." He sat up quickly, as if something in my voice had alerted him. "What is it, Kate?"

"Jaimie," I said slowly. "We have to get the police here."

He was horrified. "My dear girl, why? What's wrong?"

"I have found the body of a man in a rocky recess under the water." It sounded incredible even as I said it. Had I really seen anything or anyone there?

He responded to this inner doubt at once. "I can hardly believe it. Are you sure? What on earth were you doing swimming?"

"The reason doesn't matter now." I didn't want to explain to him the complicated state of happiness and curiosity that had sent me off. "Partly the story you told earlier. But, anyway, I found him there." I described my find, filling in the details as best I could.

Finally he said, "Look, leave it to me. I'll see the police. But I won't let him be found here, near Dragon's Eye."

"But Jaimie—" I was beginning to protest.

"No, don't you see, he can't be found here. You do nothing. Leave it all to me." He was dressing rapidly. "Don't telephone or anything. I'll go this instant and handle it. Come over tomorrow. It's Angel's birthday. There'll be a party, half a party, half a wake."

"Oh I don't know." I felt drained and deflated now.

His voice was pleading. "Do come . . . I need you, Kate."

"Yes, I'll come. No, don't bother to come and get me. I'll find the way. It's called The Grange, isn't it, your house?"

"Yes, go through Garrow and then take the left turn. The house lies off the road, but is visible across the fields. Gray stone and bleak. You'll know it by the flag on the roof."

"Do you always fly a flag?" I asked, surprised.

"I'll fly it for you," he said warmly. He kissed me and then he was gone.

I puttered around the house doing odd jobs. I could hear the wind moaning softly and hear the waves rumble and race around Dragon's Eye. The sea seemed very close. It was almost as if I could hear it rolling beneath my feet, as if it flowed under the very foundations of Markaby in some deep cavern.

My mind filled with unpleasing thoughts. It was horrible to walk around my house and know that all this time a man had stood in a grotto below, upright even in his death, with his red hair growing every day. It is said that the hair continues growing after death. I could imagine Billy English's hair streaming out into the cold, salt water.

I found myself wondering what else moved in the water where he stood. On the old map I had seen in the Berwick, the sea around Dragon's Eye was credited with monsters.

Of course, you could laugh it away as I had. I had rationalized the notion by equating it with the carved stone monster set in the wall above the main door of my house. This stone suggested, I had thought, that the so-called monsters were a distant memory of the longboats of the Vikings with their dragon prows rising out of the sea.

A reasonable answer and probably an accurate one. But now with the thought of Billy English to haunt me, it suddenly seemed just as reasonable to believe in real, living, embodied monsters, that swam and lashed their tails and fed on flesh.

I hated Markaby tonight. It was all very well for Bert, far away and safe from harm, to make jokes about my falling into a gothic dream, but I was here and the menace was real and very close at hand.

8

In the morning all traces of mist had disappeared and there was a fair wind blowing, moving steely gray clouds across the sky. Toward the horizon the sky had a yellowish tinge, most menacing.

I kept my promise to Jaimie and did nothing about the body of Billy English. I would know soon enough what he had done. I was eager to talk to Jaimie, though. There had been a wild note in his voice when he spoke of Angel and her birthday that I had missed at the time, but later, remembering, it made me anxious. Happiness seemed as fragile as the wind.

I drove to Garrow, parked my car outside the Ogles' shop and went in to see if I had any letters to collect. There was one letter and I recognized Bert's writing. When he was in the mood he was a good letter writer, using long, rolling sentences worthy of Lord Chesterfield, but also passing on the news with the skill of Madame de Sévigné. I was standing holding it in my hand, unopened, when I heard an excited conversation.

Mrs. Ogle was talking; she was in the middle of a sentence: "... washed up by the morning tide, 'un was. The coast guard was out watching the sea. Charlie Guise was with him and they spotted it. Charlie brought it in."

"What happened then?" This was a woman customer speaking.

"They laid it on the beach and waited till the police came."

"And who was it, then?"

Mrs. Ogle lowered her voice and leaned forward and whispered. But I caught one phrase and it was enough: "A body. There was a lot of red hair."

I put Bert's letter in my pocket unopened and walked over to the window, pretending to study some postcards. So Billy English's body had been found. Somehow, it had been washed out of its resting place and had drifted in with the tide.

There was no need for me now to speak. Dragon's Eye had rid itself of its unwelcome guest. I could still hear the two women.

"Been in the water some time, Charlie said. Could have come from anywhere, he said. You couldn't tell where he went in or where he was resting all this time. Farther down the coast, could be." Further whispering, then I heard: "November it would be when Billy was missed, last November, as I recall."

I found The Grange easily enough. A plain-faced, beautiful old house of dark-gray stone, it rested among quiet, rolling hills. To the right of the house was a small building with a steeply pitched slate roof and a bell tower, which I took to be the stables. I parked my car nearby and strolled toward the house. To my surprise there was a flagpole, and a flag was flying from it, just as Jaimie had said it would. In heraldic terms it must have been a banner, an oblong charged with the arms of its owner—in this case, the old English dragon now called a wivern. The creature had two legs, a green head and back, with a red chest, belly and wings. I could see why Jaimie had run it up for me: it really belonged on Dragon's Eye. I was touched.

Champagne cocktails and hot mushroom savories and sausages on sticks were to be had at Angel's birthday party that morning, together with an unmistakable air of tension. The silver platter was heavy, the glass was old and fine, and the tempers had a sharp edge to them. Angel herself (the birthday girl, as she commented sardonically) looked both radiant and amused.

When I entered, every guest turned to stare at me with one accord. There seemed to be a lot of people at first, but as I got them sorted out I saw only about thirty, and I concentrated on two faces, Angel's and Jaimie's.

Jaimie hurried forward to meet me, and seemed alert to read any expression on my face. I found it troubling. It almost seemed as if a veil had dropped between us, subtle but tangible, and for the moment we had lost some of the ease and unity we had shared with each other. Although I was adult enough to have anticipated a natural reticence after the wild abandon of yesterday, I could not keep from studying his own face with anxiety.

"We're celebrating Angel's birthday," he said, gloomily. He took a tall glass from the silver tray. "Have a champagne cocktail. We always give Angel champagne on her birthday." Under his breath he said, "I want to talk to you about your adventurous swim yesterday. Bless you, Kate."

In the background Angel laughed. In anyone of less natural dignity and force it would have been called a giggle. She sounded as free and happy as Jaimie sounded wretched.

"Thank you." I took the glass and sipped cautiously.

"About what you found in that crevice in the rocks under the sea," he began, his voice low. "A body has been washed ashore on Garrow Sands, did you know?"

"I've heard," I whispered back. "I suppose you freed the body and let the tide bring him in? I still think I should tell the police what I saw. It will help to identify him."

"Oh, everyone knows who he is," said Jaimie. "Billy English, of course. He's been missing for about two months. No, no trouble there. But don't you do anything. Leave it alone. Let us keep out of it, Kate. Billy was known to be a drunk. It's very likely that he fell into the sea in the dark one night after having one too many, then was carried by the sea to where you found him wedged, or stuck. Just as easily, he might have had a quarrel with one of the girls he was always chasing and she pushed him in in a struggle. He always did go for huge, big strapping girls—one even gave him a black eye once and the word was that *she* had raped *him!*" He poured me some more champagne. "No, take my advice, love. Leave it alone. It'll all be the same in the end. Besides, the chap's dead."

I bristled—I hate the word "besides," said like that. I always felt it was an invitation to evasion.

"Drifting onto the beach in that way," continued Jaimie, "the poor chap's no trouble to anyone. And I can't bear to think of all those people swarming over Dragon's Eye for no other reason than to complete their morbid paperwork."

I could well understand Jaimie's feelings in this regard. Dragon's Eye was a sacred, special world to both of us— had been for most of our lives, in fact, but even more so now that we could share it. I took his hand, but I couldn't "leave it alone." My conscience battled with my more selfish feelings as I squeezed his hand gently and per-sisted. "But how did he get in the sea in the first place? And how did he die? Not naturally; I'm sure he was mur-dered. I can't believe that he fell in by accident."

Jaimie did not answer. I went on with my own theory mentally before I spoke again. One thing was certain—ever since *I* had arrived at Markaby somebody had been trying to scare me away and had once even tried to kill me when I hadn't left. And I had a feeling I knew why.

All the time my mind was rapidly assembling the thoughts that followed, I was standing by Jaimie and watching Angel. She seemed incandescent with happi-ness, and the happier she seemed the angrier and more wretched Jaimie became. I wondered if it was Charlie Guise who was the cause of this happiness on her part, and of the misery on Jaimie's.

When I turned back to Jaimie, I spoke slowly and care-fully; I was so tired of fighting alone—I really needed Jaimie's support now, but I knew that my beliefs would be difficult for him to accept. "I think Billy English was killed because he'd found something on Dragon's Eye that his killer needed to keep secret. I ought to tell the police that someone has been on the island, that I think someone tried to kill me. Whoever it was will still try to drive me away, if they can—or to kill me, if necessary, as Billy English has been killed. I really ought to tell them, Jaimie, can't you see that?" I held my breath before I voiced the extent of my suspicions. "And I ought to name Angel and Charlie Guise."

As I had expected, Jaimie was incredulous. However, he considered what I had suggested carefully and I felt a surge of relief when he did not totally reject the idea, as troubling and inconceivable as it might be for him. "It might have been an accident," he muttered. "Leave Angel and Charlie Guise out of it."

"All right, I won't name names," I said quickly. "Are you a particular friend of Charlie Guise?"

"No, by God, I'm not!" The vehemence in his voice surprised me. Another sore spot had evidently been touched, and I wanted to end the macabre conversation that instant. This was a party, after all, whether or not we felt merry.

"Go away and look after your other guests," I said softly.

"I'll come back," he promised.

I tried to smile; I wanted to cling to the happiness of yesterday, but black pictures obtruded—images of Billy English tending his sheep at Dragon's Eye, images of Billy English being deliberately murdered. It was beginning to be terrifyingly clear to me that there was something on the island that no one was meant to know about.

If only I could figure out what there was on Dragon's Eye that anyone could possibly want. . . .

She drifted up to me, the only happy and settled person, I was convinced, in that entire room. For the first time I could see a look about her that suggested an angelic mood; in fact, she truly deserved her name at that moment—if the observer didn't know of the serpent in her heart. "So what you said in Newcastle is true," I said, before I could stop myself. "I believe you are in love."

"Yes. Yes, I am." Her eyes were bright and confident.

"So *that* is the decision you made. You really are going to be married?"

"Do I look so much like a bride?" She was smiling, a marvelous smile.

"Indeed you do. I can almost smell the orange blossom." She laughed aloud, but my heart was pounding. "Is it Charlie Guise?"

Now I had surprised her. "Charlie Guise? No, indeed. Why ever should you think of Charlie?"

"He's a friend, isn't he?" I was probing, curious to know if she would admit he had been more.

Slowly and soberly, she said, "He is a person to be watched. You have to know where you are with Charlie."

"Are you warning me against him?"

"No, I would not presume. It is not my business." Her tone was slightly formal, as if she were pushing me away from her. "I like Charlie, although Jaimie detests him. What he thinks of Jaimie I do not know. They do not meet as equals." I picked up the aloof little note in her voice here. "But Charlie is a naturally clever, ambitious man who will end up getting what he wants." She paused, to add: "The reverse of Jaimie."

I could see what Jaimie meant when he talked of the way Angel had imprinted her image on his mind. She was so strong and clear. Looking back, "clear" and "clarity" are the words which best summon up Angel to me.

"You *are* warning me," I said. I could see Jaimie watching me. "Because if you are, let *me* warn *you*. Leave me alone, Angel. I can be tough too. I won't be driven away from Markaby. Not by you, nor by Charlie Guise, neither by tricks of sweetness nor by show of violence."

Jaimie came over and heard the last of my speech. "Please, Kate," he implored. "Let it be. *Let it be.*"

Angel let his hand rest on her arm, her smile unwavering, and she bestowed on him a look of great patience. But it was not a look I would have wished to receive. It

196

was a look such as a saint may give a sinner just as he sets foot in purgatory: a look of love, of total understanding— but absolutely devoid of any hint that one minute of his suffering will be mitigated.

Perhaps because he felt the cool sting of her love, he turned to me and said calmly, "Trust me, Kate."

Rockets went off in my head. "I don't think I trust anyone," I almost shouted. Angel's shocked face blurred before my eyes. "Don't interfere, you say, leave it alone, Kate. It's *you* who doesn't trust *me*. All right! I'll leave it alone for twenty-four hours—and then I'm going to the police!"

A new arrival of visitors, including Lord and Lady Ranelagh, whom I recalled from luncheon at Stephanie's, allowed me to escape. Jaimie shot me a frantic glance from across the room, but I ignored his appeal. I could not help him in his struggle with Angel. I had tried and failed. They were enmeshed in a labyrinthine battle having origins deep in the Berwick family past, where I could not follow them. He was bound by it. By contrast, what freedom Lydia had given me!

Before getting into my car, curiosity prompted me to enter the small building with the bell tower. I pushed open the door.

Before me was a tiny chapel. It was richly decorated in deep red and gold and furnished with gleaming, dark mahogany pews. I stood for a moment in surprise, absorbing it all. Great bunches of white flowers were massed on the altar and down the aisle, in dazzling display. A scented breath of flowers and incense floated over me. It was positively bridal.

Seated together near the altar, deep in quiet talk, were

two people: one the frail old nun I had seen in Berwick, and the other a young priest.

As I looked, both turned toward me and gave me identical smiles. The nun bowed. I bowed back, then closed the door quietly behind me, and went to my car.

A coarse and eager wind was blowing. It blew along with it sand and detritus gathered from the beaches, so that it scraped and stung the delicate inner membranes of nose and eyes. It was a cold, erratic, wicked wind, pulling first this way and then that, and all the time rising.

I drove rapidly toward Markaby. The clouds had sunk in the sky, dark and lowering. All the way along the coast road, I kept looking toward the sea, where little white crests rose and fell all the time on the heaving surface.

There was a small figure sitting by the causeway, waiting for me. Kenny with a bird cage by his side. He stood up when he saw me and handed over Cromwell with a flourish. I had almost forgotten the parrot's existence since entrusting him to Kenny before going to Newcastle.

"Charlie Guise brought me here in his car. The bird in his cage was too heavy for me, but I thought you'd want him back." He cast a nervous look at the bird. "Charlie told me to wait and give you Cromwell. He couldn't stay himself."

"In a hurry, was he?" I asked, suspiciously. Where to and why? I thought.

Kenny shrugged. "Got business, he said. He had his mother with him and she spoke very sharply to Cromwell. I wanted to come anyway. But I'm glad I saw you coming just now. I didn't want to walk across those stones in the sea." He cast a nervous look at the causeway. "The tide's coming in and I'm frightened something might get my feet."

"There's nothing in the sea, Kenny. You know that."

"I dunno." He was unconvinced. "The bird's all right, anyway. Hasn't said much; I think he's frightened."

Cromwell did indeed look a chastened bird, and I wondered what had happened to him with old Mrs. Guise. "What did Charlie's mother do to him?" I murmured. Cromwell hung his head, unable to reply.

"She'd learn anyone their manners," said Kenny. "Frightened of her, he is."

"I'm glad to have him back," I said sympathetically. "How will you get home, though, Kenny?"

"Mum's in the village. There's a bus coming through. Charlie gave me a pound note." He patted his pocket with satisfaction. "I'll manage."

"I'll give you a lift up to Garrow. Get in." A quick look at the sea promised that if I hurried I could get back before the causeway was under water. I really would have to get a rowboat soon. And yet, part of the whole fascination of Markaby and Dragon's Eye was that I was cut off there for hours at a time.

"Aren't you frightened of being alone there?" asked Kenny, as he got into the car.

"Not in the way you think," I said. Privately I hoped I *would* be alone there. "As long as I am alone, I don't mind. I don't fancy visitors."

Kenny gave the sea and the sky an appraising look. "This weather that's coming up'll keep you alone there. There's going to be a gale."

"There is?"

"Can't you feel it rising? Slow but sure. That be the

worst sort of gale. Quick come, quick go. But this one will be a long hard pull. Battling weather, we call it." There was a certain poetry in the way he put things.

"I don't mind being on my own," I said. "I've got plenty of food."

"The sea will cast up wood for you to burn. Remember to look for some driftwood. Burns lovely when it's dry."

When we got to the main street of Garrow, he nipped out of the car. A low red bus was just drawing into a stop by the Percy Arms. "That'll be it, miss, my bus. I'll just be off." And he was running away down the street with his hair flying. My one friend, I thought. "When do you think the wind will reach its peak?" I called after him.

"Tomorrow. Day after tomorrow," he shouted over his shoulder as he ran.

Tomorrow, the day after tomorrow. It was going to be a black day, the day after tomorrow.

I carried Cromwell into the house and set him on the table in the kitchen. Then I put a match to the fire already laid there. It flared at once, but there was no warmth just yet, and I shivered.

"How do you do, my lady, and thank you very much, I've had a nice time," said Cromwell, in a gloomy voice from the table.

"Oh, you're alive again, are you?"

"How do you do, my lady, and thank you very much, I've had a nice time," he repeated. He sat on his perch, a dejected old bird.

I made us both some food: tomato soup, simply because something red is always comforting. As the fire burned brighter we grew more cheerful. One way and another I had used up most of the hours of daylight. But I wanted to do one more thing before the night came on. I dressed myself warmly and took a torch.

" 'Bye, Cromwell," I said. "I'll be back soon, I hope."

Then I set out to make a thorough careful tour of my domain. Head down, pushing against the wind, I paced the narrow track that ran around the island. I made a complete circuit before I convinced myself that there was nothing to be seen which could hint to me what this mysterious secret was that Dragon's Eye harbored. I walked around and over the pudding-shaped hill and its crest of little birches, but at the end I had to shake my head. Beyond a distinct impression that more people had walked about the island than seemed normal to its remote solitude, there was simply nothing I could put my finger on. And even this impression might have a natural explanation. I did not know, although I could find out, what surveys and inspections of the property had been carried out by the lawyers when Robert Berwick died. I could telephone Pip Naseby in the morning.

Comforted by the thought, I turned back to the house and was just facing the mainland and the evening lights of Garrow when I saw a figure waving to me from the road. It was a woman, wearing a long cloak and a hood over her hair. Her silhouette looked strange, even sinister. Through my mind flashed an impression of the Angel of Death. Perhaps it was Angel Berwick.

For the moment that we stood there, looking at each other, I was frightened. I thought that this was the crisis I had been waiting for; when I would be threatened, when I would be under attack, when I would have to stand up and fight for myself.

But I had not expected to have to fight so soon.

"Hello, Kate, can I come across?" Her voice was carried away by the wind, but I recognized it, not Angel, after all, but Stephanie Lyon.

I cupped my hands and called back. "You'll get wet; the water will be over your feet."

For an answer Stephanie wrapped her cloak around herself and picked up her skirts. I could see that she was wearing the practical sort of boots fishermen wear, and what with the wind catching at my breath and the disposition to giggle at the sight she made, I stood there without another word while she slowly crossed.

"I know I look a scream in these boots," she said, unwinding herself from her wrappings as she arrived. "But they're really very useful, these tall waders. They belonged to my mother. She used to go salmon fishing in them. I can see her now, wearing these boots, with a soft hat pulled down over her eyes and a bag slung over her shoulder, standing for hours in the Tay. I hated her catching a salmon. They're so beautiful, so very beautiful, the bravest and most gallant of fish. Perhaps we underestimate fish. We ought to think more of them. . . . I'm talking too much, aren't I?"

"I don't know," I said, feeling helpless.

"It's a bad sign. You ought to stop me. I ought to stop myself. There's old Stephanie, they say, what a tragic figure. And I *am* a tragic figure. I'll tell you why, one day. But there's nothing more comic than a tragic figure that won't lie down and die. You were laughing yourself, I saw you."

"Yes, I'm sorry."

She shook her head. "Oh, I don't blame you. It's the answer. Have a good laugh. It's better than a good cry. But

I couldn't do either." She changed the subject abruptly. "I expect you're wondering why I'm here? It's no accident, I can tell you."

"I never thought it was." I looked at her. She was shivering with cold. "Come into the house."

"I will." She followed me in a biddable way. "You've got altogether too much on your mind, I can tell. It's one of the things I learned to recognize in my years . . . in my years . . ." She stopped.

"I understand what you mean," I said sympathetically, and indeed I did.

"But you cannot know what my years were," she said sadly. "Everyone has their own bad years, but mine were terrible."

"It's behind you now," I tried to reassure her.

"So they say. I won't go on. I avoid dead ends in conversation. That is another of the things I have learned." She smiled at me, walking beside me into Markaby. "I came to tell you that while you have been away there have been people walking on your island. Yes, I have seen them. You know, I watch Dragon's Eye, and I know what it should look like in all weathers and at all times. And it has looked wrong. Lights at night, where there should *not* be light, and during the day, movement." She shook her head.

I wanted to offer her comfort, both physical and emotional. "Come and sit by the fire."

Cromwell called out from his cage: "How do you do, my lady? How do you do?"

I covered his cage with a cloth, underneath which I could hear him muttering and complaining. Stephanie I led to a chair by the hearth. She stood there, warming her hands. Such pretty, long, delicate hands. My own were quite different, being square and practical. Hands count,

I think, don't you, in establishing relationships? My hands were not like Stephanie's.

"I'm really not mad, you know. And, anyway, I can tell you from my own observation that very few people are mad on all points all the time. On this subject I am reliable. I saw what I saw."

"I believe you. You don't have to convince me." There was some coffee made; I poured her a cup. But she wouldn't settle. Cup in hand, she toured the kitchen.

"How nice it looks. Just as it always did. Hardly changed at all. And yet, you see, many of these objects are new. But they've been chosen by someone who didn't want to alter the appearances." How acute her perceptions were, and now that she pointed it out I saw she was quite right. She stood by the kitchen curtains and stroked them with one forefinger. "I remember curtains like that from my youth. How cleverly he matched them. From memory, too." She looked at me and smiled. "He did it for me, you know."

"Your husband?" I knew that for a time Markaby had belonged to her husband.

"No, Robert Berwick." She said it without emotion, even nonchalantly, as one stating a fact, something impersonal.

"Of course." Naturally. Why hadn't I thought of it? The answer was there all the time, but I had deliberately closed my mind to it.

"Everyone knows." Then she added, "Some people pretend not to. But whether they do it out of love for me or hate, I don't know."

"No one could hate you, Stephanie."

"As to that, I am not quite sure." She bent her head to study the kitchen table. "Even the kitchen table and the china on it look the same."

"So your husband did not furnish Markaby for you?" I was trying to see the picture clearly. It still had a puzzling side.

"When my husband bought Markaby from my cousin he changed everything in it. Oh, I suppose some of the old furniture, which was valuable, is the same, but the whole appearance was totally different. I never liked it. When Robert Berwick bought the house he must have tried to restore it exactly as it had been . . . for me. He hoped I'd live here again." She sounded sad. "He loved me, you see."

"He must have loved you a great deal."

"Oh yes. In the way the Berwicks do: obsessively." She said the words softly and kindly, but with conviction.

"I had noticed," I responded, thinking of Jaimie's relationship with Angel; of Angel herself (whom did she love obsessively?—someone, I was sure); and even, perhaps, of myself, if I *was* a Berwick, which I did not truly believe.

She finished her coffee. "Now I have told you what I came to tell you. And I expect you are saying to yourself, if she is so sane, why did she not use the telephone?"

Truthfully, I said, "I never thought about it."

"Well, I could have, but I am not fond of the telephone. It changes voices and you cannot read the face behind the voice. I suppose it is a little legacy of my madness. And what a trivial one. No, I don't mind having it." She was winding herself into her outer clothes. "It is even a comfort to me. To know the *area* of one's madness—that is something, after all."

When she had finished wrapping herself up, she said, very quietly, "You must not think because of the way I speak that I did not love Robert Berwick." She smoothed her hair, and in the firelight I could see the warm and pretty girl she once had been. "I fell in love with him after I had been married about five years. I think it does sometimes happen that way if the marriage is not a success. Robert was a good deal older than I. He had his own tragedies. His wife and one married son were killed in a plane crash. The other son died young; Robert was left with only grandchildren. But he said he'd watched me grow up and loved me all the while. I didn't know." Her voice was tender.

I could picture Robert Berwick saying these words to her. From what I remembered of him he was a man whose strength responded to young things growing. Something of the feeling he had offered to her had washed over me.

She continued. "My husband was away a good deal. Robert and I became lovers. I realized I was going to have a child. In these days one would think poorly of oneself allowing an unwanted pregnancy, or letting it go on. But twenty years ago it was not so easy. And I suppose I wanted the child. I *think* I did. It is so hard to be sure now. I told my husband, of course."

"Better to be honest, I suppose," I said, wondering if indeed honesty in such circumstances was worth it.

"I had the child in a little local nursing home—it's closed now. It was a difficult birth," she said. "I don't remember much about it. When I was properly conscious, my husband told me about the child. . . ."

"Yes?" I waited.

"We told people the child was stillborn. It was not; it lived and was a monster," she said. "I never saw it, but my husband told me. 'Born a monster,' those were his words. I say them to myself sometimes. I can never forget them. It was so terrible to me that my child and Robert's should be a monster. It destroyed me, really," she said simply.

"I left it all to my husband. He managed everything. I saw no one, not even Robert. My husband kept Robert away. I was grateful to him for that."

"What happened to the child?"

"My husband arranged for it to be placed in a special home. It had little real identity, poor creature."

I paused, then I said, "He told Robert Berwick that you had given birth to a daughter, a beautiful child, and that he had arranged for her to be adopted into a family Robert would never know, and to which Robert could never trace her."

Stephanie stared at me. "Did Robert believe that?"

"I think so. I think he *did* believe what he'd been told. He must have—he spent a lot of time and money trying to find the child he believed to be his daughter. You believed what your husband told you, and so did Robert Berwick. But you were told different stories."

Stephanie stared as if she did not understand me. Or understanding, did not believe.

I tried again. "Your husband told you one story: that the child was a monster. Robert Berwick was told another version: that a daughter had been born and put out for adoption. And your family solicitors got yet another version: that the child was dead. Think about all that for a moment."

Stephanie sank down into a chair as if her heart and brain were suddenly demanding an unfair share of her body's resources. Her face first flushed, then the blood drained away. "A lot of people believed the child was dead," she murmured. "It seemed an easy lie." She looked up at me, her face drawn. "But now . . . I don't know what to believe. And he told Robert that the child was a girl, and adopted? Robert must have hated that."

"He did," I said, with conviction.

"And I? Oh God, how I felt." I could see that she was beginning to understand what had been done to her, and not only to her, but to Robert Berwick. A peculiarly delicate and clever punishment had been handed out to them both. "To each of us the story that would cause most pain," she said. She put her head down on the table and burst into tears. Even when she raised her head presently and looked at me again, she was still crying.

The storm of emotion that burst within her did not easily die down. She sat there, tears streaming down her face. They seemed to well out uncontrollably from some deep source inside her.

"All the time I was so wretched, I never cried at all," she said to me. "I was dry, dry. Every opening, every orifice became dry, the skin inside them paper-thin and cracked."

"Yes, it was a terrible punishment you gave yourself," I said.

"Gave myself?" she cried, and I could tell now that she was angry. "It was given to me. On purpose, by my husband, out of hate and jealousy."

She was still crying; not even anger stopped her tears. I let her cry. Quietly I made up a bed in the big bedroom upstairs and put in a hot-water bottle to warm it. I let her cry herself into exhaustion. My heart went out to her, but it seemed better to let the emotion run its course.

In a little while I put a fresh cup of coffee in front of her and she began to drink it, mechanically at first and then with enjoyment.

"Thank you, Kate, for what you've done."

"I don't know if you do owe me any thanks," I said.

"Yes, there are still problems, aren't there? Including

which of the three stories is the truth. Is there a child born to me still alive? Do I have a daughter?" She looked into my face. "Is it you, Kate?"

I shook my head. " 'Who bolted the door and for what purpose, I'll never know, there's a story for you,' " I said.

"What's that?" she asked.

"It's a quotation."

"Where from? I don't know it. Should I read it?"

"I wouldn't try. It's a story about nameless people. It's called 'The Unnameable.' I suppose what I'm trying to say is that life doesn't resolve all problems, does it? We don't get to know the answers to everything. Life isn't like a well-structured play."

"Oh, you are too much for me." She buried her face in her hands and said, "I don't want to admit that."

"No, neither did Robert Berwick."

"Poor Robert, oh poor Robert. Oh God, how tired I am."

"You'd better stay the night with me." I stroked her hair, so soft and fine. Mine felt coarse and thick beside it. Surely I was never her child? But then I remembered how Robert Berwick's hair had sprung so vigorously from his head.

She stood up. "Dear child, no. Thank you, but no. I must get back. There's my little dog to begin with, besides the hens and other mundane things like that. Oh, I have a lot left to live for, never fear."

"You can't go home," I insisted. "It's too late now, and the weather is too bad." The wind was still moaning round the house. "You *must* stay the night. Stephanie . . ." I stopped. "I think I *may* be Robert Berwick's daughter. He thought so. And what he believed I would like to accept. There are so many things about me that I feel I inherit from him. I feel it in my heart. There is no logic about it. How can we ever know for sure?" I ended slowly.

"Will you be content, half knowing, half accepting?" asked Stephanie. "I would be."

"I can never give up Lydia," I said quickly.

"No, indeed." She came up and kissed my cheek. "Why should you? What she has been to you I could never have been. But may I claim a small share of you? I promise not to be greedy." There were tears in her eyes. "Good night, my dear child. How proud I am to say it: my dear child." She savored the words. "It's time I left now."

"You can't go back through this weather." Alarmed, I glanced toward the window visibly shaking in the wind.

She was suddenly practical. "Oh, I'll ring up Charlie Guise and get him to come across for me."

"Not Jaimie?" I asked. Surely Jaimie would be the one?

"Oh no." She was powdering her nose, miraculously restoring her appearance with the skill of one of her generation. Now I and my contemporaries would wait with red nose and bleary eyes till nature cooled us down, but not Stephanie. "Charlie's much more help on this sort of occasion," she said.

"But what about the causeway? It'll be under water."

"It's never very deep, my dear. Haven't you noticed? Anyway, Charlie has a little boat drawn up on the sand above high-water level."

"I haven't noticed that, either," I admitted.

"It's always there."

She did telephone Charlie, then, and I heard her asking gently, but without apology, if he'd come and fetch her and take her home. I couldn't hear his side of the conversation but it must have amused her, because she smiled and even gave a soft little laugh. "Yes, I know I'm awful, but do it, Charlie," she said. "There's a love."

He came quickly, almost as if he had been waiting for a call or at any rate had nothing better to do on a cold evening than to wait for one. In what seemed a very few minutes there he was, banging on the front door of Markaby.

"I think I'll carry you across, Steph," he announced briskly. "There's not much water. Wind still rising, though."

"I noticed." They looked at each other. "I hate the wind on the sea. Do you think there'll be a storm?"

He shrugged. "Storm season."

"So it is." I noticed that she in no way resented his free and easy manner with her. Grace Beanley had affirmed he had a way with women and this judgment was obviously well founded. Me he more or less ignored.

Stephanie put her arm around me and kissed me gently, before she departed. "Some time soon, my dear, we must talk again. But meanwhile, thank you. And you'll remember what I said about Dragon's Eye? What I saw?" She studied my face. "You believe me?"

"I have every reason to believe you," I said.

"Good. Come along, Charlie, then, I'm ready. You must keep an eye on this girl, Charlie, she needs it."

He didn't answer. Instead, he busied himself with getting Stephanie on the way. "Come along, then. You'd better take my arm as we go down the path, and then when we get to the causeway, I'll give you a hoist."

Stephanie giggled and together they set off. The clouds had parted and a moon was sailing high in the sky. I watched them till Stephanie turned and waved her hand, and then they were gone, out of sight. It was a wild, wild night.

9

I went inside and took the cover off Cromwell, hoping for a little light conversation. I got nothing from him, though; he seemed sleepy and cross and barely opened his eyes. Instead, I listened to the drone of the wind and the steady threnody of the waves.

Finally I checked the fastening on all doors and windows and went to bed. I read for a little, and then tried to sleep. I lay there for what seemed a long while, listening to the noises of the night. Perhaps I did sleep lightly for a while. I had the impression of time having passed. I heard Cromwell call out from downstairs in the kitchen. I didn't take any special alarm from this. I had noticed that he was a strange old bird, almost human, and often talked in his sleep.

But I pulled on some trousers and a thick sweater and went downstairs. I had left a small lamp burning in the kitchen, and the fire was still glowing. Cromwell was clearly visible in his cage. I had covered him up, but probably some light was coming in underneath and disturbing him. His head was on his chest and his eyes were closed, but suddenly he raised his head, opened his eyes wide and looked at the door. I too looked around. There had been a noise from the hall.

Someone was inside the house.

I suppose I had known all along that if some intruder wanted to get into an old house of this sort there would be no keeping him out. Without a moment's hesitation I moved across the room and put out the lamp. Now there was only the light of the dying fire.

I stood listening. Silence, absolute silence from the hall. Even now I was not sure what I had heard, but I thought it was the noise of somebody banging into a piece of furniture. There wasn't much in the hall, except a table and a chair, both lined against the further wall. If I was standing here, frozen, it was possible my opponent was immobilized in the hall.

I was at a disadvantage, however, because I was only guessing, whereas the intruder must have heard me come down the stairs and go into the kitchen. The telephone was in the old drawing room, if I could get there; but it meant crossing the hall.

There was a telephone extension in what had been the main bedroom, next to where I now slept. If I slipped up the back stairs which led to the upper floor, I could get to this instrument without crossing the path of my unknown enemy.

I left the kitchen by the back door and slipped up the stairs. A quick look around the upper landing and I was into the big bedroom. The bed was still neatly turned back as I had arranged it for Stephanie. Heading for the phone, I decided I would call the police and summon help.

I picked up the telephone, alert for any sound of movement from below. The telephone was dead. It must have been cut off. Slowly I replaced the receiver. Still slowly, feeling as if my limbs were very heavy, I moved into the upper hall. It was empty. I walked to the head of the stairs and looked down. I saw him. A tall dark figure was outlined against the faint light from the kitchen. Then the figure melted into the depth of the kitchen.

Without hesitation, I rushed down the stairs, pulled at the great front door and ran out into the night.

At first I just ran blindly, desperate to put distance between myself and the stranger. I stumbled up the path that led away from Markaby toward the hill, where the ragged thicket of birch trees and brambles crowned the summit. I crouched here, catching my breath and listening. The noise of the wind and the sea made it difficult to pick out other sounds. I could hear nothing, but the instant the moon came out from behind a cloud I saw movement close at hand. A gentle bleat floated over to me and I realized that I had entered the world of sheep. My eyes were finally getting used to the dark. I could see that there were about half a dozen animals sheltering here, some standing, others asleep. The ewe I had disturbed was heavy with lamb.

I sat down on the ground under a tree, breathed deeply as I counted twenty, and then tried to use my mind sensibly. It had been stupid to run up here; I should have made straight for the causeway and got across it, somehow. Now I had to find my way to it without my pursuer getting to me first. I couldn't know what was planned for me, but I could guess that the sea and death by drowning were a likely fate.

A waving circle of light showed itself. He was searching for me. Slowly, methodically, the ground was being covered. I moved deeper into the trees. The searcher drew closer. I could make out a tall figure. Since I was not likely to give up without a struggle, the attacker must surely be armed.

I stared about me, seeking refuge. Someone, probably Jaimie, had provided winter fodder for the sheep, and this was piled up beneath the trees. I pushed my way between two sheep who were sheltering close together and tried to burrow into the hay. It was easier than I had thought, because, in fact, the fodder had been tossed into a slight hollow.

I crawled into the dip, pulled the hay over my head, and hoped I had disappeared completely. Sundry tiny movements and sounds suggested that I shared my hiding place with various other little animals of a retiring disposition. I longed to scratch.

In the dark, sounds from above were more muffled; yet I became conscious of movement close at hand. I could sense the sheep moving about as if troubled. The hay covering me was rumpled, as if a hand was searching it. A tiny creature ran down one leg, my nose tickled so that I wanted to sneeze; but I clenched my teeth, forcing my body to obey my order of silence and immobility. A sheep trampled very close to the hay; I felt the pressure of its sharp hooves. I think this animal's movement may have saved me. I lay undisturbed.

I lay as long as I could bear without moving, then I cautiously stuck my head out and took a look. Nothing was visible except the trees, the sheep, and the wild night sky.

I stayed where I was for what seemed like hours. Gradually, because of the peaceful stance of the sheep around me, I became convinced that the searcher had gone—from my immediate neighborhood, at least.

Stiff, aching, and frozen, I crept back to Markaby.

The front door was open, just as I had left it. The night seemed darker than ever. Dazed and tired as I was, the blackness of the hall inside Markaby seemed impenetrable. I put out my hand to feel the way like a blind person.

My fingers touched another hand, which at once seized mine in a dry firm grip. I screamed once loudly and then again and again.

"Stop it, stop it at once!" A light switch was snapped on.

Charlie Guise stood there, one hand holding mine, the other on the light switch.

I stopped screaming, my breath coming in a series of shuddering gasps.

"Thank goodness. I thought you'd do yourself an injury. That's better. Are you all right? Can you speak?"

After a minute I could. "What are *you* doing here?" What was he *always* doing here after an attempt had been made on my life?

Before he answered, he made me sit down; then he went away, to reappear instantly with a glass of water. Finally he sat down on a stair and studied me. "I stayed with Stephanie for a good while. You didn't think I could leave her? She told me what she'd seen happening on Dragon's Eye—lights and so forth. I gather she'd told you. As I drove home from Stephanie's, I kept an eye on the island. When I saw pinpoints of light moving, I got suspicious and rowed over."

It was a good answer. Whether it was true or not, I could not decide.

"And when I got here I found the front door open and no one about. And then you, screaming your head off."

"There *was* someone here. I was frightened and ran to hide. If you don't know the background, it sounds ridiculous of me, stupid even. But I thought I had reason. Billy English . . ."

"Oh, you know about him?" He made it a question, but he did not even try to sound surprised.

"I found him." There, it was out.

"You?" Now he did sound surprised. And not too pleased, either. "Go on," he commanded. His voice was stern. It put me on the defensive. Unfairly, so I thought.

"His body was hidden in a rock crevice, put there either by chance, by the sea itself, or more likely on purpose, to hide it. I believe he was murdered. Anyway, I found it."

"And what did you do about it?" He made it sound, if not exactly an accusation, then certainly a sharp question. "Nothing? Anything?"

"I did something. I told Jaimie Berwick." There was a silence. "He moved the body. I don't think he should have done that, but he says he doesn't want the body associated with Dragon's Eye." It was a relief, in a way, to have told him. I took a deep breath.

"You sound nervous." He was still studying my face.

My eyes dropped. "I've been frightened. I was frightened sometimes on Dragon's Eye before I found a dead body, and now I'm even more frightened. I don't want to share Billy's fate."

"Sounds reasonable." He kept his voice cool. "Why not clear out? Go away? Go back to London?"

"Yes, that's been the suggestion all along." I was better controlled now. "From every side that's the suggestion I get: clear out, go away. Well, I won't go. I said just now I was afraid. It was true. I have been afraid. I don't like what's going on here. Who could? But *I* will be the one to choose when I leave here and why. It's about time

217

everyone understood this." I had made quite a speech out of it. I stood up. I was feeling stronger and, oddly, more confident. "I was going to be killed. I'm not sure how, but the sea came into it."

"There are many ways of arranging a mortality at sea," he said.

I saw a bit of white fluff on the floor. I picked it up, and found I was handling a small piece of cottonwool. From it floated the sweet odor of chloroform. Without a word I handed it to him. He sniffed. "At least we know which method was to be used this time." He made the gesture of smothering my face with a pad, and then mimicked my fall, unconscious, into the sea.

I was silent. It was unpleasantly vivid to me without his help. This must be the manner in which Billy English had been drowned. Only a few feet of seawater would be required, and then the body could be discarded at will. Where I would have been found, I didn't know. My unspoken question was answered for me.

"You would have drifted far away from Dragon's Eye," said Charlie, "the way the tides and winds are running tonight." He got up from the stairs and strolled over. "You'd better come with me."

Oh, right, I thought. I said, "I'll make my own decisions."

He said irritably, "The way the wind is rising and the sea with it, you could get cut off here."

I said pointedly, "As long as I'm alone, I'm safe."

"I could make you come. Take you."

"Try it. I should certainly fight."

He eyed me. "I'm twice your size. You wouldn't fight long."

Deliberately I turned on my heel. "Somehow I don't think you'll risk a fight in which you might get marked, but I certainly would. Cuts and bruises have to be explained away."

I allowed myself a look at his face. It remained dark and expressionless. I hadn't got a reaction; I give him that.

"I suggest you go to Stephanie Lyon. Or to my mother." He came over and took me firmly by my wrist. "If you won't go easy, then you'll have to go hard," he warned pleasantly.

"No chloroform?" I taunted.

"I wish I had some," he said, still pleasantly.

Both of us heard it at the same time; above the wind and the waves, the sound of a bell, a single tolling note, constantly repeated.

"What's that?"

"It's the bell from The Grange." He dropped my wrist. "Ringing to call out the boat."

"The lifeboat?"

"Of course, what else?" He spoke impatiently, as if it were a fact too obvious to state. He stared at me for a moment. "I must go. Will you come or will you stay?"

I rubbed my wrist. The bell was still tolling.

Outside, following the darkness of the hour before dawn, a gray light had appeared. Charlie Guise looked a figure of black and white, all color drained away. I suppose I looked the same. In the grisaille landscape the dim sea rolled, shifting great masses of water with casual abandon. The wind had raised itself to a wail.

"How will you get across?"

"I have a boat tied up below. I can row across. It's still possible, just." He looked at the sea appraisingly. "Well, how is it? Will you come with me?"

"No." And, after all, it cost me something. "I'll stay."

"Right." And he walked away, without a backward look.

I thought he might be going to his death. That he was personally brave I was obliged to admit, but trust him I could not.

As the light grew stronger with the break of day, so did the wind. I stood on Dragon's Eye and looked out to sea. Mere minutes had elapsed since Charlie Guise's rapid departure, but already only a fool would have tried to cross the causeway.

The surge was dashing itself against the rocks, sending spray leaping higher, ever higher, and then falling back into the elemental force below from which it had sprung. I was hypnotized by the stern vigor and energy of the scene before me. This boiling sea looked capable of mastering any human strength. If there was a ship in trouble out there, then its position was fearful.

The bell had ceased to toll its summons. For what it was worth the boat must be on the point of launching. Surely no boat could survive in such a sea? I couldn't see anything but the tumbling waters and the gray sky. I couldn't hear anything but the steady roar of the sea and the wind tearing past. Suddenly from the south I heard a gun. It came again, a distress signal booming. Fixing my gaze in the direction of the sound, I could just make out the shape of a small vessel. A tiny lozenge of black, intermittently visible through the heaving seas. On board, her men must be sweaty and frightened. The black lozenge did not move. I guessed she had run aground on one of those dangerous ridges of rock that ran out from this coast. I could never see the ship distinctly for long, as great seas constantly rose between us.

I knew the lifeboat must now be pushing out from

Garrow. In my memory, she seemed too fragile a shell to propel herself out to rescue anyone. But I knew that she was sturdily built in fact, and specially designed to withstand heavy seas. I thought of the men who would sail in her. I thought especially of Charlie Guise; I might suspect him of violent crime, yet never for one moment considered his turning back or failing in courage in the Garrow lifeboat. He was my oar; he would do his bit. Jaimie, too, would be there. The bell had rung from The Grange. He was not a man to evade his responsibilities.

I turned toward Garrow. I could just detect a group of figures huddled together on the edge of the cliff that ran like an apron down to the sea. Here the boathouse stood, although the building itself was out of my sight. None of the tiny figures I could see seemed to be moving about— all were simply standing, staring out at the water. If they turned to look at me, I suppose that was how I would appear to them as well: remote and motionless.

A huge sheet of spray rose up before me, blotting out what I had been able to see. By the time the air cleared, the scene had changed. The group of watchers had scattered, the sea seemed temporarily calmer, and the wind abated. Suddenly, there she was—a small craft thrusting gallantly through the waves. I could see her lights.

The lifeboat was out. I had this one glimpse, then a great sea rose up and the sight of her was again lost.

When the sea leveled off, it was empty. Nothing was to be seen except a moving mass of water. I thought the lifeboat must have sunk already—until the seas parted, and I saw the boat climbing up the side of a wave. Up she came, wavering for a second on the crest, and then was gone. Time had stopped, but my vigil must have lasted hours.

Even I could see that there was a strange quality to the sea. The wind and the racing tide were meeting each other head-on to produce an explosion of energy.

Straining to see the stranded vessel, once again just visible through the spray, I noticed that now she seemed to have shifted her balance and to be listing slightly. What looked like a small angle to me, at this distance, was probably acute and terrifying to those on board. She could not last long under those conditions. Even as I watched, she lurched again. But the lifeboat had now appeared out of nowhere and was close at hand. Unbearably, the drama was interrupted as once more a great gap of water had opened up between them. Then I saw what was happening—the lifeboat was swinging round in an arc to approach the stranded ship from the other side.

A new sound had entered into the wind; it was screaming on a higher, wilder note. A strange, dark belt of cloud was coming in from the seaward side of Dragon's Eye. The dawn light faded fast. I just had time to see a mountain of water rise up and cover ship and lifeboat when that cloud opened. A handful of hail struck me savagely in the face. Then more, and still more. The force of the hail pressed me to my knees so that I crouched, head on my arms, trying to shut everything out. In my emotionally exhausted state, the storm seemed to possess the primeval force that might have beat on this planet when the mountains and seas were mating. I have never felt so far away and lonely—before or since—as I was there.

I do not have any concept of how long I remained, oblivious, in this position. But when I looked up the sky seemed to have lightened magically. The hail stopped, the cloud had passed over. The waves stretched before me, suddenly calmer, rolling now with arithmetical steadiness across the seascape. One after the other, as far as the eye could see, they rose and fell, rose and fell. The watchers at Garrow had gone away. I was alone with the wind and the sea.

I watched as long as I could bear to watch, the cold eating into my bones. But of the two ships, the one little, the other large, there was no sign: only the empty, rolling North Sea waters.

Cold, wet, and utterly wretched, I walked back to Markaby, took off my soaked clothes, rolled myself in a blanket and lay down on the bed. There was no need to look for monsters in the waters around Dragon's Eye; the sea itself could be a monster whom the storm called up.

I don't think I slept for long, but I awoke refreshed and alert. I immediately tried the telephone. It was still dead. I dressed and went down to the kitchen to make some coffee. While I drank it I listened to the radio, hoping for a news bulletin from the local station at Newcastle. But nothing more than light music was played, with occasional cheerful comments from the announcer. Nothing about the wreck of a ship in that storm or the loss of a lifeboat.

Outside, a great peace lay over land and sea. The sky was a tranquil arch of pale blue. We had passed through the storm and emerged on the other side. I would never get used to the sudden changes of the weather on this coast. I walked along the path toward Dragon's Hill, on which I had hidden in the dark with the sheep, all the time keeping my eyes on the sea. But Dragon's Hill remained calm and empty. The tide was very high, higher than I had ever seen it before, and the causeway was deep under water. I thought I would leave it for a while longer before trying the crossing.

I was still undecided about what to do and where to

go. I decided that a sensible plan would be to call on Phillip Naseby in Berwick. He would, I hoped, offer sound advice, and perhaps I could convince him to come to the police with me.

The sheep were still grazing on the hill. A few had wandered away and were standing in a group nearer the sea. As I looked at them they moved off, as if my approach had alarmed them.

My attention elsewhere as it was, I almost stumbled. Lying in the grass, face hidden, was a man. He was lying, legs drawn up, hands together under one cheek, like a child. It was Jaimie Berwick.

I knelt down beside him. "Jaimie?" I said softly. He was wearing a thick dark-blue sweater and an oilskin jacket. His feet were bare. Everything about him was soaking wet and decorated, here and there, with seaweed. Unbelievably, he had come out of the sea to Dragon's Eye.

"Jaimie!" I gave him a shake. He couldn't just lie there exhausted, as he obviously was, or pneumonia would result. "Jaimie, wake up."

He opened his eyes, but soon let the eyelids drop again. I could see that he was at the end of his energies, so tired, so spent, that nothing was real. I took his hand, and, cold and flaccid, it rested in mine. Probably his temperature was dangerously low, and this accounted for his sleepiness. Could he have swum ashore to Dragon's Eye from a sinking lifeboat? I had to get him inside, quickly.

I slapped his face, first one cheek, then the other. "Jaimie, Jaimie Berwick. Wake up." He slowly opened his eyes, and this time they stayed open. "Can you put your arm around my neck? Good, now try and stand, and I'll help you up."

I hauled him to his feet; he winced as I tugged and pulled, but eventually we stood upright, swaying together. My fear was that he would fall and drag me down with him.

"Start walking, Jaimie," I said. Somewhat to my surprise he managed to obey, and, yoked together, we traveled slowly down the path to the house. We took our time, but we made it.

As we walked, I made my plans. I wouldn't let him rest in the kitchen. I'd force him to walk upstairs, and then I'd get him into the bed I'd made up for Stephanie. I'd make him drink something hot. . . .

The exercise was helping; he was more conscious as I pushed and coaxed him up the stairs. He even had strength enough to try resistance as I pulled off some of his wet clothes and swathed the blankets round him. He looked much better, but a great bruise was starting to appear down the left side of his face. I was beginning to suspect that his left forearm was broken; the hand and wrist were red and swollen.

When I came back with some hot tea, he spoke to me. "It's Kate, isn't it?"

"Yes, of course."

"Sorry to be stupid." It was an effort for him to speak. "Not quite sure where I am."

I said eagerly, "On Dragon's Eye. You're in Markaby. In bed. You must have swum here. Did you swim?"

"I did swim," he agreed, after thinking about it.

"Did the lifeboat go down?"

He looked at me vaguely. "No, I don't think it did. Don't remember."

"Well, you've swum from somewhere," I said. "Here, drink this."

"What is it?" He stared at the cup with suspicion.

"Hot tea."

"Never drink it." He closed his eyes.

"You're going to drink this." And he did, urged on from sip to sip by me. When he'd finished, I put the hot-water bottle in beside him and, at last, let him sink into a sleep which looked a good deal more natural than the one in which I had found him.

I went back and studied him once or twice, as the morning wore on. Somehow, soon, I must find a way of getting into Garrow. Angel was bound to be sick with worry about Jaimie. I was myself, although, as time wore on, he began to look much more normal. Perhaps I could run up a flag which would be seen from the mainland. Or, as it grew darker, I might light a bonfire. I think I was a bit mad myself during this time.

He was muttering in his sleep when I next looked, so I woke him. "How are you now, Jaimie?"

"Not bad. Not bad at all." He answered me without really opening his eyes.

"How did you get here? Do you know?"

"I swam."

"So you did. You said that before. And you've hurt your arm. And your face. What hit you? Were you hurt as the boat went down?"

"The sea hit me. Or something in the sea hit me. Can't remember."

"No." I accepted this as a fact. He had certainly tangled with something. "What happened to you, Jaimie? Can you remember anything more?"

He opened his eyes and looked at me and frowned.

"I remember falling into the water. Or jumping. Not sure which."

"The lifeboat must have gone down. And the other ship, did that sink? And both crews? What happened to them?"

He shook his head.

"Perhaps you're the only survivor. I have to get you some help soon, Jaimie."

"Later. Tired now." He closed his eyes. "Lost you, Kate, haven't I? My own fault. Gold from dross, I never know it, really. Always went for the wrong things. Except with you."

Not knowing how to answer him, I put my hand on his, and we sat there silently together. It was true that so much had happened in so little time that I barely had any idea where my heart lay, and the time of our loving seemed a fleeting memory. I would have to wait until things calmed down before I would be able to reassess my feelings for this handsome young man. Nevertheless, my fondness for Jaimie as Robert Berwick's grandson was undiminished, drawn as I had been into his circle of danger. Presently, I realized that his hand seemed very hot as if from extreme cold he had now swung toward fever. I had to get help.

I went outside, intending to see if there was any means by which I could send a signal to Garrow. I had even cast a desperate glance at Cromwell's cage, but this look was enough to convince me that he was not the bird to send out as a dove over troubled waters, or as a carrier pigeon. I doubted he could even fly.

A sheep had grazed its way to the vicinity of the house, to stand alone about twenty yards away. But there was something about the way it stood there that drew my attention to it. The creature was moving restlessly from foot to foot. I went over for a closer inspection. One sheep looks very like another, but I believed that this was the ewe I had seen when I hid from my attacker in the dark. It was on the point of lambing, and, from the way it was behaving and its unusual proximity, something must be badly wrong.

"Oh God," I thought. "And now I've got to be midwife to a sheep."

Easier said than done, I decided a minute later. I could see the animal flinch and quiver, but I had no idea how to help her. A very timid and tentative investigation had revealed no sign of a lamb's head appearing. I supposed it did appear head first like a human baby. But was it born in a sac or not? I had no idea.

I went back into the house, and met Jaimie coming shakily down the stairs. He had his oilskin jacket on. "I'm just pushing off," he said.

"You can't go now. I want help with a ewe that's lambing."

He kept on walking down the stairs. "You sound nervous."

"I am." I put my hand on his arm in entreaty. He turned and looked at me.

"You are a funny girl. You withstand I don't know what, without turning a hair, and you start shaking when a ewe starts to lamb."

"I'm sure this one is in bad trouble and will die without help. Besides . . ." I paused. "She's a sort of friend. Will you help me?"

He hesitated. "Well, I've only got one good hand, do you see?"

"I know that." He had the arm held into his side. "You should let me bind it up."

"No need, no need. Where's the ewe, then? Give me a look." He marched impatiently out of the door, followed by me.

He was gentle with the creature. "What is it then, old lady? Let me see you." Then he turned to me. "I'm no vet, but it looks to me like the presentation is wrong. Coming feet first, should be head first."

"What's to be done?" I tried to sound confident, as if I was sure something could be done.

"It ought to be shifted. Moved to the right position."

"Will she die, otherwise?"

He hesitated. "She's a hardy old thing. All these cross-breeds are. But yes, she will die in the long run, of septicemia. The little beast will rot inside her, you see. She needs professional help."

"Won't she die if we wait? Can't we help?"

Again he hesitated, and then said reluctantly, "Yes, she might. We can try. But I've only one good hand."

"I'll help, of course. I'll help. I'm another pair of hands." I was pleading.

He looked at me and gave his head a slight shake, as if the sight of me was not reassuring. "Help me out of this coat, then," he said. He went white with pain as I did so. I took the scarf off my own head to make a sling for the bad arm. It left him with only one hand free. I would have to make up for the deficiency. "Hold her then, Kate, and don't bother stroking her head. She's not a cat."

It was the only trace of irritability he showed; otherwise he was marvelously patient and gentle, with both me and the ewe.

"Get me a bucket of hot water," he said, over his shoulder. "And some disinfectant, if you've got any. And a stool to sit on, if there is one."

I labored back and forth with the things he wanted, glad to be helping, anxious to do right.

"The beast keeps slipping away again," he said, removing his hand. "The thing is, I'm awkward, and my hand is too big. I'm not doing a neat job. We need a lady's hand." He looked at mine.

I swallowed hard. "I wouldn't know what to do."

"I'll direct you. Go on, have a try."

Slowly I inserted my right hand into the birth channel It was warm and slippery, very muscular too. I tried to think of it as a dark tunnel at the end of which was life waiting to be born.

"Now feel carefully. What can you feel?"

"A leg. A tiny, fragile leg."

"What else?"

"Another leg."

He frowned. "Try again."

"Still another leg." I had been doing a little gentle investigation on my own account. It seemed to me there were too many legs. I raised my head. "I think there are twins."

"Could be. Well, in for a penny, in for a pound. Do what I tell you and work in time with the contractions of the uterus."

"I have no choice!" I replied. The old ewe had strong muscles. My hand and arm were going to be black and blue. I wondered what it was doing to the tiny lambs. For the first time I realized what a painful business birth must be for those waiting to be born.

He was precise and meticulous in his instructions, and he had an imaginative clarity that made me understand what I was about.

Slowly, step by gentle step, I maneuvered the first little creature into the correct position to be born.

"Now, wait. I think the other might follow naturally, once this one gets out. They'd be a bit cramped in there, and until there's more room it'd not be able to right itself naturally."

The ewe gave a heave and strained. To my pleasure a tiny face appeared, then a waving foreleg, and then the complete lamb was on the ground at my feet.

I was triumphant and turned to Jaimie to share the success. To my surprise, he had sunk to his knees, his face white. I supposed it was the pain of his arm, but as I rushed to help him, he muttered, "Never could stand the sight of blood."

I laid him out on the turf and returned to my other patient. A second lamb, and then the placenta appeared rapidly; but the ewe by now was taking an interest in affairs, and gratefully I left her to it. The twin lambs were already nuzzling her for food.

Jaimie was sitting up. I went and sat beside him and put my arm around him. "It was a shepherd and his lass," he murmured. "Am I drunk or do I dream?"

"Neither. It really happened." We sat beside each other on the rough turf of Dragon's Eye, at peace again and happy.

The air was growing mild and tranquil; the storm of last night was a million years away. I could smell herbage and sea and even sheep, but it was all innocent and sweet. It was a dream of happiness.

"I ought to push off," he said, after a while.

"Stay." Now he put his good arm around me and we leaned together.

"I know I ought to go," he murmured. "For every reason, I ought to go."

"Stay. The water's still well over the causeway. Stay till it's quite safe," I answered from the depths of my dream.

"Safe? Who knows what's safe?" But he did not go.

We went back into the house; the hours passed dreamily. We talked, ate some food, talked again, and sometimes kissed. I didn't know what to make of myself. I didn't seem the girl I had been. For that matter, neither was Jaimie what I'd known before.

We both had our confessions to make. He told me about Angel.

"It's time you knew. She's going to be a nun. She's going to take her vows."

I must say I could hardly believe it. "Angel, a nun?" I was incredulous. Was this what had lain behind her radiant happiness? Marriage, yes, but not the lover I had expected.

"Yes, it's always been her intention. She waited till her twenty-fifth birthday before going ahead. She knew I didn't want it to happen."

"But you didn't want to marry her? You never did?" Was it from anger at and jealousy of Angel's dedication that Robert Berwick had asked me to save Jaimie?

"No, but it's her money, you see. She'll take that with her to the convent; it will be her dowry. That's only right, I see that, there has to be one, but I wanted the money to work The Grange. I need it." He was in earnest. "A place like The Grange eats money."

"I wish I understood you better, Jaimie." Love you I

always will, I thought, but the manner of it is changing. My conversation with Stephanie Lyon had to be considered also. Were we blood relations? "You do look tired."

"I'm glad the lambs are all right," he said absently. "You've changed your mind about marrying me, haven't you?"

"This isn't the time to talk about it."

"There'll never be a better."

For a little while I had been living another life, but I was coming back to earth now.

"I've got to get you home, Jaimie," I said uneasily. "You look rotten. Do you think you had a bit of concussion?"

"I can't remember a damn thing," he said, gloomily. "I remember climbing up onto Dragon's Eye after swimming, and that's it."

"You were knocked about." I studied his face where the bruise was turning blue.

He stopped. "That was underwater. Something hit me."

"Something?"

"Yes, I was swimming; I was coming up through the sea, when it happened. I'm clear on that." He didn't go on.

I thought he was beginning to remember quite a lot, but did not want to talk about it.

"Is it possible," I said slowly, "that someone attacked you?"

"Who? One of your criminals? I know you're imagining a gang." He was skeptical.

"Could it have been Charlie Guise?"

"Why Charlie Guise?" Now he was alert and looking at me intently. "Why Charlie, for goodness' sake?"

"I think he's mixed up in it all. Did he go out in the lifeboat? Can you remember?"

234

"No, I can't."

I stood up. "We have to find out." I felt compelled by a sudden urgency. "You stay here. You're not well." His face was drained of color and looked pinched with pain.

"My arm's not too bad," he said. "I can move the fingers. I think it's only bruised. But I feel sort of sick inside."

I helped him to a chair. He lay back, eyes closed. "Don't leave me, Kate."

"No, I won't." I let him hold my hand. We sat together quietly. He seemed to drift to sleep. I tried to release myself so that I could make him more comfortable. Then I saw his hands. All the time we had been helping the ewe I hadn't got a good look. Now I did.

"Jeez!" I said aloud. I don't usually swear. I know plenty of the required words, having been in the theater, but I don't use them much. Now I could have used a whole stream.

Both his hands were torn and scraped. The nails were dirty; here and there his fingertips were raw. I winced just looking at them. But what I saw on closer inspection was a surprise to me. The condition of Jaimie's hands looked like the result of hard manual labor. Beneath the neck of the oilskin, where it touched the skin, he had knotted a silk scarf. It was a scarf of plain white silk, slightly luxurious, but unmistakably masculine. From it came the faintest whiff of that perfume of verbena and lime, touched with lavender, that made the scent Le Jardin mixed for Angel so individual. Of course. With all the hints I had of their closeness, with all I had seen of the duality between them, why had I not guessed that Jaimie liked it, too? A dry, astringent scent, it was not unsuitable for a man.

I sat there gazing at his face, which in repose looked

drawn. I know my own was sad, for I saw it in the mirror. I thought quietly for a while, then I got up and went to my room.

When I came downstairs I was dressed ready for North Sea swimming. The water looked a pretty blue today, almost as if it might be warm. But I knew it was not.

I thought Jaimie might hear me going out, but he didn't. He stayed where he was, still slumped in a chair, eyes closed. I didn't expect to be gone long. Too long in that water and I'd be dead.

I chose my spot, reckoning to go into the sea as close as I could to where Jaimie had climbed out. Where he had climbed out, I would go in.

Underwater I looked around; the sea was dark and cloudy, the consequence of the storm. I made out that I was very near where the body of Billy English had been trapped. I couldn't be quite sure, but to me it looked the same. I moved on, flashlight in one hand.

Ahead, I saw an opening like the mouth of a tunnel in the rock face. Seaweeds grew around it, and it looked like the entrance to a watery hell, but it interested me. I had considered the possibility of something like it existing.

I made for the opening, entered the tunnel and slowly swam along it, touching the rock face at intervals with my fingertips. It was widening every minute, but the flashlight was not yet showing up anything of interest, and the cold was penetrating my suit. Soon I would have to turn back.

I paddled forward a few more feet. There must be something down here.

In the dark water ahead of me, there was movement. I

stopped. Yes, there it was again. A dark shape, rippling slowly through the water toward me.

Now I could see it in the light of the torch. A great dark form about eight feet long and thick as a tree trunk. It was no vegetable, however, for it was moving toward me purposefully. As it swam into the light I saw the head: long, bevelled, and with teeth like a horse. I don't remember noticing the eyes; all I could see were the teeth, and the muscles of the body, as it propelled itself forward. I could guess now what had hit Jaimie; one lash from that body could break a man's arm.

It was coming toward me with the steady intent of malice. Acting instinctively, I put out the flashlight and forced myself upward at an angle. I rose above the creature and swam away fast. Underneath me I felt the water vibrate with the creature's movement. I could feel the angry lash of its body. Then it was gone.

My head was above water. I had swum through the mouth of the tunnel into a rocky passage. My knees scraped on rock. I stood up and walked out of the water onto solid ground.

I looked about me, shining the flashlight this way and that. The passage led into a cave, which itself was dry and cool, and which had obviously never been under water.

I sat down on the floor, placed the flashlight beside me, and waited for my nerves to steady. This cave could be entered only from the sea by an entrance which was under water at high tide. I had approached it that way. But I could see from the watermarks on the side of the passage and from the way the seaweed grew that at times, according to the tide, it might be possible to walk through rather than swim for it. When the tide was out and the stone track along the causeway was bare, this tunnel was open.

I stood up. I had met the monster of Markaby. Or one of them, for possibly there were others. I judged it to be a giant eel—of no friendly disposition, either. Probably a colony of them had always lived among the caves and passages of Dragon's Eye. It was a likely habitat. Was this Grace Beanley's "Old Bluetooth"?

Thus, deliberately and reasonably, I slowed my pulse, and forced the adrenalin level in my blood down. People in panic may act fast, but they are seldom acute and accurate observers of what lies about them. I knew that I had to make a careful viewing of what lay about me.

The light of the torch had shown me that preparations of some sort had been started here. A man had been working down here and had left his equipment about. I saw spades, picks and a big lamp with its own container of oil, as well as a small radio.

I thought I could guess where Jaimie had been; but I still had no idea what he had been doing here.

I wasn't cold in the even temperature of the cave, but I could have done with some other clothes, for the sake of my appearance. The diving suit clung to me, so that I looked like a fish with feet. I felt clumsy and inelegant and awkward.

God knows why that should have mattered down there —until I turned my head, and knew why it mattered. A man was watching me. I suppose any woman any time can sense that sort of look.

I faced him completely, trying to look arrogant. I knew that I had succeeded, because as my flashlight dipped across his face I got a reflection of my own look back from him.

Like calls to like, and between Charlie Guise and me there was more than one point of resemblance.

He had on blue jeans and a dark-blue cotton shirt, so although wet and I hoped uncomfortable, he was more conventionally dressed than I was. In fact, he looked tiresomely normal and matter-of-fact, as though he had every right to be where he was. I, on the other hand, felt at once ridiculous, a girl making a fuss and creating a stir where no stir need be.

"How did you get here?" I said; it came out in an even more unfriendly voice than I'd expected or planned.

"The same way you did. I swam."

He'd been here some time, I thought, because he was not dripping wet.

"I wondered if you'd gone down when the lifeboat sank."

He said: "But the lifeboat didn't sink. Instead, it picked up all the survivors of the *Anstruther Star*, the ship in trouble."

"And so what are you doing down here?"

"I might ask you the same question." He put out a hand and easily took my flashlight from me. "Do you mind, you're shining that in my face. But I'll tell you. I was waiting."

There's a way of responding to people that isn't a true response at all, but simply a turning back toward them of what they've already said. Policeman and psychologists find it very useful. I used it now. "Waiting," I repeated.

"Yes, I wanted to see who turned up here."

I still didn't understand.

"*I* arrived," I said.

"So you did," he agreed.

"I swam up the channel and met a sea creature on the way that was about ready to eat me up."

He responded at once. "You met old Jumbo. I used to swim here a lot as a boy and often met him or one like him. Conger eels of a big sort. Harmless enough, if you don't interfere with them."

"This one thought I had," I said grimly.

While we were talking he had moved across the cave, adjusted the oil lamp, and lit it. A mild yellow light flooded the whole area. It showed the cave to be about nine feet high by twelve feet long, hollowed by the sea out of the living rock. But the wall at the end had an arranged, man-made air. The stones, although ancient, had once been worked. One area of stone, about eye level, had been removed, and then been partly stuck back again.

This was how Jaimie had injured his fingers. He had tried desperately to fill in the hole in the rock wall. He had hurried in vain. Either something had interrupted him, or someone—it had to be Charlie Guise—had made a fresh aperture. For me it was just above eye level. I am tall, but Jaimie Berwick was taller.

I turned to Charlie Guise. "You didn't really answer my question. Why are you down here? Not just waiting."

"No. Distrustfulness is written all over your face, did you know that?" He seemed to find this amusing, rather than otherwise. "And you have a quite remarkably expressive face and voice. To tell you the truth, I expected to find someone already here."

He pointed about him. "There are signs that someone has been here."

"He was here, of course," I said slowly, my fears confirmed. "Jaimie Berwick." I hated to name him.

"Where is Jaimie now?"

I didn't answer. I couldn't. I thought back to some of the episodes in which Jaimie was involved with me, and in which I had trusted him. Our meeting in the museum at Berwick. My conversation about my discovery of Billy English. No wonder things had gone subtly wrong with everything I had entrusted to him.

First he had tried to frighten me away from Markaby, then he had tried to kill me, then he had fallen in love with me—or had he? Pride made me want to believe his love had been as real as my response. But even then, when I had threatened to go to the police, he had come to Markaby again in secret. I think he had meant to kill me, or in some way silence me, but he had found it impossible to do so.

He had never been on the lifeboat.

He must have been down here, tidying away all the traces he had left when he was caught by the storm.

It would have been dangerous to leave till the seawater subsided. Even so he had been knocked about. He had pretended to forget, but I was sure that any lapse of memory had been only temporary. Jaimie knew. Looking back, I realized now how tense and weary he had been all through our reunion on Dragon's Eye.

"All right. You needn't tell me. On Dragon's Eye. Take that look off your face, I can read it better than any book."

I covered my face with my hands. "I've betrayed him."

Charlie came up and put his arm around my shoulders. "You've betrayed no one. He betrayed you."

I took my hands away and stared at the cave. "What is there here that all of them want so much?"

He said: "Go and look. Look through the hole in the wall. I have looked."

I walked over slowly, stood on my toes, and looked in. It was hard to see at first.

"Use the flashlight," said Charlie patiently. He brought

it over to me and presently, since my hand trembled, focused it for me.

I don't know what I expected. The glitter of gold, the sparkle of diamonds, anything but what I saw.

Sand had silted up inside the cavity, covering the objects within, but although the centuries had passed, the air here was clean, and not enough dry earth had fallen to mask the essential character of what lay hidden—buried, rather, for I was looking at a tomb.

There was the unmistakable proud outline of a Viking ship. I could see the dragon's face on the prow, with its fierce smile and arrogant head. I could see the outline of a carved wooden cart, and what looked like a sledge.

I was looking at a Viking invader's burial chamber. Here the Angel of Death had brought him, together with armor and swords and axes, his dogs and horses, his sons and his slave woman, all entombed in his ship.

I remembered the story that Jaimie Berwick had told me in the museum; the story of how such a Viking leader was buried, and of the strange and savage ritual that went with it. Then it had seemed distant, an archaic event that could enchant me but that I could dismiss. Suddenly it had come very close. The strange tension and nervousness that had touched me in the boathouse came back, only with a very much stronger force. Death and sex and violence suddenly seemed very close. I could almost smell it in my nostrils. Sometimes they burned the ship with the dead man in it; this one they had buried and raised a memorial mound above. Now I knew the origin of Dragon's Hill. I had walked on the island, and all the time the old Viking had lain beneath.

I looked again at the chamber in the rock. Briefly I wondered how long the ship and the grave goods would remain without disintegrating, now the sea air had penetrated the once-sealed chamber. At the moment they appeared solid, but I knew that old wood, however robust its appearance, is really as fragile as puff pastry. I took one last look. As I shone the flashlight along this way and that, vestiges of color seemed to come to life. I saw stripes of green and blue on the rugs covering the sledge, a hint of gold from the wooden cart as if parts of it had once been gilded, and from the wooden prow a glow of defiant red. Before my eyes the scene seemed on the brink of returning to life. It was a marvelous moment, the sort one dreams about and never thinks to witness. Such moments can hardly come very often or to many people. I made it last as long as I could before I turned away.

I stepped back and Charlie came up beside me. "You know what you've got here?"

"Oh yes. Yes."

He looked through the hole. "My own ancestors must have stood on the sands and watched this chap's ships come at them over the sea. Well, here he is and here I am." He sounded satisfied.

"Yes, you're one of the dark ones, aren't you?" I said.

"That's right. And you're one of the fair invaders. By the look of you."

The enmity between us had suddenly faded, as some emotions will when reality comes in. But I had nothing ready to take its place. I rested my forehead against the cold, dry stone. "Oh God, I'm so tired. So deadly tired."

"Come on," said Charlie. He put his arm around my shoulders. "Let's get you back."

"I don't fancy meeting Jumbo again," I said, my face still hidden.

Comfortingly, he said, "I'll see he doesn't worry you."

"And Jaimie? What about Jaimie?" I still didn't look at him.

"Does it matter to you so much?" His grip tightened. "Come on, tell me, my girl."

Instead of answering, I said, still without looking up, "Whatever was he trying to arrange? What did he hope to gain?"

"Look around you," he said. "All this, of course.

"It's a marvelous and beautiful collection of immense value. A national monument. People would flock here to gaze at it. Not just scholars and students, but ordinary people. I've never seen anything like it, have you?

"And it belongs to whoever owns Markaby. It would bring prestige and even wealth. But it's more than that— it has a sort of magic, this site. Even I feel it. I think Jaimie wanted desperately to own it."

"Yes, I can understand. I feel the same. But I would have let him have it."

"He'd already killed Billy English," Charlie reminded me. "And you would not have let him make money out of it, would you? I think I read you better than that, Kate. You'd have thrown it open to everyone for free."

"Yes, you're right. I couldn't profit from it. To me, Markaby and Dragon's Eye are almost a sacred trust. One with L'Anse aux Meadows and Novgorod and Vinland the Good—magic, magic names. But exploit it? No, I couldn't do that."

"As Jaimie knew. It's over now, though. You stood in his way. You and Robert Berwick, because he left Markaby to you, and with it this undiscovered, secret treasure."

"Poor Jaimie," I said. There was a moment of silence. I was the one to break it. "I'm not in love with Jaimie Berwick. I thought I was, though. It was like being on a merry-go-round. Round and round, up and down, all to the music of the fair till you roll off."

"Fall off and I'll pick you up," he said steadily.

"Thank you."

"It's not thanks I want."

"Robert Berwick asked me to save Jaimie. I didn't know from what. At first I just thought it was from Angel's ruthlessness. Perhaps it was that, too. But now I think that Robert caught a glimpse of the violence in Jaimie in those weeks before he died and became frightened."

"I know he did," said Charlie Guise. "Jaimie was furiously angry when Robert told him Dragon's Eye was not part of his inheritance. I think that scene helped kill Robert. Oh, not directly, but it was added stress to a sick old man."

"I haven't managed to save Jaimie. I wish I could have. Perhaps no one can. All I can do now is to give him a chance to save himself."

"Yes, it's up to him," said Charlie gravely. "And what about me? Come on, now, a straight answer and a straight look, please. Where do I stand? Or do only people in need of saving interest you?"

"You don't need saving, you devil," I said, beginning to smile, in spite of myself. "I do."

I was starting to move on again when he held me back. "There's something I want to say, need to say, and I want to do it now, down here. It's my secret. We met once, a long time ago, you and I. You may have forgotten, but I have not. I was working on a boat on the beach, and you were watching. You watched for ages, and I waited and waited for you to speak to me, longing for you to do it, and then when finally you asked if you could help, all I could do was to growl that it was no work for a girl. That was our first meeting. I longed to say, yes, please stay, but I was awkward, stupid."

"Rude," I said, remembering the dark-haired boy.

"So you *do* remember. I believe you've remembered all the time." He caught my hand. "You always knew who I was."

"Grace Beanley thinks I've dreamed about you," I said. "After some sorrel tea. That's her secret."

"Oh, those Beanleys," he said, with a groan. "They know everything, see everything. Did you dream?"

"I shan't tell you," I said deliberately. "That's *my* secret." I moved away. "Come on, let's get back."

The journey back was managed more easily than the journey out. Even in this short time the water level had dropped and we were able to walk through a good bit of the passage. Charlie supported me and I felt brave enough to face even Jumbo and his peers. There was one point, where the water deepened, when I saw a dark flicker of movement approaching. We were still wading, up to our thighs, through the passage toward the mouth of the tunnel, where it would be necessary to jump forward and swim. I saw the movement again. I looked anxiously toward Charlie. Had I imagined jaws and teeth showing close to me? He pushed me away and kicked vigorously.

"Jumbo?" I said apprehensively.

"He's in a rotten mood." Charlie gripped my arms and rushed me forward.

The creature slid through the water, teeth showing. Its teeth were more for display than for use as a weapon; it was the movement of its body that it used for attack. Not that I liked the teeth, and the head looked as big as a horse's.

"I thought you said Jumbo was harmless?" I said, with what breath I had left.

"Must be a female," grumbled Charlie, taking evasive action. He seemed to know exactly what to do, but I supposed with his job he would.

But we made it, swimming vigorously through the few yards of water that remained. Charlie helped me scramble back up onto Dragon's Eye. I had met the dragon, face to face, and survived.

"You might say, 'Thank you for your help on a smooth passage back,'" he said. "I was clever, I thought."

"Oh well, after all you are a fisherman," I pointed out. "It is your job."

He gave me a surprised look, and then started to laugh. He was still giving small, cheerful hoots when we got to Markaby.

Jaimie was standing at the front door watching us. He took in the situation between me and Charlie Guise in one luminous, comprehensive glance. Jaimie was never stupid. "I shouldn't have gone to sleep," he said.

"I've had a look around down below," I said awkwardly. "The island's just a great funeral monument, really, isn't it? I suppose he must have been a great leader to get such a resting place."

"One of the greatest. But nameless now. You needn't go on talking about it." He turned away. "I knew as soon as I came here to Dragon's Eye and found that I could not, could not," he shook his head, "harm you in any way, that it was all up with me. I wanted to stop you from going to the police. Frighten you away, anything I could. But I was helpless. So I went down below. I was going to clear away all traces; I was afraid I'd left a lot that people would find once they looked."

Charlie said, "You were in the cave when the storm broke?"

"Yes, it caught me there. Shouldn't have. I know the sea, I could read the signs, but I just did not bother to look until it was too late. Eventually I did struggle up to the surface and crawl up to Dragon's Eye. Kate found me. She thought I'd been washed off the lifeboat."

In a slow voice, Charlie said, "I should go home now, if I were you."

He and Jaimie exchanged looks. "Yes," said Jaimie, thoughtfully. "I will. That was my intention. I'll walk across the sands to Garrow. The tide is going out fast now."

"You do that, then," said Charlie. "But watch out, while you're doing it. There's a sea mist coming up."

Jaimie nodded.

To me, he said, "I want you to know: at first it was only money, but later the feeling for Markaby became a sort of obsession. I was under the spell of Dragon's Eye. I felt like a Poet and a King. Do you understand me?"

"Wasn't it the same for me then, Jaimie?" I asked.

He came over and kissed me on the cheek. "Goodbye, shepherdess."

We watched him out of sight. "There goes an old-fashioned honorable man," said Charlie. He seemed quite serious. "In his special way."

Charlie took me and my parrot to stay with Stephanie. I must say a few days away from Markaby suited me. Apart from anything else, I needed a rest. I packed a few clothes and we set off straightaway. "I'll telephone from the village," he said. "I'll also report your telephone out of order."

We picked up my hired car and used it to drive to

Garrow. I was tired, and glad to let Charlie drive. I was also glad to sit in the car while he went into the post office to use the telephone.

The main street of Garrow, usually so empty, had several groups of people standing around and talking. The events of the last couple of days, what with the storm and the shipwreck, not to mention the previous finding of Billy English's body, had provided them with the drama of a lifetime. Hands were waved to Charlie, and voices called as he walked along. "Ca' canny in there, my lad," called one old man. "Your mother's little dog has been in there, afore you, and took a piece out of Ma Ogle's skirts."

Mrs. Ogle was on the pavement talking to one of her woman friends, and she was not talking about the storm. Her voice carried easily. "The old dowager's a tartar and no mistake. But I made her pay for the damage, that I did."

I listened absently. Her tone was admiring, not hostile. Whoever the old dowager was, Mrs. Ogle liked her.

I could still hear her every word. "Charlie's the spit and image of the old lord," she went on. "The brother's a poor sort, he won't make old bones, but Charlie'll be the old lord over again, you'll see." She gave a ribald laugh. "Ay, he's a devil, is Charlie." Then she lowered her voice to continue the conversation. I could fill in this bit for myself.

Charlie was gone a longish time. When he came back he apologized for the delay. "I met my mother in there," he said. "And she'd been having some sort of a row with Mrs. Ogle. I had to soothe her down. Not that she needed it, as she'd won her argument. She said you could come to stay with her, if you wanted. But I'd already rung Stephanie, so I left it like that. I thought you'd prefer it, anyway."

"I would, really, if her ladyship's as much of a tartar as Mrs. Ogle believes. Although I gather she admires her for it."

"She is much admired," said Charlie. "I admire her myself. You will, too, when you know her."

"So you're not just a poor young fisherman? You're going to be the old lord over again, are you?"

He started the car, not noticeably fussed. "You began all that about the fisherman," he said. "Not me."

"I overheard Mr. Ogle asking you about the fish prices, the very first time I clapped eyes on you, remember?" I said. "Of course I thought you were a fisherman."

"I do indeed have an interest in the price of fish. At Seahouses I have a new freezing plant, into which I put a lot of money and work. Of course, they joke about it around here, but they like it all the same."

"And you don't live in a fisherman's cottage?" I asked.

"I live in that house I once heard you so vividly describe as a gaunt old barracks. It is an old barracks." He took his eyes off the road to look at me. "You weren't just interested in me as a poor fisherman, I hope?"

"There's a truck straight ahead, so keep your mind on your driving," I said placidly. "The answer is, no."

With a touch of irony, the first telephone call I received, when established with the welcoming Stephanie, was from Bert. Without preamble he said: "The operator told me I'd find you at this number."

"Well, you have," I said.

"Did you get my letter?"

"Yes." I remembered I had and it was still in my pocket.

"Have you opened it, then?" He sounded cross. "I thought I would have a call from you, once you'd read it."

"It's in my coat pocket. I'll read it now, this instant.

Things have been happening here. If it's about work, Bert, I haven't forgotten."

"Glad to hear it. I had Dickon Marlow up here." Bert lived on the top of the nearest to a skyscraper he could get in London. Reaching for the sky, he always said he was. "Wants a job out of me. Might give him one. There's a walk-on in that piece you've got."

"He won't like that much," I observed.

"No. Good for him, though. Too pretty. Needs it knocked out of him. Like I did with you." Then he got down to business.

"He picks things up. Says he thinks you're contemplating love and marriage. I don't know where he gets his information, but I've noticed there's usually something in it. Never said this before, but for someone like you it could be dangerous. You don't want to get caught up in a tight situation. Work first, dear. You're susceptible, see." For the first time in all the time I had known him there was genuine concern in his voice. But probably all he had in mind was protecting his production. "You learn how to look after yourself."

"Thanks, Bert," I said, somewhat sadly. "But I already know all about it."

"You do? Fine." He dismissed the subject. "Right, then, get back to work, Kate, d'you hear? Work."

I did not stay long with Stephanie, but during that visit a great affection grew up between us—not motherly or daughterly, those words were never used between us, but fond and true. I told Lydia all about it when I got to London and she never grudged me one bit of it. There has never been a mite of selfishness or possessiveness in Lydia. I would like to see her look happier again.

Though I did get the part, my project with Bert was put off again, and then again; that's Theater Street. We will get down to it one day, I suppose, but I have been lucky. Other work has come my way.

I go back to Markaby constantly. The Beanleys are in residence, supposedly caretaking for me and looking after Cromwell. "You should have asked me about Mr. Jaimie," said Grace Beanley one day, "and I'd have told you. All of us knew about him and Miss Angel and Markaby we did, couldn't miss." The Beanleys know everything, of course, and if they don't, they know how to find out. "Did you a good turn, didn't I, miss," went on Grace, giving that ribald laugh, "with my cup of sorrel. Didn't you dream, eh? Old Grace knows," and she winked. "Dreamed of Charlie Guise, didn't you? So do we all. But take my advice; don't give that one too easy a time."

Charlie Guise has become part of my life, both here and in London. I may say that I didn't forget Grace's advice about him and I struggled to carry it out. He conducted his courtship in a characteristically straightforward and determined way, one day filling my room with flowers, and the next offering me a choice of diamond, ruby, or sapphire as a betrothal ring. I refused all three gems. "Charlie," I said once, "how did you come to be so interested in it all? You were there, watching, right from the beginning, long before you knew me." He answered simply: "The same reason as you; Robert Berwick asked me to look after him. He knew, he knew that Jaimie was headed for trouble."

Jaimie never arrived back at The Grange. The sea mist had swept in, blotting out coast and water. It was presumed he had somehow lost his way in the obliterating fog and been drowned. Later, when his body was washed up farther along the coast, it seemed to confirm this judgment. But I knew, and Charlie knew, and the police knew that it had probably been a deliberate act. He had let himself drown.

"It was just as well," said Charlie sadly. "It is almost certain it was Jaimie who killed Billy English. The police know it, and could have proved it. This way he saved Angel and The Grange some terrible publicity."

Personally I wondered if it mattered to Angel. She was untouchable. Far away from human emotions. But I was glad for the memory of Robert Berwick.

And perhaps I do Angel an injustice. The Grange was turned over to the teaching sisters of her order, and a small school for handicapped children established there. The chapel at The Grange remained the private property of the Berwick family, and it was there that the memorial stone to Jaimie was to be erected and a service held. What Angel does not get one way, she gets in another.

Almost a year had elapsed since Jaimie's death. The memorial service took place on a fine autumn day. After the solemn requiem mass held for Jaimie, I stood looking at the simple stone which bore his name, set in the wall of the chapel. It was then I had my conversation with the old countrywoman.

After her comment on my gold ring with the sheep's head on it, she moved away with a puzzled look, although there was, in fact, a good reason for the sheep, even if she never knew it. Charlie joined me while I was standing there.

"Come on, Mrs. Guise. I must get back to work and so

must you." He took my arm. "So that we can keep the werewolf from the door."

This was a reference to my latest film, which had indeed been very successful, but Charlie (and Bert, too, for that matter) thought I ought to aim higher. Be more serious, Bert had said, in spite of the fact that I was and always had been very serious in my application to my craft.

"Charlie," I said, still full of my own thoughts. "Had it been you in Jaimie's position, would you have gone away like that, so quietly and without a word?"

He thought about it. Finally he said, "No, I would have put up more of a fight, wrongly perhaps, but there it is. I know I would."

"Me, too." I said. "That's the essential difference between us and Jaimie. We're fighters, and he wasn't." But I said it sadly, and I put my hand gently on my ring. "I remember the old ewe and the day of the lambing."

Nothing much has been changed at Markaby. Charlie and I have left things as they were through the centuries. A shame, some archaeologists might say, but it seemed right. The old Viking still sleeps where he has always slept, in his burial ship beneath the hill, and above him the sheep still graze by the North Sea.